MURDER BY LACE

An animated crowd had gathered at the nearby coffee truck, and there was no mistaking its excited chatter for the usual buzz. Something big was happening. Since I suffer from a terminal case of nosiness, I moved toward a fellow whose histrionics had attracted a crowd of listeners.

"The guy was murdered," he said. "At the back of that field."

Several others had joined the crowd, and he turned to face us. His gestures became even more exaggerated as he attempted to dramatize a struggle that included strangling himself until his eyes bulged. Then, in a hoarse whisper, he delivered his trump line. "He was strangled with a piece of lace."

"Lace?"

I was dumbfounded. Few places felt safer than Brimfield. There have been a variety of flare-ups through the years, but no real violence.

"He was found at daybreak," someone put in.

And then I heard who it was. My God, Monty Rondo. I felt the breath get knocked right out of me.

A KILLING IN ANTIQUES

A Lucy St. Elmo Antiques
—Mystery—

Mary Moody

AN OBSIDIAN MYSTERY

OBSIDIAN

Published by New American Library, a division of
Penguin Group (USA) Inc., 375 Hudson Street,
New York, New York 10014, USA
Penguin Group (Canada), 90 Eglinton Avenue East, Suite 700, Toronto,
Ontario M4P 2Y3, Canada (a division of Pearson Penguin Canada Inc.)
Penguin Books Ltd., 80 Strand, London WC2R 0RL, England
Penguin Ireland, 25 St. Stephen's Green, Dublin 2,
Ireland (a division of Penguin Books Ltd.)
Penguin Group (Australia), 250 Camberwell Road, Camberwell, Victoria 3124,
Australia (a division of Pearson Australia Group Pty. Ltd.)
Penguin Books India Pvt. Ltd., 11 Community Centre, Panchsheel Park,
New Delhi - 110 017, India
Penguin Group (NZ), 67 Apollo Drive, Rosedale, Auckland 0632,
New Zealand (a division of Pearson New Zealand Ltd.)
Penguin Books (South Africa) (Pty.) Ltd., 24 Sturdee Avenue,
Rosebank, Johannesburg 2196, South Africa

Penguin Books Ltd., Registered Offices:
80 Strand, London WC2R 0RL, England

First published by Obsidian, an imprint of New American Library,
a division of Penguin Group (USA) Inc.

First Printing, July 2011
10 9 8 7 6 5 4 3 2 1

For Terry

Acknowledgments

My gratitude to Rod Kessler, Michelle Gillette, and the workshop folks, for the early encouragement to keep on writing while I was still trying to figure out how to tell this story.

Many thanks are due to my agent, Nina Ryan, for her insight and guidance whenever I painted myself into a corner. Sincere thanks to Kathy and Tom Tetro for their help in navigating Brimfield's rules, and for patiently answering my many questions about both Brimfield and antiques; any errors that remain on that score are mine. To Joan Haynes, thanks for the cell phone. Special thanks to my husband, Terry, who read this book in every incarnation and was supportive and understanding nevertheless.

My mother, Babs Kittredge, instilled the thrill of the hunt in all four of her daughters and was the inspiration for the story—she would have changed everything.

1

Most treasure hunts are fantasies. Not mine. I hunt treasure for a living, leaving me plenty of time to fantasize about other things. Like the fantasy that some-day all my kids will have jobs.

That Tuesday in early May, the alarm clock woke me at two o'clock in the morning, exactly when it was sup-posed to. The alarm clock has become an artifact in my life. I rarely need it because I awaken earlier with each passing year, but I'm grateful that I still need it to wake me for two a.m. treasure hunts.

This was the big one. I pulled on my hunting en-semble and ran my eye over my gear, streamlined for greater efficiency. I want to drag the least amount of paraphernalia around with me while still being able to carry the big prize, should I find it. I also need the means to haul my booty carefully because most of my treasure is fragile. Supercart, stashed in the van, was ready and up to the task.

For this trip I had pulled out all the stops. It's my most important hunt of the season. I had emptied the van of extraneous items, something I rarely do, since I consider my van an extension of my purse. I felt good. Successful.

My garb, too, was the product of much forethought. I'd put it together to make me look invisible, and it did. Well, not exactly invisible, but like the kind of woman you look right through when you meet her. When I first realized that I came by this look naturally, it was a painful insight. It had, unlike lightning, struck me at the same time as the realization that I was middle-aged. I haven't learned to enjoy being invisible, but I have come to find it useful.

Two items keep me from total invisibility. First, I wear skirts rather than the compulsory sweats necessary to complete an invisible uniform. Skirts allow me simple encounters with the only negative element in this treasure hunt, the Porta-Potty. I hate Porta-Potties. My other exemption from invisibility was the sudden turning of my faded straw hair to a rich shade of #35s Sunlit Blonde.

My recently overhauled purse completed the ensemble. Crammed with paper products cozied up to a hundred dollars' worth of ones and fives, the purse contained no real money, just the hundred. I keep the real money elsewhere. I belted the purse around me and waited for the coffee to gurgle through the machine before I could head for the granddaddy of all treasure hunts. Brimfield.

I'm Lucy St. Elmo, antiques dealer, and I was ready for the first Brimfield of the season. The Spring Brimfield. The *best* Brimfield. Say "Brimfield" to any antiques dealer in the country and you'll get a reaction. Dealers love it and dealers hate it—sometimes the same dealers—but they all understand that as a treasure hunt it's unsurpassed.

"Pandemonium," Mr. Hogarth had muttered, shaking his head during the last antiques dealers' meeting, "and it gets worse every year."

Mr. Hogarth is the only person I know who has attended every single Brimfield since it began in 1959. He must have been mature even then, because he's older now than many of the beautiful antique lamps in his shop.

"Prices soar, they want an arm and a leg, and for what?" he'd asked.

"Junk!" he had answered himself.

I, about to mention my excitement that Brimfield was almost upon us, reconsidered. Mr. Hogarth is a nice old coot, and if he felt like grumbling a little, I could listen a little. Grumbling is not his usual style. He's usually a joy-filled pedagogue. And, though he specializes in old lamps, he's known for his instant, fact-filled lectures on any aspect of the antiques trade.

"People throng together, clogging the pathways," he complained. "They pay no damned attention to what's going on around them." His own patina seemed a bit tarnished that day, his disposition curmudgeonly.

I've adopted many of his techniques for plundering Brimfield, but I don't have the nerve for his crowd-scattering technique. He lopes along, wheeling his cart ahead, looking deep in thought. In his oblivion, he's ready to plow right through people standing in his path.

I'm not sure that he is oblivious. I have a feeling that he's fully aware. He rolls directly toward the one causing the bottleneck. But wait. He stops, a fraction of an inch from the hindrance, now a sitting duck.

They jump out of his way, often making gestures of offense. At that point he reawakens as Mother Teresa, and with a beatific smile and bowing head, he mutters, "Sorry, sorry," and, waving a little benediction, he continues on his way. Something about the old man's attitude seems to soften people.

He was whiny at that meeting, though. "Half of the good stuff is gone before they open."

That's an oft-heard complaint, and on occasion there is more than a kernel of truth in it. He's the one who taught me how to grab the good stuff early, particularly before the openings, and I often get the drop on other shoppers by using his methods.

I wondered if his age was catching up with him; he's well into his eighties. He frowned and muttered something about how "It used to be good out there." I asked if he was thinking of giving up Brimfield.

"Good gravy, Lucy, what is the matter with you?

I'll never quit Brimfield. I love Brimfield. There is no place else in this country where you can find the kind of antiques that are out there just for the taking. I've told you, Lucy," he sputtered, "Brimfield makes the market."

He looked at me, and my amazement at this response must have registered with him, because he flushed, and grinned, and said, "Lucy, sometimes it's a strain, waking up early, walking miles through the fields, trying to mine gold from stuff that belongs in a landfill, but if you're in the antiques business it's easy to become an antique yourself, and Brimfield is where to have your cobwebs removed."

That's *my* Brimfield. Officially known as "The Brimfield Antiques and Collectible Shows," but referred to simply as Brimfield. It's the antiques marketplace to beat them all. And, in spite of his complaints that day last year, Mr. Hogarth would be where he belonged: absorbing yet another infusion of the vitality that overtakes him, and the rest of us, during the Spring Brimfield.

It's located in a lovely old town in central Massachusetts, which, coincidentally enough, is also called Brimfield. Close to thirty-five hundred people call it home. They think of it as *their* Brimfield. I'd never dispute that; the town is theirs. It's just that they sometimes get overly sensitive. Claims of trauma are trotted out regularly by the offended. The town gets overloaded, okay? The spectacle of forty or fifty thousand people flooding into a town of thirty-five hundred is daunting, I agree, but who brought us there?

Right.

Brimfield appears like Brigadoon. Suddenly, in a magical moment on the appointed day, it's there. Rather than once every century, it materializes three times each year, in May, July, and September. And the May Brimfield is peerless. Where before there were tree-studded fields and meadows sprinkled with occasional barns or buildings, there now stands an enchanted territory. A tent town packed to bursting with treasures. After six days of revelry, comedy, and tragedy, the phenomenon vanishes.

The fields line both sides of Route 20 for more than a mile, some as small as five acres, others ten acres or more. Within each, hundreds of tents are arranged into streets and alleys in a higgledy-piggledy imitation of city blocks. Gathering places have sprung up, perfect for eating or resting or socializing.

Big tents and little tents, in a carnival of colors. Yellow and white stripes predominate lately, looking far more festive than the army surplus colors of the old days. Each tent is an antique shop.

Imagine four thousand antique shops and only six days in which to examine every item in each one of them before those fifty thousand or so other buyers get all the good stuff.

My heart beats wildly. My adrenaline surges. My systems galvanize. The hunt is on!

I feel taller during the hunt. I feel thinner during the

hunt. I'm convinced that, during the hunt, my eyesight improves. Hamp, my husband, has assured me that I'm deluded, but when I'm hunting I even forget that I have a fiftieth birthday chasing me. Tell me that's not real.

By twenty past two, I was ready. I had spent the night alone in our tiny apartment in Boston. This put me closer to Brimfield. It's a little more than an hour away from the apartment, and close to three hours from the Cape. It was easier for me to pull myself together here, since my stumbling and clunking about wouldn't wake Hamp and the family, all snug back on Cape Cod.

An ironclad lease ties us to the apartment, which was a source of much anxiety in our family. We had rented it for our younger daughter, Nancy. It was adorable, safe, near school, and best of all we could almost afford it. Several months passed before we realized that she didn't live there. Even before the hand-wringing and recriminations abated I noticed how much I liked the funky little place, and I began to find reasons for staying there with Hamp. We use it as a refuge.

We love our large, rambunctious family, who keep bouncing back home to us at the Cape, but we slip away to the little apartment whenever we get the chance. That's how we remind ourselves that we love each other, too. Alas, this week I'd be here alone.

The coffee was ready. I poured an inch of it into the

dearest treasure that I keep here, my Rozane mug, and sipped at the scalding coffee. I let myself dream, for a moment, about the possibility of acquiring a match for it this week.

Enough. I poured the rest of the coffee into my thermos and hurried away. The drive was an easy one from the apartment. The sky in Boston was clear and starry. Traffic was light, and at that hour the Mass Pike had no construction bottlenecks. I approached Exit 9, where the slight increase in traffic hardly made a ripple, then sailed down Route 20 for the final ten miles. There were enough vans and trucks and RVs going in my direction to assure me that the plunge in the economy wouldn't be fatal for this year's antique shows. We were all making the pilgrimage to Brimfield.

I found a good place to park, right off Route 20. Stepping out of the van, I felt the cool air, ripe with the smell of spring, and I sensed, *knew* really, that this was going to be one of those special days. I rolled Supercart out of the van. It was folded into its smallest position, but still it took up a good chunk of the van's space. I headed for the parking attendant. I wanted to see if I could strike a deal with him for later in the day.

Parking at Brimfield is inexpensive. Arrive early enough and it's convenient, too. The space is yours, but on a heavy day, if you move, you lose it.

I wanted a guaranteed parking space, and a little more. If I can fill my van several times a day, and drive to a barn nearby where I store things temporarily, it makes the day perfect. But on top of that perfect day,

I'd like just a little more space, preferably near the parking attendant, where I can drop off large pieces of furniture that I acquire. I'm happy to pay for this convenience, but some parking attendants just can't see it my way.

This one, a kid wearing a broad smile and a Boston cap, listened intently, nodding and "Yes, ma'am"–ing me as I told my story. He was young, and in charge, and he could give me the old "Sorry, ma'am, but rules are rules." Instead, he asked, "What time will you make your first trip back to the parking lot?"

I looked at my watch; it was almost four o'clock. "I'd like to be back here to empty my first load before the six a.m. openings."

"Great!" he said. "I'll take your offer, but I'll need a signing bonus. Bring me a coffee and something good to eat, and you've got yourself a deal."

I would have hugged him, but I didn't want to scare the kid. It was shaping up to be a wonderful day.

2

It was still dark. Official opening time for the first day of Brimfield was still minutes away. Daybreak, it was called; the term is relative around here, but I was already in clover. Most of my take so far was of the bread-and-butter variety, but it was all I could do not to prance my way through the people streaming into the area early, trying to do a little preopening shopping. Naughty, naughty, that's against the rules. May they get what they deserve. Unless I see it first.

Yes, yes, and yes again. In less than an hour I had Supercart half filled. I had lucked into a collection of art pottery almost as soon as I stopped at my first field. I paid three hundred dollars for the collection of eight pieces, less than I'd be willing to pay for one of the items, a pedestal.

There were three pieces of Rookwood and three pieces of Roseville, one of which was the top prize, a

Normandy pedestal, just what I love. The sale included two McCoy flowerpots that I could have left behind. I didn't really want them, but the dealer wanted to get rid of the whole group, almost as if it would sully his collection of primitive kitchen utensils.

It's been said that you can get a bargain from a dealer who specializes in something other than the item you're buying, implying that the dealer doesn't recognize it or value it. But now there are books that help identify an unfamiliar object and give some idea of its current value.

If this guy did any price checking, he used information that's long out-of-date, because this stuff was increasing in price even as we were completing our sale. If he'd waited until his field opened, he'd have been able to double his price within the first few minutes. There could easily have been a bidding war for that Normandy pedestal, even without the jardinière. Jardinières are easier to find than pedestals, and though Normandys are relatively rare, I knew that in time I'd come across one.

I walked along Route 20 and entered the flow of people heading toward the dim lights of the next field. The bare lightbulbs were slightly brighter than candles. No one at Brimfield has ever overspent money for lighting. It's to no seller's advantage to illuminate the chips and dents and cracks, nor to spotlight the outright fakes and forgeries.

Dark as it was, I nevertheless spotted Natalie Rosen ahead of me. Her athletic stride was easy to recognize, and her dark hair caught the scanty light. Natalie's an old friend, and I hurried to catch up with her. Another of the pleasures of Brimfield is the renewal of old friendships.

Natalie and I met soon after we started our businesses in the same wretched building in Worcester fifteen years ago. The fact that we operated on shoestring budgets, had no idea what we were doing, and had opened businesses that were only slightly more advanced than lemonade stands might have been thread enough to weave us a friendship, but something else happened in that relationship.

We became learning systems and support systems and a mutual admiration society for each other. We were intricately linked providers of exactly what the other most needed, which was often just to be taken seriously.

"I hope you've had better luck than I," she said when I caught up with her. "I've been here an hour and I haven't found a thing."

I immediately launched into a detailed description of my loot, but stopped. "Have you really not found anything?"

Natalie had turned to antiques far later than I, but she's a much better shopper. She can see possibilities quickly, make decisions quickly, and strike deals quickly. I was surprised that she hadn't found any treasures; there were lots of goodies around.

"Not a thing," she said. "I wasted too much time trying to make a deal on a pickle castor, but the price was outrageous and I walked off in a huff. I can hardly keep my mind on what I'm doing. I'm going home." She sounded angry. Her steps pounded along the gravel path. Her hair, a glossy mahogany helmet, shot forward at every step, then slipped back into its allotted place. Every hair on my head was jealous of its behavior.

"Don't be silly, Natalie." We pushed our carts along, Supercart rumbling a rich baritone, her smaller metal cart twittering timpani. "It will be daylight in a few minutes. You'll get your bearings, and once you've bought that first trophy, you'll feel better."

"No," she said, "I'm giving up and going home. The day's hardly started but it already feels like a total loss."

"Don't go home, Natalie. If you're down in the dumps, you're better off here. You'll see old friends, and you'll get involved in this circus. It will be good for you."

We didn't see each other as often these days because our businesses are now at opposite ends of the state, but our friendship is still deeply felt. We missed the daily details of each other's lives, but we picked up old conversations comfortably and somewhat regularly. I suspected her old scars were acting up. In the dim light her dark eyes glistened. I was afraid she might cry.

"I'm interviewing," she said.

Well, I'll be draped! This was Natalie's code for saying she was dating.

When we met, Natalie, a fragile young widow with

two small children, was still reeling from the loss of her husband. She had nevertheless created her odd little business. She plunged all of her energies into the business and the children, and they'd responded. Each had teetered precariously on occasion, but had adapted and developed. In the end, though the business and the children had changed, all thrived and grew.

Slowly but inevitably her healing took place. I like to believe I played a part in it. She mended and gathered strength, and her recovery progressed. I'm only half a dozen years older than Natalie, but I mothered her quite a lot. I sometimes sensed that her recovery was stalled, but I saw, too, that she was resilient and that she could work her way through the damage. It's a fact of my life that the most interesting people have all had to work their way through the foulest damage.

She began to date. That was when I noticed that she had created her obscure code of euphemisms that I call Natalieze. I watched her "interviewing" with intense interest. I couldn't wait to hear what she'd dream up to call a boyfriend once the interviews got serious. But I'd be waiting still, because things never got that far. Natalie dismissed all her suitors before they reached boyfriend status.

"Who's the lucky fellow?" I gushed. "Do I know him?"

"Don't get excited, Lucy. This may just be another bit of research."

"I know, I know. So why don't you stay here and shop around? You may find another pickle jar."

"It's a pickle castor, Lucy, sterling silver, with a mother-of-pearl insert. I'm sure it's like the one I saw at the McGirr Museum a while back, so I don't think there will be too many of them around."

She was put out with me. I think she needed comforting, but I didn't have time to comfort her just then. This early part of the hunt must be done quickly. The competition immediately following opening time is vigorous, and for good reason. The unusual stuff goes fast. You can wait years before seeing its likeness again. Could we meet later for coffee? She hesitated, then agreed. I thought I knew the cause of her jitters. I'd calm her later. She was just worked up about the d-a-t-e.

"Good," I said. I was happy that she wouldn't go home and fret, and only mildly guilty over my relief in not having to take the time to console her. "You'll find something you like better, and you'll make a killing on it."

We hugged, said our good-byes, and I rushed off. More fields open on opening day than on all other days. Efforts to stagger the opening hours and monitor the selling hours are imperfect. Plenty of deals are made before the listed business hours, and I intended to make as many as I could.

I was flying. Supercart was holding up well. This was its sixteenth year of Brimfield. When filled, it has been the object of much eye rolling by onlookers. Made for me by my oldest son, Philip, when he was fifteen years old, it was built to be a repository in transit for my lovely treasures, and as I go along buying more and more goodies I can keep raising its sides and its supporting shelves higher, and wider, until it's packed six feet high and about four feet wide.

I like Supercart so much because it makes me feel like Superman as I roll it around the fields. I used to be called petite, sometimes even tiny. That was okay. But over time I've acquired some age, and some mass, and now I'm more often called short. I don't feel short, and I don't like the term.

Each and every one of the twenty-seven definitions in *my* edition of *Webster's* implies that "short" means not enough. I see Webster as a trifle dogmatic, but his work has caught on in our house, so it's hard to argue with his decisions. With Supercart I feel that I'm showing the world that I'm *more* than enough. It's perfectly balanced, has springs, and its nice fat wheels are nifty for keeping my stuff from getting jounced around on the rutted gravel paths and lumpy fields.

Its weathered wood has never been painted, if you don't count the two blobs of bright red paint that I dabbed on one side when I was testing colors for my shutters at the Cape. Despite the fact that it looks, when full, as if I am wheeling a small storage shed around, it's a dream to push. The pièce de résistance is the hinged counter that pulls down along one side, convenient for lunches, conferences, or writing checks or receipts.

Of all the conveyances, carts, and carriers you see at Brimfield, either handmade or commercially made—

and there are plenty of both—Supercart permits the biggest loads to be carried with the least effort. The fact that people find it funny-looking when it's full still bothers my son, Philip, but not me.

Philip takes everything seriously. He once told me that we live in a dysfunctional family. I think he meant crowded. He just married a woman he's known for three weeks. Don't get me started on the possibilities for dysfunction. They're living with us.

The crowds, the disorder, and the confusion of Brimfield have never unnerved me. I find it more peaceful than the crowds, the disorder, and the confusion of home.

My next field keeps close tabs on its sellers. Now I wanted to shop in a place that hadn't been cleaned out by someone like me. After all, I had just acquired the art pottery from a guy who was selling before his field opened.

A crowd had gathered at the gate, and though the formation of a line would have ensured them an even-handed entrance, they jostled and jockeyed and formed an unruly mob instead. Through the judicious use of Supercart, I found myself at the front as the first scant rays of light touched the edge of the sky. It was five a.m. and dark turned to light. In less time than it took them to open the gate, it became daybreak. Brimfield had officially opened.

I abandoned Supercart as soon as I was inside the fence. I left it next to the gatekeeper, and I ran into the field, scanning each booth. I moved as fast as I was able, stopping only for the unique, the pristine, the exquisitely designed objects.

This early run is not when I look for special bargains, nor when I do heavy negotiating or dickering. That comes later, on the second run-through. Right now my purpose was to find, and buy, extraordinary antiques and premium collector's items. If lucky, I might also find a museum-quality piece or two.

Each time my arms were full, I returned to Supercart and spent a minute packing the treasures I'd culled. I wasted no time; still, I couldn't help but admire again a perfect Grueby paperweight, a Weller pitcher delicately painted with dew-drenched blackberries, and the signed Dresden lamp that had never been converted to electricity. These, and most of my harvest so far, are the quick turnover stuff in my shop. I arranged things and rolled on.

Some of my purchases had to be left behind. A China cabinet with a curved glass door and a chunky oak kitchen table were too large and too heavy for Supercart. If I continued accumulating treasures at this rate, I'd hire a mover to help me pack and move everything into my temporary storage nearby, in a friend's barn.

I had no helper today. TJ, my latest and most unlikely Sherpa, was back at the Cape. He'd drive up to Brimfield twice this week, tomorrow and Friday. We'd load up a big rental truck, packing it tight for the trip back to the Cape. Then, on a quiet day next week, with

Brimfield over, we'd return once again and empty the barn.

It wasn't until I was once again gathering and safely repacking my booty in Supercart that I noticed the sound of sirens coming from the other side of Route 20. In fact, it dawned on me that the sirens had been there for some time, but I had been communing so perfectly with my greed that I had blocked nearly everything else out.

It was time to head for the van and unload. I wanted Supercart empty for the six o'clock opening. Three fields opened at six o'clock this morning, and I had found premium goods at each at one time or another.

But first I stopped at a truck that had been tantalizing me with its aromas. I decided to join the parking attendant for breakfast, and chose an exquisite pair of Italian sausage subs smothered with onions and peppers. An unusual offering for this hour of the morning, but the maître d' had no trouble accommodating the crowd, many of whom had been working here since before midnight.

An animated crowd had gathered at the nearby coffee truck, and there was no mistaking its excited chatter for the usual buzz. Something big was happening. Since I suffer from terminal nosiness, I moved toward a fellow whose histrionics had attracted a crowd of listeners.

"The guy was murdered," he said. "At the back of

that field." He was pointing in the direction of a field across Route 20, slightly south of us.

Several others joined the crowd, and he turned to face us. His gestures became even more exaggerated as he attempted to dramatize a struggle that included strangling himself until his eyes bulged. Then, in a hoarse whisper, he delivered his trump line. "He was strangled with a piece of lace."

"Lace?"

I was dumbfounded. Few places felt safer than Brimfield. There have been some flare-ups through the years, but no real violence.

The leading man seemed to have exhausted himself and his information. A woman nearby pulled a mahogany Regency chair out of her cart. She offered it to him. He sat down, breathed deeply, and some color came back into his face.

Meanwhile, bits of information trickled through the gathering.

"He was found at daybreak," someone put in.

And then I heard who it was. My God, Monty Rondo. I felt the breath get knocked right out of me, and I must have teetered, because the woman with the Regency chair said, "Do you need a chair, too? I only have the one, but I think this fellow has recovered."

3

Monty Rondo. Dead. I stood, gaping. The two huge sausage and pepper sandwiches trembled in my hands. This can't be. Monty murdered. The jolt was too terrible to absorb. What should I do?

What I *did* do is try to deal with the sandwiches. I made a nest for them in Supercart's cache. My hands shook as I tucked paper around them, and I made a pretty good mess of the job. I pushed Supercart to the parking lot, and all of a sudden it weighed a thousand pounds.

I stopped and leaned against it.

"Was he a friend of yours?"

It was the parking attendant. Word of the murder had spread, and the kid seemed to realize that I was shaken.

Was Monty my friend? I hadn't thought about it. He'd been part of my life for fifteen years. We'd done business together. We'd come to know each other, know *about* each other. I'd looked forward to his off-beat chatter, to the prizes he'd picked for me. He was more than just a business connection.

"Yes," I said. I just hadn't realized it before.

"So what happened?" he asked.

"Someone strangled him with lace."

The kid looked at me, eyes wide, mouth a perfect circle. "Lace? You mean, like, a tablecloth?"

"More like a strip of lace. It could have come from a tablecloth, maybe the edge of an old tablecloth, I suppose."

"But wouldn't an old piece of lace fall apart when you pulled on it?"

"Old lace looks fragile, and with some kinds you can pull one thread and have it unravel, but a strip of lace itself is as sturdy as a rope, even after it's been laundered and bleached for years."

He assimilated that information, and I handed him both sandwiches, apologizing for forgetting the coffee, but he stopped me.

"I'll help you load your stuff into the van, and you can tell me about it. I'll get coffee later."

I nodded. The kid—he called himself Coylie—moved my things out of Supercart, and I arranged them in the van. I told him about Monty.

The first thing you noticed about Monty was his voice. His thundering voice. "Even when you couldn't see him, his booming voice announced his arrival," I said. He talked nonstop, and at full volume. "He had stories for every situation."

The kid nodded; I think he listened the way my kids sometimes listen. Nodding and saying "uh-huh" occasionally. But I went on anyway. "He could be so irritating, you could strangle the guy sometimes." I stopped, realizing what I had said. The kid looked up and smiled. Just as well if he wasn't paying too much attention.

When Supercart was empty we closed the van. Coylie slid his cap off and fanned his face with it. He ran the other hand through a mass of orange ringlets that sprang to life and caught the sunlight. He motioned me toward the lawn chairs he had set up at the entrance of the parking lot. There, he picked up both sandwiches and held one out for me. I shook my head but sat down in the other lawn chair. While Coylie ate, I babbled on; I couldn't help myself.

"He was very kind to me when I was starting out," I said.

"So why'd someone want to kill the guy?" Coylie asked as he started on a sandwich.

"He could be a nuisance sometimes," I said. "He never knew when to stop. He had no sense of what was playful teasing and what was a pain in the neck."

"You think someone'd kill him for that?" Coylie asked.

"No, it was probably his cash. There's a lot of cash around here today."

"Not in my pocket," he said. Then he nodded and started the second sandwich. He checked his watch and reminded me that I wanted to be at a six o'clock opening. I pulled myself to my feet and headed toward Route 20. It would be good to keep busy. I rolled my empty cart in that direction.

In spite of his colorful ways, or perhaps because of them, I had enjoyed Monty's company. He had acquired a partner of sorts, called Silent Billy. The man was as quiet as Monty was noisy. Monty was high-spirited, traveling in his own uproar. Silent Billy was devoted to him. I met Monty shortly after I opened my first little antiques shop in Worcester.

That was when I still thought there was no more to the antiques business than opening a little shop and giving it a cute name. I wanted one of those darling little shops, a sort of antique boutique. I had been a collector of antiques since childhood, but I soon learned that the business was a whole different ball game from collecting pretty things.

When the youngest of my brood entered high school, I opened my first shop, Olde Stuff. It was wonderful. I loved that shop. I thought of it as the fulfillment of a dream in my lifelong pursuit of antiques. But it was just the beginning.

Monty was an early caller. He admired my shop vigorously, which brought his good taste to my attention. He also welcomed me into the antiques trade, and though he may have had an ulterior motive, it was nice of him and made me feel good.

"I, myself, am in the junk trade," he boomed.

"Junk trade?"

"Yes. Junk is the first level of the antiques business," he said. "I, myself, find many beautiful objects that I bring to the auction houses and the antique shops. Yes, you people love to see me coming."

Well, well, well. What an interesting point of view.

"I buy contents," he said. "You got a cellar? I buy the contents. You got an attic? I buy the contents. You got a barn? I buy the contents." He flung his arms around my splendidly crowded little shop. "I, myself, clean out your junk pile. The bitter with the sweet. I'll even pay you to let me take it away.

"People love me," he said with a slight bow of his head and shoulders. He said it often, and it always made me smile. But not everyone smiled at Monty's diamond-in-the-rough candor. Some found him irritating, and others found him downright rude. That first day he explained in great detail how he purchased various contents, "and in tough times, I, myself, have even been known to buy out garage sales."

His practice was then to sift through the contents for the treasures. After all, how did I think that all of those wonderful antiques were found in the first place? It was Monty, he himself, who found them, and sold them to the breathlessly waiting antiques dealers.

Ah! Monty was a picker. At the time I didn't even realize that pickers existed. He was a good one. He knew who was selling what. He made it his business to bring exactly the right thing to the right dealer. Monty rarely missed a sale; he delivered the kind of thing that his customers enjoyed handling.

His day-to-day business occupied a small ware-house from which he sold the rest of the contents as used furniture. Though named Warehouse Used Furniture, it was known unofficially in the trade as Monty's Contents.

The warehouse had two particularly interesting features. One was the little workshop in which the repair and restoration work went on, and the other was the room in which he stored antiques not yet passed on to dealers. The used furniture business was open only three days a week, but it was busy and looked to be thriving. The workshop and the antiques rooms were not open to the public; they were entered by invitation only, and Monty was surprisingly selective about invitations.

I came to understand that he had a system for choosing which dealers were to buy his wares. His system seemed, to me, more selective than his method for acquiring the antiques. I didn't know the process, exactly, but I did know that when a chosen buyer failed to live up to Monty's expectations, he was in for a long and complicated procedure before earning his way back.

The first few times that Monty visited my shop, I couldn't wait to go home and report his pronouncements to Hamp and the kids. Hamp didn't find my Monty stories as fascinating as I did, and the kids soon referred to me as being in the junk trade. So I curtailed the stories, but I was overjoyed when I met Natalie and we discovered that we both took great pleasure in knowing him.

Natalie and I came to view Monty as a stroke of

luck. Our early dealings with him had met with his approval, and there was a big payoff for that approval. He took an interest in us, brought us special items, nurtured us. I suspect that my part in all this was to ride Natalie's coattails. Monty had a soft spot for her. He'd been instrumental in redirecting her efforts toward more profitable ends. Natalie had understood and transformed her odd little business into the success it has become. Monty enjoyed Natalie's good fortune, and basked in her rapt attention.

Now he was dead. Brimfield buzzed with the news. He was killed, I supposed, in a robbery. Monty carried a wad of cash with him that he flashed indiscriminately. I think he felt that it impressed people.

Cash is a useful tool. Buyers at Brimfield this week would be carrying large amounts. Sellers were more apt to sell at a discount, and sell quickly, when they knew that they would walk away with good old unreportable currency. I, and the rest of the antiques world, had often seen Monty pull a roll out of his pocket that he could hardly wrap his hand around.

I gently patted the wad I carried, and was reassured knowing that it was safe. Each morning at Brimfield, I start off with thirty one-hundred-dollar bills. I fold them and paper clip them together by fives so I can reach into my stash and remove as many, or as few, as I want, without fumbling. The stash, along with my credit card, my ATM card, and a few blank checks, is usually enough for anything I run into around the fields.

Occasionally I run into something requiring more cash than I have on hand, but usually I can produce enough earnest money to hold the deal down until I can come up with the balance. For years now banks have decked out vans and set up ATMs as portable branches; I use them infrequently. They're never handy when I'm making a deal.

I drifted along, going through the motions of shopping, picking things up and putting things down, but I couldn't concentrate, and my mind turned again to Monty. I left the field without a single purchase. I looked up and realized that I had been heading all the while toward the back of the field where his body had been found.

Silent Billy, Monty's helper, stood at the edge of the activity. I watched him shift from one foot to the other. He drew his hands out of his pockets, chipped at the air, and then put them back in his pockets, where they found coins and stuff to jingle. He stepped forward and back, and then he rocked from side to side. Hands out again, he took off his cap. He ran his fingers across his hair and beard. I could hear the scratching sound his stiff fingers made against his stiff white hair.

Several varieties of policemen busied themselves at the scene, in addition to the town police. State cops, plainclothes cops, cops from nearby communities, and security company cops milled around. The earth, soft and damp in the spring, had been trampled. Tracks from a number of shoes and vehicles had pressed their patterns into it. Trampling the clues?

I moved toward Billy. He looked up and recognized me with a curt nod. What should I say? I'd known him for five years, maybe longer. The name Silent Billy is a slight exaggeration of the man. Almost anyone standing next to Monty for several years would appear to be silent, but in fact Billy really is as tight-lipped a man as you can find. He responds to questions, but he is a master of the one-word answer, and I never saw him initiate a conversation.

I walked over and asked if he was all right.

"All right," he said, looking dazed. His voice, a gruff low rumble, always sounds as if he's recovering from a cold. Whenever I hear him I fight the urge to clear my throat.

"What happened, Billy?"

"Murder," he said.

"Do you know how it happened?" I said.

He looked at me. Always loaded with nervous energy, this morning he snapped with static. He leaned back on his heels, then rocked forward; his head bobbed as he looked over one side of the hill, then the other.

"Billy, I know Monty's dead, murdered. Do you know what happened?"

"Don't know," he said.

It wasn't a surprise. What did I expect?

Billy's jaw moved, he looked at me—I thought he'd

say something, but no words came. Nothing. Just silence.

That's when a boy dressed as a policeman approached us, stood at attention, locked his eyes into a space just over our heads, and announced that this was a crime scene, in case we hadn't noticed the twenty-five or so policemen, the vehicles with flashing lights, and the yellow tape strung up as if another war were over.

Dismissed, and moving along as instructed, I turned, expecting Billy to drift along with me. The cop, growing into his role, took a breath and announced that Billy should come along with him for questioning.

Billy hesitated, looked over his shoulder at me, and said, "Help!" He looked afraid. The way I figured it, the guy doing the questioning would have more problems with the interview than Billy would. And then the cop amazed me. He put handcuffs on Billy. It took a minute for the idea to sink in that the cop was going to question Billy as a suspect, not as a person with information.

That made no sense. I knew in my gut that Silent Billy didn't kill Monty, and I knew it without a doubt. Billy is a truly gentle soul who was far more than a Sherpa to Monty. He ran the workshop, refinished furniture, and made spectacular repairs. I watched their friendship deepen over time. Billy was the only helper Monty ever called his partner, and I truly felt that Monty had mellowed because of Billy's ability to turn a blind eye to Monty's irritating behavior.

4

Unnerved by this turn of events, I drifted by tents thronged with people but didn't hunt for treasure; I couldn't really think. The idea that Billy was accused of killing Monty was incomprehensible. My mind stuttered with a flood of information and contradictions. I walked along faster.

Billy joined Monty after we'd moved to the Cape. He went about his business, helping Monty and fixing furniture. Monty said Billy could fix anything made of wood, could bring it back to life.

But Monty complained about Billy's judgment. He told me that Billy spent as much time and effort repairing the old cheap furniture that came under his hand as he did on the fine stuff.

"If I tell him to repair five items down at the warehouse, he'll start with the one closest to where he's standing, and he'll spend as much time on a piece that will earn us five bucks as he will on one with a hundred-dollar profit."

I thought about their relationship and continued along the fence until I approached the front gate. Monty's criticism hadn't seemed to bother Billy. At the gate, I parked Supercart, walked out to Route 20, and turned west. I moved along, increasing my speed until I was going at a pretty good clip. I don't walk often enough, and after a while I began to enjoy it. It calmed me, made me feel better. I decided to walk the length of the marketplace along Route 20.

Billy usually came along when Monty delivered goodies to his customers across the Cape. He never said much after hello, but that was hardly noticeable since Monty filled our visits with stories, gossip, and news about what was happening in shops across New England. Billy once interrupted Monty to point to the pieces of a small Dunhill humidor stand that I'd acquired for a pittance because it was in extremely poor condition.

"Good stuff," he said.

I laughed and agreed. "I've been fiddling with it for months. I'm not even sure that all of the pieces are there."

Billy looked it over, turned to Monty, and said, "Can do."

Monty told me that if I liked, Billy would fix it for a nominal bench fee. I have a little workspace in an alcove by the shop's back door. While I cleared the workbench, Billy went out to the truck to get his tools. He returned with a long, heavy-looking metal box and an old black leather bag reminiscent of a Norman Rockwell doctor's bag.

"Let's see if Billy can work it out," Monty said.

Billy worked something out that I still have trouble believing, even though I watched. In about twenty minutes Billy had the humidor back together. It was fine-looking. Its legs took it up to about three feet high, with a small drawer as well as a sealed cabinet. Each piece fit into the next perfectly.

As the wood came to life under his hand, Billy came to life, too. He even chatted a bit, explaining in his scratchy delivery what he was doing. There are people who can't imagine that a man can have a relationship with wood, but watching Billy, anyone could see it. He took jars and rags out of his doctor's bag, and he cleaned and polished the humidor, which finally looked like the masterpiece it was meant to be. But he wasn't finished yet. He took a small pocketknife and made a tiny mark under a corner column.

"Mine," he said, and dabbed over his mark with his special polish.

Monty and I applauded the work—it was beautiful—and Billy mentioned that he signs everything he works on.

"If he fixes it, he signs it," Monty agreed.

"The used furniture, too?" I asked.

"It's all used furniture to Billy," Monty said.

I thanked Billy, and he looked pleased. Monty told me to pay Billy directly. But he didn't leave it at that; he made one of his annoying little speeches advising me not to begin buying junky furniture for Billy to fix.

As if I would do that. At any rate, Monty went on a bit, telling me that if I wanted to have Billy fix anything, I had to go through Monty to make the arrangements. He turned it into one of his little jokes: I was not to take advantage of Billy; the only one who could take advantage of Billy was Monty himself. I thought about that day, remembering that both he and Billy stood smiling at me while Monty announced his silly rules.

I had walked a little over a mile to the end of the last field, so I turned around, and before long I became interested again in what was happening around me. Brimfield was buzzing with sound and movement, and full of treats for the eye.

Some Limoges dishes caught my eye. Pink flowers, lovely, no price tag. I can always sell Limoges, and pink flowers are the easiest to move. These were in fine shape. No chips or cracks, no scratches from an indifferent dishwasher, mechanical or human. There were eight small plates and one dinner-sized plate.

"How much for the dishes?" I asked, pointing. I didn't refer to them as Limoges.

"They're Limoges," he said.

"Pretty," I said, and drifted to the next table.

The dealer, sensing that I was losing interest, named his price.

"A little high for odd pieces," I said.

"That's a cake set."

Surprised, I laughed out loud. "Good save," I said,

and it was good. Sets of anything have a higher value than odd pieces or singles. I've created sets on occasion myself. Depending on which pieces of China or porcelain have survived, they become a soup set, a sherbet set, a salad service.

Grinning, he said, "I've been toying with calling the ashtrays that are going for almost nothing wine coasters."

I rolled my eyes and pointed to the Limoges. "Can you do any better than that?" I often ask.

He could, and I took them. It's no trick to ask for a better deal. The trick is not to come on like gangbusters. He wrapped my Limoges in newspaper, and because I was without Supercart he gave me a plastic grocery bag, along with a witticism warning me not to swing the bag. I moved off toward Supercart. With a calmer mind, my thoughts returned to Silent Billy.

The shopping was therapeutic, but I was stumped for a way to help him. I knew he was incapable of killing anyone. I also knew that the police were unlikely to find my opinion that he didn't any more valid than I found their opinion that he did.

Billy had asked for help, and I struggled to figure out a way to help him without getting into trouble myself. I'd promised Hamp I'd stay away from crime; let the police handle police business. It's not a problem that comes up frequently, but I had, on occasion, helped a friend or two out of trouble. Minor scrapes. I'd been successful, too. Except for the time I got shot.

Prior to that Hamp had paid little attention to my

forays into "helping people." In an emotionally weak-
ened condition, during my recovery, he'd extracted my
promise. I'd caved. My pain and embarrassment at letting myself be shot had magnified the tiny kernel of
truth to his claim that I'd drifted blindly into a fool-
hardy adventure. It wasn't that way. Not really.

But Billy had asked me for help. So I needed to figure out how, then get the right people involved, and
then bow out. I was stumped. I have trouble talking to
the police, because I usually see things a different way
than they do.

I do know Matt Whitney, but I hesitated to use that
connection. Matt is a customer of mine. He's a big defense attorney, and a big customer, and a Big Man. I
couldn't ask him to help Silent Billy, but maybe I could
ask his advice on how to *get* help for him. Otherwise, I
didn't know what to do next.

Matt is a hard guy to talk to. He's impatient and
somewhat curt, and conversation with him is a little
like being cross-examined. Then, too, I had the feeling
that he was unlikely to help anyone who couldn't help
him in return. I searched my mind for other options,
but decided, by default, that I had to call Matt.

I hate to talk on the phone. I don't like telephones. I
don't like being connected to another person by a de-
vice that's smarter than I am. I'm uncomfortable when
I can't touch the person I'm talking to. And phones are
like dogs, you know—they can tell when you don't
like them.

I realize I'm going against the grain here, and it has

nothing to do with the mechanical aspect of telephones. It's just the power that telephones have over people that bothers me, and now they even have power over other machines. My kids have tried to convince me to get a cell phone—for emergencies, they say. So far their emergency calls have been for me to run some errand they don't have time for. A cell phone would only keep me on duty 24/7.

So where were these phones when I needed them? Brimfield was becoming more crowded by the minute, but I didn't see a single soul with a phone, not even a stranger. I might have to ask to borrow one.

It's hard to find a public phone lately. I walked along, and was relieved to find a phone-on-a-stick, one of two planted side by side along Route 20, convenient to the thundering compressors of the nearby food concessions. People were shrieking into both when I arrived. Trucks slowing to a crawl on the overburdened road added their rumble to the growing din. When I took my turn, I could hardly hear the dial tone over the noise. The man on the next phone was shouting something about a trapunto quilt.

I had my List in my purse. There were only twenty-five phone numbers on it. The paper was cracked where it had been folded, but I had folded it carefully, so I could read the numbers without trouble. I keep this List between my driver's license and my ATM card. It gives me great comfort. Names are added slowly. This is the List that's at the core of my business.

Matt Whitney is on my List because he wants me to

call him anytime I have some fine American Chippendale furniture. Matt wants the good stuff. So do I, but I can't get my hands on it as often as I'd like. Despite the way I feel about telephones, I call him whenever I can get what he wants. I go out of my way to find what he wants, and Matt goes out of his way to buy what I find for him.

Occasionally people ask to be called whenever you have a certain object they collect. I always agree, and sometimes, if it's convenient for me, I follow through, but usually what people really want when they ask for a call is the right of first refusal. Meaning that when you call them, they want all the details, such as condition, price, measurement, style, and history if there is one, and then they tell you that they don't need that particular thing. These are not List people. What they want is a picker, and I'm no one's picker.

So, when I finally called Matt's number, my mind was aswirl with all sorts of fact and foolishness. I expected to reach Ellie, his secretary, and when the phone was answered by Matt himself, I was so surprised that I didn't know what to say.

"How come you're there?" I asked without introduction.

"It's nine a.m., Lucy. What's on your mind?"

Matt's not interested in any of the long, involved stories I end up telling. I'm not interested in them myself sometimes; it's just that they issue forth, explaining things to me at the same time that I explain them to someone else.

"How did you know it was me so quickly?" I asked.

"Lucy, are you in trouble, or do you have some Chippendale?"

"I have a friend who didn't murder someone," I said, "but the police think he did, and he has no money, and . . ." I would have quavered on, but Matt stopped me. I wanted to be concise, but I was truly quite nervous.

That was when Matt changed. He began to behave in a way that I had never observed in him before. He asked me several questions in a most gentle tone of voice, and he talked to me for the first time ever as if he had all the time in the world. Gone was the interrogating attitude that I had come to expect.

He asked me about my friend, and when we both found out that I didn't know Silent Billy's last name, he didn't make any of his caustic comments, nor did he question my "friendship" with Billy. The only time he seemed to stop cold was when I mentioned Monty's name.

"Monty Rondo?" he repeated. "I knew Monty Rondo. I defended him years ago. I got him off a handling stolen antiques charge when we were both starting out in Worcester."

That was news to me. I told Matt that in the fifteen years I had known him I had never heard anything about Monty being involved with stolen antiques. The antiques world is rife with gossip, and the grapevine is healthy indeed, but I had never heard rumors that would connect him with stolen anything.

"It was more than twenty years ago," Matt said, "and maybe he wasn't guilty, Lucy. Some of the folks I defend are actually innocent." A hint of the more familiar Matt had come creeping back.

"I know, Matt, and I'm sure Silent Billy is one of the innocent. He's a nice quiet guy who does most of the furniture repair and restoration work in Monty's workshop. He does beautiful work."

"A carpenter?" he asked.

"Better. He's more like an ace cabinetmaker. Monty used him for repairing some of the junky used furniture he dug up, but his work is much finer than most of the furniture he gets to work on. As a matter of fact, I think you have a piece, a dining room chair, that he worked on."

"Remind me."

"A late Newport Chippendale with a restored arm. I showed you where he signed it."

"A stylized W?"

"Yes."

"Exquisite workmanship," he said. As a collector, Matt's had more experience with the other side of that problem, fine furniture that has been badly repaired by someone whose work actually cuts the value of the piece.

"Lucy, do you know who murdered Monty?" That came from left field. If I knew who killed Monty I would have gone directly to the police. But, since I didn't want to blight my newfound pal-ship with Matt

Whitney, I answered, sans wisecrack, that I had no idea who killed Monty.

Matt, to my great relief and surprise, said that he was interested in Billy's case. That he would find out if Billy had been charged, and that he would talk to him. I could feel my tension drain away. I had done my duty. I could get back to the treasure hunt.

And that's just what I intended to do, but first I'd go to the police station and let Billy know that a good lawyer was on the way. It wouldn't hurt for me to see what was going on there, just in case. . . .

5

I couldn't recall where the police station was so I asked for directions, and was surprised that it was in Town Hall, less than a mile down Route 20. I decided to walk. Before I set off, I went back to the van and rolled Supercart into it. It was beginning to be a tight squeeze, but it would be easier to move along without it.

I walked through the crowds clustered along Route 20 and sensed a different feeling. Sounds were muffled and people seemed subdued. The dynamics of the place had shifted somewhat, and people seemed to be adjusting. My own sober mood was pierced by qualms as I approached Town Hall.

It's a modest wooden building painted an off shade of peach and trimmed with reddish brown slats. The building evokes a wistful desire to be a model of Victorian architecture, but a number of Tudor effects also decorate its façade. It's neither Victorian nor Tudor.

Like many other confused municipal buildings, it's designed to accommodate the tastes of warring factions that crop up in towns.

I went up the stairs and read the sign fastened to the front door. It announced that the public would *not* be permitted to use the bathroom in this public building. I'd forgotten the attitude. I went in and entered a long, narrow hallway with a high ceiling. The lights were off, but daylight filtered in through dusty windows.

I rummaged around in the hall trying the doors. All locked. I scanned the hundreds of notices posted on the walls. No sign of a police station here. The stairway leading to the second floor ended in a locked door. The building was quiet. Had I misunderstood the directions?

A short stairway led down to an emergency exit at the side of the building, then turned and steeply descended into a basement. A circle of light showed at the foot of the basement stairs.

I went down the stairs and heard sounds of activity. The light came from a door that was ajar. I pulled the handle gently, and the door screamed a hideous creak that announced my arrival. Two heads, behind a high wooden counter, swiveled in my direction. One, swathed in a stiff black beehive, gasped. "How did you get in here?"

She gulped some air and clutched at her narrow breastbone. Her face, in sharp contrast to her inky suede hair, was a shade of white that may never have been exposed to daylight, a slice of ripe Brie.

"Through the front door," I said, pointing toward the general vicinity of the front door. "Can you tell me where the police station is?"

"That door should be locked," she said.

"It's not," I replied, and asked again about the police station. Now I could hear voices and movement coming from a hallway to my left. Maybe it was here after all.

"Normal hours for the police station are seven to nine on Monday evenings," she said.

Huh? "Seven to nine on Monday evenings," I repeated. Today was Tuesday. "The police just took a friend of mine in for questioning." I hesitated, and both women sat up straighter, pursed their lips, and said nothing. "They'll probably want to talk to him today."

The women looked at each other. Then Snow White turned and said, "The police have special hours during Antique Week. If you're going to see the police, you'll have to use the police entrance, in the basement."

"Is it in this building?" I asked.

"That's what I said," she told me. "But you have to go around outside and use the police entrance in the basement." She turned back to her work, and I slipped out of her coven, back into the hallway.

We were in the basement, so the police were probably on the other side of that wall. It might be blocked from here for reasons of security. Or maybe not. I looked around a bit, and was just about to try my luck at another basement door when Snow White poked her head out of the creaking door and said, "This is a private area. Exit by the stairs." She had tuned her voice to the door's pitch, and she didn't need a crack team of attack dwarfs to encourage me to move on.

So, back up and out and around I went. From the bottom of the driveway I saw the large parking lot in back. Except for a dozen or so police cars crammed up close to the back of the building, the lot was empty. The police cars bore an assortment of insignia. A tiny sign near the corner of the building murmured POLICE.

I entered and descended a few stairs into the basement. The room was about five feet wide by ten feet long; in a previous life it had probably been a hallway from the back door to the utility area. Now it was the police station.

The tiny space was filled with official-looking equipment and official-looking people. Maybe two people could work, seated, in the room if they didn't mind tripping over each other to get to their workspace. A television set, tuned to a daytime talk show, played, but no one appeared to be watching it.

Within this space, several policemen and policewomen stood toe to toe. There was no room for any other arrangement. Silent Billy was not in the room.

The conversational rumble in the room made no allowance for eavesdropping. I couldn't pick out anything specific as I worked my way into the mass of people in that small space. I asked a heavily decorated policeman if I could speak to Billy.

"Billy who?" he asked.

"He has white hair and a white beard and I only know him as Silent Billy."

He smiled and said, "He's silent, all right. What do you want him for?"

What should I say?

"I'd like to know if he's been charged with a crime," I said. I meant to be brazen, but my voice sounded timorous as I continued. "And I'd like to pass a message on to him."

We stood maybe five inches apart. He looked straight down at me from his great height. My eyes were level with an elaborate arrangement of ornamentation over his chest, and I caught the ghost of a smirk playing at one side of his mouth. Icy suspicion crept along the back of my neck and slipped down into my spine. He wore his height like a man who believed it was an achievement.

I felt myself slipping into a familiar emotional quagmire. I try not to be overly sensitive about my lack of height. The older I get the easier it is, but sometimes I'm too watchful. I start looking for signals, maybe imaginary signals, that say I'm about to be discounted. Referred to in some diminutive form such as "little lady," the blackboard scraper of my mind.

"So, how do you know Billy?" he said.

"Through Monty. I did business with Monty."

At that moment the outer door opened and two more uniformed policemen entered the tiny room. There was a pause, during which everyone in the room avoided looking at everyone else in the room, which was now crammed. People shifted from one foot to the other, some squaring shoulders, others puffing, making themselves larger somehow, marking territory. My embellished blue knight gave it an instant's thought, and then solved his part of the problem.

"I'll tell you what," he said, without diminutive. "Why don't we just step into the parking lot out there for a minute, and I'll see what I can do for you?" He gestured toward the outer door with one arm and made a sweeping movement toward it with the other. This created the illusion of a pathway. I took my cue and turned toward the door. Everyone near us, realizing that we were leaving, squeezed together slightly, expanding the opening another three inches. He moved toward the door, leading with his shoulder, and I followed in his wake. In a few steps we were out in the brilliant daylight.

"What kind of business did you have with Monty?" he asked, settling his bulk onto the fender of a dark blue Crown Vic and still managing to look down at me.

"Antiques. I had an antiques shop in Worcester for eight years. Antiques is a tight community, and everyone knows everyone. We all know Monty."

"Knew. You knew him," he corrected me.

"He visited me after I moved to the Cape, too. He stopped at antiques shops all over New England."

"When did you last see him?" The brass decorations on his chest sparkled in the sunlight.

"A week ago, maybe more."

"What did you talk about?"

"God, who can remember? Probably—"

"Did you argue?"

"Of course not."

"You don't remember what you said, but you're sure you didn't argue?"

"Oh, Lord." Surely this guy doesn't think . . . No, he doesn't think that at all. He's just being a cop. "I never argued with Monty."

He didn't exactly roll his eyes, but his face managed to convey disbelief. "I heard Monty argued with everyone," he said. "Was there some particular reason why you're the only person in the universe that he never argued with?"

As I stood in the parking lot, the bright spring sunshine had, at first, warmed me, but now I felt my body slip into overheat. I hate this. A *flash*. My ears sizzle. A spot in the center of my chest spreads heat lightning outward until sweat spreads dampness as far as it can, and I'm covered with a warm clamminess.

He was serious. My face, neck, and ears were fried to a crisp, and I was irritated as well as hot. I stiffened my neck, aligning it with my already straight spine, and said, "I know I didn't argue with Monty then, because I never argued with Monty, ever. And I know any number of people who never argued with Monty." Why isn't he out chasing bad guys?

"Any number, huh?"

"Yes," I said firmly. Heat still radiated from me, but it was coming under control now. This guy expected some explanation regarding why I was here to see Billy.

"Your relationship with Billy . . ."

"I don't have a relationship with Billy. He's a friend of mine."

That stopped him. It stopped me, too. The sweating had made me feel uncomfortable, but there was no need for me to be intimidated by this sparkling fellow in uniform. So why was I babbling inanities? I squared my shoulders. I felt my bones locking together in the process that turns me rigid.

It took all of my concentration to speak quietly, and slowly, and to remember not to clench my teeth. "I mean, he's a nice man that I know. A good person. He was usually with Monty, or doing some errand for Monty, and *that's* how I know him."

"That's your motive," he said.

"My motive?" He's off his rocker.

"Hey, you got your disgruntled employees out there, killing people all over the place. Monty didn't have a wife to kill him, did he? So Billy's *my* candidate. He's a good one, too. That's my position."

He paused for a second, moved his bulk off the Crown Vic, and nodded his head. But I knew he hadn't changed his position. I'd just heard him work that theory out, and I still couldn't quite believe it.

"Has he been charged?" I couldn't even say "with murder."

"Hmmm? Well, I'll tell you what. I'll have you wait in this here parking lot, and I'll go back inside and check out the situation. Why don't you stay here and I'll get right back to you."

He went into the building. Relief skimmed through me. I needed a minute or two to myself to figure out the right way to approach this thing. Maybe it made a certain kind of sense for him to believe that Billy was guilty. All I needed to do was point out the flaws in his thinking.

Maybe he'd come to his senses. I walked the length of the parking lot, pulling long breaths of fresh air into my lungs. I paced back to the spot where he'd left me. I worked out questions I hadn't thought to ask. I mentally scripted the way our conversation should have gone, the way I wanted it to go when he returned.

I stood for a while, and then I paced for a while. I conducted an animated conversation with myself. Yes, this whole mess could be worked out. I'd help the police figure it out. All I needed to do was figure it out myself. That's where I ran out of steam, and where I noticed that half an hour had passed since the Big Sparkler had returned to the police station. I went back inside.

He was embroiled in an intense conversation with a fellow wearing plain clothes and an attitude that said "in charge." I couldn't hear them over the rumble of talk within the room, but I could see that they were serious. Sparkles gave the appearance of listening intently. The new man pointed his finger, jabbing it toward Sparkles's chest. He did most of the talking.

Sparkles nodded affirmatively. Definitely in a deferential position, I thought. I took this for a good sign and began to form the points I wanted to make when I met the new man. He'd probably welcome my thoughtful analysis after speaking with Sparkles.

I worked my way over to them. They both turned toward me. I detected the slightest bit of annoyance at the interruption.

"This here's your dowager lady, from the parking lot," Sparkles said.

Dowager lady?

The new cop shot me a smile that flashed on and off in an instant. I prepared to speak. He beat me to it.

"We transferred your pal over to the state police as soon as he arrived here, ma'am. He was out of here an hour ago."

I was astonished. "But he's not guilty," I said.

He nodded his head once, flashed his on-off smile again, and said, "Thank you for bringing that to my attention, little lady."

He turned back to Sparkles. I was dismissed.

6

When I left the police station I decided against taking the time to get Supercart from the van. I had lost an hour, missed some of the best action in the fields, and worse, I had missed coffee with Natalie. I headed toward the Patio in case she had lingered, visiting with anyone there. I needed to figure out what to do next. Coffee might help.

There are few restaurants in Brimfield during the other forty-nine weeks of the year, but when the antiquers converge, a wide variety of temporary food enterprises surface. Not too many years ago your only choice in cuisine was the toppings offered for your hot dogs. Now, ethnic, exotic, and a wide variety of deep-fried foods are featured everywhere.

Attempts at serving healthful offerings are becoming popular, too, but snacks totally devoid of nutrients still do the best business. Food is served from the trucks and tents and temporary stands scattered throughout the fields. They stand alone or cluster together in twos, threes, or more. Some offer seating, and part of the Patio's appeal is that you can sit and visit awhile. It's a good place to gather.

At the Patio, a wagon train of food trucks circles the edge of a pebbled parking lot. Picnic tables and an assortment of other outdoor furniture fill the space within. Some of the tables sport umbrellas. The Patio is comfortable when the weather is good.

Nothing at Brimfield is comfortable when the weather is bad. Fortunately, it's rarely bad during the selling season. Rainfalls, high winds, occasional snow flurries, and ice storms are forgotten the instant the treasure hunt resumes. Today was balmy, developing into one of those glorious spring days that fatten a poet's portfolio.

As I got closer, the smell of food whetted my appetite and I realized that I was hungry. I had left the sandwiches with the kid in the parking lot when I was still stunned by the murder, but now my stomach was sending messages about not being fed since the coffee on the drive here at two thirty this morning.

The day was getting away from me.

When I reached the Patio, I didn't see Natalie, and I stood at the truck with the shortest line. One couple was ahead of me, a matched set. They were of similar shape: pearoid, with low centers of gravity. Both wore black sweatpants and sweatshirts printed with pink poodles. They carried large nylon tote bags embossed with dancing pink poodles. Both wore visored caps embroidered in pink poodlery. She wore earrings from which pink poodles dangled. His ears were nude.

They gave the man in the truck a complicated order that called for deep-frying spiced chicken wings, but without the batter that was the specialty de la GMC. The wings were to be accompanied by what sounded like batter-dipped, fried sneaker sandwiches.

The man who took their order grunted and without comment began preparing it. While he worked, they discussed their safety in the wake of today's murder. The woman was fearful. I wondered who she was and eavesdropped.

"We should leave. This place is creeping me out," she said.

"Let's not be hasty," he said. "We've come this far, so we might as well see what's being offered."

"Murder is what's being offered," she said. "And I'm not risking my life, or my collection, with some nut running around murdering people."

She felt that Brimfield was dangerous because of Monty's murder. The man appeared to realize that while it had certainly proved dangerous to Monty, the murderer was unlikely to drift by in the sunlight, randomly strangling yet more victims.

Minding my own business has always been difficult for me. I had just about decided to keep my mouth shut when the woman turned around, looked at me, and said, "Aren't you afraid to be here alone?"

I knew I should respond sensibly, but I had used up

any sense I had left back at the police station. I knew she needed reassurance about her safety, but I couldn't think of anything reasonable to say, and the most neutral response I could dredge up was a lie. "I'm sorry. I've been daydreaming."

"Don't you know there's a murderer running around loose here?" the husband asked.

Whatever happened to "let's not be hasty"? They both looked at me. None of this was their fault. I wondered if a diversion might be a good tactic to keep me out of trouble. Diversions don't work on my kids anymore, but occasionally I can still sidetrack my husband with them. I asked if they were poodle collectors or pink poodle collectors. I hit pay dirt, because their concerns about danger and murder were set aside, and both responded to my non sequitur.

"We're pink now," she drowned him out. "We began with anything poodlish, twenty-three years ago, but we've had to specialize in pink because we've run out of space twice."

"Did you buy a bigger home?" I asked, managing not to smirk.

"We put an addition on our first home, but when we ran out of space again, we decided it would be easier to move rather than to build another addition."

Mrs. Poodle described the changes in their homes as their collection grew. Her husband continued speaking at the same time. I couldn't quite hear his words, but every so often he repeated his leitmotif, "Our house is a museum."

I smiled a lot and murmured comments like, "How true" and "*um-hmmm*." I didn't know which face to focus on; they both looked at me while they spoke.

I realized that I had opened myself up for further enlightenment in the Art of the Poodle, and I gazed around the Patio looking for an out. Within my view were a few people I knew, and one of them was heading my way.

"Lucy," he said, his rich voice carrying from several tables away.

John Wilson could have stepped out of an ad from a gentleman's magazine. As always. His features are plain but his grooming and attire are meticulously detailed, in the tweedy manner of the English soap operas on PBS. His look evokes an image of fine old museums, and in fact, he is a curator at the Jeffries Jade Museum. The Jeffries is a little too new and a little too small to suit him for long. Wilson moves from museum to museum.

New England is loaded with wonderfully esoteric little museums. Wilson has worked, in various capacities, at a number of them, always moving upward. These museums are generally endowed by someone with scads of money, but on occasion they're founded by someone who is merely eccentric.

The founder of Wilson's current museum, Conrad Jeffries, may have been both, but his extravagant bequests have culturally enriched a number of communities in New England. It's located in a depressed mill town north of Boston, which assures that Wilson will be off to greener pastures before too long.

I was surprised to see him here. Generally, when I bumped into him these days, it was likely to be at one of the high-toned auction houses. I visit them regularly, to see what's going under the hammer in the big time. I also like to see who's buying. It gets harder all the time to figure out who's really buying. Even the new rich are getting cagey. But I'm good at it.

Wilson, with a healthy budget from his trustees, didn't have to set his refined foot into Brimfield's bedlam. He was very likely doing the same thing here that I do at the swanky auctions: checking out the trends, watching the movers and shakers. He's not exactly a snob, but I think Brimfield is a bit uncivilized for his tidy nature. I suspect that he may not care for the salt-of-the-earth flavor of the place.

I'd sensed, over time, that he's not able to make up his mind about my flavor, either. He often finds me invisible, but not today. Today he must have noticed my transition into dowagership.

He took my hand. His smile, practiced and professional, swept over the three of us at the stand. He leaned toward me and spoke softly.

"Natalie was looking for you," he said. "She left just after I arrived, about fifteen minutes ago."

"Damn." I never should have waited for that silly cop.

Mrs. Poodle stood back and admired Wilson openly,

taken with his well-cultivated looks and the charming way he was able to dismiss her with a smile; she even nodded her approval to me.

"I missed her," I said.

"We only spoke briefly," he said. "She seemed unsettled, distracted."

"Did she say why?" I asked. She was probably upset with me.

"Who knows with Natalie," he said. "She runs hot and cold."

"Oh?" I wondered briefly if he was one of her rejected swains, but I was saved from asking.

Mrs. Poodle, smiling hugely, tapped Wilson on the arm and advised him that he shouldn't leave me here alone, that she had just been warning me about the murderer.

Wilson turned to her, surprised by the intrusion. He took in her full measure, and I watched him decide to bestow some of his grace on her.

"Let me assure you, my dear," he said, "that we are all safe from the murderer."

His declaration took the rest of us by surprise, and we sent up a dissonant chorus of "Whys?"

Wilson replied gently, his pleasure at being the bearer of glad tidings evident, that the murderer was now safe in police custody and that we could all rest easy. Oh, God, he meant Silent Billy.

Just then the man in the truck handed their order out to the Poodles. I glanced at the sandwiches. There actually could have been a sneaker under all that puffy batter.

I began to explain that Billy didn't do it. But the Poodles, who seemed overjoyed with Wilson for bringing news of their safety, were thanking him, as if he had single-handedly captured some lunatic mass murderer who'd been chasing them. Wilson was accepting his due. I was invisible.

The Poodles scampered happily over to a table and pounced on their chow. I stood transfixed.

"Why did you do that?"

"Do what?" he asked.

"Why did you lead them to believe that the murderer was Silent Billy?"

"Good Lord, Lucy, the police caught him—they have him in custody. I'm sure they've found out how badly Monty treated Billy. I wanted to assure those poor souls that they were safe, that we're all safe."

"Billy didn't kill Monty," I said.

Wilson's eyebrows rose. "What on earth makes you say that?" he said.

He walked away shaking his head when I replied, "I just know it, that's all."

7

Silent Billy was in big trouble if the rest of the world were as easily convinced of his guilt as those three. I turned back to the food truck and saw that several new people were now in front of me in the line. I was ready to begin squawking a loud objection when I noticed a fluttering from the side of my eye.

It was Baker Haskins waving a napkin at me. Baker was mouthing my name, too, as if calling me, but, with his mouth full of food, his calls were a pantomime. He was *silently* calling me and waving his napkin from several trucks away. The fact that he had caught my attention this way tapped a vein of silliness in me, and this chipped a crack in my bad humor.

Baker is fascinating. He's the subject of much conjecture in the antiques world, and in other worlds as well. I strolled over to where he stood. He's a tall, awkward-looking man, and he was eating a huge piece of pastry. It was shaped like a cow patty and had been liberally dusted with powdered sugar. As Baker nibbled one end of the pastry, the other end sprinkled powder over the front of his clothes. The sugar did no damage; it merely masked previous spillings. It looked like he'd been here awhile, but that was not so, and it turned out that he had missed Natalie, too.

Baker is one of the few friends that Hamp and I share, but know separately. Hamp knows him from the halls of academe, and me from our shared passion for antiques. Well, we know him together, too, but it's a different relationship than with our other friends. Hamp has little interest in antiques, and I have little interest in intellectual pursuit, and Baker thrives on both.

For almost thirty years we've enjoyed his company as if he were another couple, perfectly matched to us. Somehow, when he's been one-half of an actual couple, it hasn't worked. We'd seen less of him both times he'd been married. But when he was single, as now, and as most of the time, we saw him often.

He wore a wide-brimmed straw planter's hat that shaded his pale eyes and protected his huge shining head from the sun. Numerous bags hung from straps crisscrossing his chest and shoulders.

"I didn't want to lose my place in line," he explained with his mouth still full, "and anyway, you were in the wrong line, Lucy."

"Why?" I asked.

"Because the food over there tastes like an old

sneaker, and because that's where Wilson caught up with you."

"So what do you prescribe, Dr. Haskins?" I asked.

He was, after all, a doctor of the PhD variety. He had, I knew, a collection of PhDs.

"I recommend the souvlaki and a chat," he said. "Eating and talking will make you feel better, and it'll give me a better feeling for what's really been going on around here." Bits of pastry flew from his mouth and sugar continued to drift into the air between us as we progressed to the front of the smoothly moving line.

Baker ordered for both of us, then popped the last bit of cow patty into his mouth. He told me that when he'd arrived at Brimfield, barely fifteen minutes before, he'd heard rumors of the murder. He'd then spoken to a police officer directing traffic. The cop told him that Billy had been taken into custody, charged with murder, and handed over to the state police.

I'd been buzzing around Town Hall for over an hour, killing precious time, learning nothing, and Baker had stood on Route 20 for a few minutes getting the official story. We carried our food over to an empty table, and I asked Baker what he meant by the Wilson crack.

"Not much," he said. "He's been overbearing when I've worked with him, but as long as he stays out of my face I can handle it."

"You guys work together?"

"Occasionally. Museum galas, fund-raisers, that sort of thing. Temporary situations. The man has trouble letting go," he said.

I nodded. "He had no trouble letting go of me," I said.

"A run-in?" Baker asked.

"A misunderstanding. When we first moved here I answered a call for volunteers for the Storybook Ball. I presented myself to Wilson, told him that I'd been a board member, a fund-raiser, and a very active volunteer at the Ruby Museum. The man fell all over himself welcoming me to the fold."

"Sounds like a good beginning."

"Well, it turns out that Wilson mistook me for a heavy donor type of fund-raiser. When he realized that the Ruby was a tiny museum that our local historical society had put together to honor the memory of the Ruby family, and that our fund-raising consisted of bake sales, car washes, and flea markets, he dropped me with a thud."

Baker laughed. I joined him, but in fact I had been embarrassed, and could still feel the sting of being dropped all those years ago.

"He raises funds for a number of good causes," he said.

"Yes, and to give the devil his due, I've found him to be pretty knowledgeable about antiques," I said.

"Don't count on everything he tells you," Baker said. "He has a need to be seen as an expert, but he's lazy. If he'd cut out the Machiavellian behavior, and worked a little harder at actually learning something, he could be a true authority."

When we were seated he crossed his long legs and

said, "So, what gives?" I filled him in on what I knew about the murder and Billy's trouble. He nodded and chomped and sipped until I wound down. It turned out that he was right; I did feel better eating and unloading my feelings.

"I agree with you, Lucy. The police have the wrong man. Silent Billy doesn't have it in him to harm anyone."

"I'm sure that sooner or later the police will realize that," I said. "But in the meantime Billy's in trouble."

"Don't be so sure the police will discover their mistake, Lucy. When they have a suspect, they've been known to build a case around him."

"They can't—" I bit the words off. I know they can. They didn't know Billy. If they believed he was guilty, why should they look for someone else.

"I saw Billy just yesterday," he said. "When he delivered a candlestand to my office."

"Something Monty picked for you?"

"I'm not sure," he said.

We finished the last morsels of our yogurt-soaked bread at the same time and leaned back to savor the rest of the coffee.

I reached into my purse for some foil-wrapped wet napkins to wipe our fingers, and Baker reached into one of his bags for a cigarette. I held my tongue about the smoking. Baker is an adult. I had a tired old speech about the evils of smoking, but I had listened to myself once, and it stunk worse than the smoke.

"I used to ask if people minded if I smoked," he said, "but now that the whole world has seen fit to become sanctimonious about it, I've quit asking. Besides, this is a roller-coaster business for many of us, Lucy, and smoking helps to even out the jolts."

I suppressed a laugh. It's true that we're in a wildly bumpy business, but Baker is well cushioned from jolts. He's richer than God. He has old money and new money and in-between money, and he has lots of it. The media records its fluctuations. Baker manages the managers who manage his money, but he finds none of it as interesting as antiques.

Baker's true love is his *Learned Informer's Antiques Review*, a trade newspaper that he founded, on a whim, when he was still in school, years ago. The *LIAR*, as it calls itself, chronicles the happenings in the antiques world with more excitement and wit than is usually found in the antiques trade's press. It is a weekly newspaper, and though it is heavily subscribed to, and packed with advertising, its likely contribution to Baker's wealth is minor compared to his other assets.

"Did he say that the candlestand was something you always coveted?" I asked. That was one of Monty's standard marketing ploys.

"No, that's what I expected when he called, but it's a Shaker piece, and I've never collected Shaker furniture. So he must have been telling the truth. Unless he developed a new selling technique."

"What do you mean, 'telling the truth'?" I asked.

"Well, Monty called me early yesterday and told me he had something he wanted me to see. I tried to dust him off, Lucy. I don't want any more stuff. I'm trying to weed out, and get rid of my extra stuff, so I discouraged him."

I nodded. I knew that nothing could discourage Monty, but I also knew that Baker was always trying to "weed out" his extra stuff.

"Did he tell you to reserve judgment until you saw it?" I asked.

"That's what I expected, but he was very mysterious, told me he only wanted me to hold the piece for him, that I couldn't *buy* it if I wanted it. He said that he'd try to deliver it personally."

That certainly sounded like a new gambit for Monty. "But he sent Silent Billy instead?"

"Yes, and naturally Billy didn't say a word about it. He came in, put it in my office, tipped his cap, the way he does, and left."

"Was there anything unusual about the candlestand?"

"I don't think so, Lucy. I hardly looked at it. It doesn't fit in with my other furnishings, so I wasn't interested."

We sat quietly for a minute and thought it over.

"I wonder if it has anything to do with his murder. Do you think it could, Lucy?" he asked.

"Baker, I think he was murdered for his wad of cash, and I think that the candlestand is just a candlestand.

It's something that Monty thought when you saw it, you would want it."

"But Shaker isn't me," he said.

"Baker, you're all over the place. It's hard to predict what you'll be into from one week to the next."

He smiled sheepishly. "You're right, Lucy, but I'll give it another look-see when I go back to the office tonight, to figure out why he found it so interesting."

With that settled, he turned to other issues. "Would you like anything for dessert? There's a strawberry shortcake stand."

"No, you enjoy it, Baker. I've just missed another opening. I'd better be on my way. I'm sure I'll bump into you regularly this week."

"Believe it. I'll be here every day. Are you planning the picnic for Friday?"

I hadn't been planning the picnic at all. The picnic had expanded. Once a pleasant little luncheon among friends, it had lately taken on the features of a big-time tradition, and for me it's become cumbersome. When it was smaller, just half a dozen or so of us, we'd gather up food from the marketplace, squeeze into someone's car, and find a nice spot to stop and eat.

Friday afternoon is a great time for visiting. We entertain one another with stories of the monstrosities and masterpieces we've spotted around the fields. We compare *this* Brimfield with previous Brimfields. We socialize. It is a nice way to visit and gather energy before the arrival of the amateurs over the weekend.

Lately, though, I spend more time and energy on the preparations. Scouting a place takes time. It has to be conveniently located, but suitable for accommodating at least fifteen, sometimes closer to twenty of us. And with interest growing, there is another problem: With the increasing crowd we have to choose a place that's public property.

When it was a smaller event, we'd often picnicked on privately owned land. We'd feasted, visited, and carried out our trash in the same bags we'd brought the food in, leaving little or no sign that we'd been there. No one had ever raised an eyebrow at us. Now, just carrying out the trash had become a major job.

All of this finding, and fetching, and carrying has traditionally been done by me, with help from Mr. Hogarth. It takes time and expends energy. By Friday I usually find that my time, and my energy, are lagging a bit. I try not to show it, since Mr. Hogarth, more than thirty years my senior, takes it all in stride. But I've been finding it tiring. Not to mention that with all of the housekeeping duties, I do less visiting, and visiting is my main reason for having the picnic in the first place.

"I'm not sure I even want to bother this year, Baker." I was about to explain, when his expression stopped me.

"That's where I hear my best reports of the Spring Brimfield," he said. "That's where I decide what tone to take in writing about the events here. Why, that little picnic mirrors the Brimfield phenomenon exactly."

He couched his words in theatrical body language, but I could see grievance in his face, hear plaint in his voice.

Rats. I liked the picnic, too. But with the added preparations and cleanup, it was getting to be more work and less play than I wanted.

"Okay, Baker, fine. You want the picnic, we'll have the picnic, but you, and anyone else who shows up, will have to get involved in the preparations."

"Okay."

"I mean it, Baker, I'm getting too tired to put that sort of thing together."

"Okay, I'll help."

"Just a nice, simple picnic. That's all I'm up for, Baker. No extravaganza."

"Sounds good to me."

"What sounds good?" I asked, suddenly interested.

"Helping with the arrangements," he answered. "I've wanted to get involved, but you've been so proprietary about it that I didn't want to usurp your turf."

Proprietary?

"Friday afternoon?" he asked, grinning.

"That's still a good time. We can firm up the details as the week progresses." That satisfied him.

I gathered myself together and took my leave. In fact, the picnic was a fun event. Sheesh! I liked it, too. I'd walked halfway to my destination when I remembered that I'd forgotten to ask Baker if he knew anything about that old trouble that Matt had handled for Monty long ago. I'd ask him next time.

On my way, I stopped at a mover who works the Brimfield show. I've used him regularly to move my heavy furniture into my storage space. He turned me down for a better deal on a long haul. I'd have to look for another mover later.

8

I'd missed the opening minutes at Dealer's Choice, and the best finds would be gone, so I walked toward my parking lot intending to pick up Supercart. People crowded the paths on both sides of the road. Route 20 danced with color and movement.

Things were somewhat of a jumble in the back of the van. A pair of old wooden shutters, in an Art Deco style, leaned against Supercart. I pushed them back with one hand and jiggled Supercart's handle with the other, to free it. In the process I grazed an elaborate metal floor lamp, and its arm hooked over Supercart's other side. Irritated, I gave Supercart's handle a jerk rather than take the time to free it manually.

The lamp instantly came loose, and the sudden motion sent Supercart, and me, sprawling out the back of the van and onto the ground. I landed on my bad hip and struggled to get to my feet before an audience gathered, but I was too late.

"What's going on?" It was Coylie, the parking attendant.

"I'm resting on the ground here, gazing at my cart." I heard the sharpness in my voice. What did he think I was doing?

"I heard a yelp that sounded like trouble."

Mortified, I dismissed the incident as I struggled to one knee.

"Are you hurt?" He held a hand out and helped me to my feet. "Come over to my office and sit a minute."

The kid wanted to help. Supercart looked okay, so I limped along behind him, brushing the dirt from my clothes and checking my landing site cautiously, subtly.

He'd added an old spool table between his lawn chairs: his office. I sat in the chair he indicated, shifting my weight to the right as I did so.

"I'm fine, really. It's the day that's all wrong. The murder and Billy's arrest. Then I managed to make it worse by missing a friend in need, botching a moving problem, and falling."

"Well, you have plenty of company. I'm lower than whale shit myself," he said. "Oops, sorry." He began fumbling an apology.

"This is a bad day," I said.

"Make that a week," he raised me.

"How about a lifetime?" I offered, getting into it.

"We could rue the day we'd ever been born," he said, grinning.

"I'm no good at ruing, and the day I was born was probably one of my better ones. But, okay, I give up. It's been rough for you, too. So what's your complaint?" I asked. Might as well give him a chance to whine, too.

He swung himself out of his lawn chair, hesitated a moment, rubbed his palm against his chin, then began pacing.

"I'm not going to make it in this business," he said. "And I'll never survive if I don't do it here."

"What business?" Running this parking lot's not much of a career. The kid seemed bright; he had a lot going for him; he'd find something better.

"This business, antiques," he said, gesturing around us, waving his arms wide. "I'll have nothing. I'll be nothing."

"How are you in the antiques business?" I had missed some vital part of his problem.

"I'm here for the flea market. The parking lot just earns me a little survival money until Thursday."

"Aha! Thursday. I'll bet you want a place at May's, and you didn't reserve it ages ago, so when you got here all of their spaces were taken."

That field is a top draw at Brimfield. About six hundred dealers sell there, many of whom have kept those spaces for years. And there's a waiting list of names lined up to take the place of anyone who drops out.

I dismissed his problem. "It's not the end of the

world," I said. "There are plenty of other places to sell from. Lots of good places are still available."

"That's not quite my problem," he said.

"Well, you've got a whole lifetime," I prattled on. "You're young. I wouldn't worry about it if I were you."

"I'm twenty-two. And age is not my problem."

"Oh?"

He paused and pulled the bill of his cap down over his eyes, releasing bright orange curls that sprang from the back of his head. He leaned his head back and looked out at me from under the cap's deep arch.

"No, in fact, I do have a spot at May's, and I managed to get it without reserving in advance, and I'm still twenty-two years old." He looked at me.

Cocky. Was he bluffing? "How did you do that?" I asked.

"Guy I know, Frankie, claims he's doing me a big favor. He's full of big favors, old Frankie." Coylie pulled his cap off and tossed it from hand to hand. "Gonna show me the ropes, gonna help me out, gonna put me on the map. Left me in the lurch this morning."

"What happened?" I asked.

"I moved some of his stuff here from Scottsdale, where I met him at a flea market. Frankie's been in the business a long time, and he had some great advice. I've been struggling to make it, and he gave me some good ideas."

"Sounds okay so far," I said.

"It sounded good to me, too. I'd help him drag his stuff here, and help open his booth."

"Then he'd let you sell your stuff from his booth?"

The kid grinned. "Yeah, how'd you know?"

"Half of the folks here have that deal," I said. "So, you agreed. That still sounds good to me."

"Yeah, both of us would make out."

"But what?"

"But he had to leave here in a hurry this morning. He didn't want to lose his spot by turning it back in. So he sublet it to me. I'm taking it in his name."

"What a break," I told him. "That field has hundreds of buyers lined up. They wait in line for hours for that field to open. He did you a favor."

"I'm not so sure," he said. "I'm here alone, and Frankie has my cell phone, and most of my cash."

"Do you mean that he took it without asking?"

"No, he asked for it as a loan. I'm to pay myself back when I sell some of his inventory."

"Coylie, that seems fair enough. That field is a premium place to sell antiques."

"But their rules," he said. "I just read the rules Frankie gave me, and they're impossible."

They do have rules. They even have some enforcement.

"But sellers love that field," I said. "They come back again and again. There must be a way to keep within the rules and sell your stuff without having to quit the business."

"I wish," he said. "But the silliest rule is the one they seem most serious about."

"Which one is that?"

"The one that says that I can't set up and unpack my stuff until after the buyers have been let in. Meaning that I'm unpacking my truck, and setting up for display, while customers pile up in front of me. I can't do that. I have to at least set up my tent in advance, so I can get my inventory where the customers can see it, and I can see them."

"But, Coylie, the buyers know you'll be setting up."

"Yeah, right," he said. "And they'll be right there to take advantage of the chaos."

"It is chaotic. That's part of the fun."

"You call that fun? The sellers aren't even allowed to set up the damned tents until the customers arrive. Then we can take our stuff out of the truck and display it. What if it's raining? I've got Frankie's paintings and my rugs to display. I have jewelry to show. Am I supposed to do that in the rain, with a crowd piling up in front of me? This place will be a mud hole in five minutes."

"Well, the same rules apply to everyone."

"Well, I'm not everyone." He had been pacing back and forth in front of me, and now he threw himself back into his lawn chair. "I can't do it, and I can't afford to have a helper. I can barely make it myself, and antiques are supposed to be my livelihood, what I've committed to."

He looked miserable. "What made you choose antique shows, Coylie?"

"I've noticed," he said, holding up a hand and counting on his fingers, "that you can get into the antique business without having any diplomas. That you don't need to pass any tests. That you don't need a license, and you don't need a lot of cash to get started." He raised his eyebrows and looked at me for verification.

I nodded; everyone thinks they can be an antiques dealer. "That's technically accurate, but it's not exactly the whole story." This business is loaded with people who jump in without experience. Then jump out soon after, when they've had "bad luck."

"You're thinking about experience? Reputation?" he asked. "I figure I'll gain plenty of experience following the flea market circuit, and I can build a good reputation, too. Not only that, I can look around, see if there's anyplace I'd like to settle, when it comes time to settle down."

It sounded like a plan. I wondered if the kid had an interest in a particular type of antique, or had just decided, out of the blue, to be in the antiques business.

"What kind of antiques do you like?" I asked.

"That's easy," he said. "I like old Navajo rugs, and I like Navajo jewelry. As a matter of fact, I like just about any kind of Indian jewelry. The old stuff, mostly, but I occasionally pick up something new, if it has a particularly good design."

"I like jewelry myself," I said. I'm not too familiar with Indian jewelry, but I know people who love it and collect it. "Anything else?" I asked.

"I pick up punched tinware when I can find it, especially lamps and lanterns."

He thought a moment and told me that he collected other things as he came across them, with leanings toward rustic furnishings.

"The jewelry is a particular problem," he said. "Some of it is valuable, and most of my bankroll is tied up in it. I'm afraid to turn my back on it while I set up the rest of my inventory." He looked deflated.

"How would it be if you did have a helper?" I asked.

"I told you, I can't afford a helper," he said.

"I heard you, but if I volunteered to help you out, at least during the unpacking and setting-up stage, would it help?"

"God, I can't ask that," he said. His face flushed and he looked embarrassed.

"You're not asking me. I'm volunteering," I said.

I gave him my best smile, a pillar of innocence, hiding, I hoped, the hidden agenda that had instantly occurred to me. There's a rule against dealers selling to anyone, including other dealers, before a field opens. But enforcement is tricky, and if buyer and seller are subtle enough, a few quiet deals can be made without fear of trouble.

Coylie was overjoyed. I savored the moment. I'd be inside the field before it opened, before legitimate buyers were allowed in. I couldn't believe my luck. Sure I'd help the kid.

"So what's your moving problem?" he asked.

Startled out of my selfish reverie, I turned my attention to the problem of moving the furniture.

"I have some furniture stashed around the fields. Things I've bought and paid for. There's too much to fit in the van. When I don't have my regular helper with me I usually hire one of the movers that hangs out here. I have him cart it over to a friend's barn nearby. But he balked on the small load that I've gathered so far today, and made a deal taking another load on a long haul."

"When do you have to move it?"

"Sooner is always better," I said. "Dealers hold a large piece, paid for in advance of course, for a short time, but real estate is too valuable here. They usually want to replace a sold piece with inventory stockpiled on their trucks."

"Well, you've already paid for it, so it's pretty safe," he said with a big grin. "What are they going to do if you don't come back fast enough to suit them? Sell it to someone else?"

"Yes," I said. "That happens."

I watched the grin on his face freeze as dismay snatched it away. Now it was my turn to laugh.

"Yes, it's true," I said. "Sometimes if the dealer is ornery enough, and if he has an interested buyer, he'll sell an item he's already sold to you."

"They can't do that," he sputtered.

"They can, and they do," I said. "And sometimes it goes fast, especially if you've bought something very special. Say you've only left it for a few minutes while you go back for your vehicle. Another buyer may ask the dealer how much you paid, then offer a higher price. Bada-bing, it's all over."

"That has to be illegal," he said. "It's unethical; it's irresponsible."

"Maybe it is, Coylie, but try and make a case of it."

"But if you paid for it, and they give it to someone else, that's gotta be illegal!"

"Oh, they give you your money back, and sometimes with apologies that may be sincere." Maybe. But I'm sure I've also seen the smirks of a sly deal on occasion.

"I have a truck," he said. "I'll give you a hand."

"Oh, Coylie, no. I'm sorry. I wasn't angling for your help, truly. I'm sure I can get a mover. I just hate to pay top dollar for the pitiful load I was able to gather today."

"You're not asking me. I'm volunteering," he said, repeating my earlier words. "I can't take big loads, because my truck is full of Frankie's stuff."

"If it's full, how can you carry my stuff?"

"Easy. When Frankie had to leave, we tossed a lot of his stuff into my truck, without arranging it. If I take the time to rearrange it, I'll end up with lots of space."

I hesitated. I truly didn't want to exploit the kid any further. Our deal for Thursday was already nudging my guilt button. I was about to put my foot down about moving when he interrupted my thoughts.

"How about you pay me? I won't gouge you. We won't be able to tell who's doing who the favor here."

"Perfect."

"I get off at two," he said. "I'd like to be back here by four o'clock, to get paid for another job."

We firmed up the time, the place, and the price. Revived, I grabbed Supercart and headed toward Dealer's Choice. I was far too late for the opening; I'd be going in just when everyone else was halfway through their second run.

I rambled through the field, trying to keep my mind on what was going on around me, but I couldn't get into it, and considered quitting for the day. When I saw Mr. Hogarth at the coffee stand, I joined him, and in telling him that I had Coylie lined up to help me move my things, I had a flash of insight. What a match those two would be for each other!

And I was right, so the day turned a little better, and I did fairly well at the one o'clock opening. No one-of-a-kind treasure fell into my hands, but I did acquire some first-quality stuff that suited my shop perfectly.

My second run-through was also productive, and it took the curse off the rest of my day at Brimfield. I had acquired far less than usual for the first day of the spring show, but the worst was behind me, and I could now concentrate on the treasure hunt.

I was back to Coylie before two, and helped him finish consolidating things in his truck. He packed it right up to the roof. My role was merely to hold a stack in place while he fastened it with straps and netting to keep it from falling when the truck moved. This arrangement opened up plenty of space.

"Is this yours?" I asked, as he stacked some of the inventory in the truck.

"The painted woodenware is Frankie's. It's not his thing, but he carries it because it's available, and it sells. Artwork is what he likes to carry. Southwestern art. That's packed tight at the other end of the truck."

I took a close look at the woodenware, signs, decorations, and weather vanes painted in what must have once been bright colors. The even patina didn't look right to me. It looked "antiqued."

"Is this old?" I asked.

"It depends," he said. "The wooden pieces are old, but the paint is new."

I wondered how the folks that run May's would like that. With all of their rules, they've fought the good fight to keep it an *antiques* marketplace. At one time, there was more effort to keep the whole Brimfield market vetted. To keep the goods sold here if not antique, then at least collectible.

Though their efforts were not completely successful, it has kept out most of the tube socks people and their ilk.

He showed me some of his inventory, and would have showed me more, but he was concerned about the time.

"So, what happened? Why'd Frankie have to rush home?" I asked.

"He didn't say," Coylie said. "But it was probably lady trouble," he said. "Frankie has a lot of lady trouble."

The truck was organized, and we had plenty of free space ready, so we set out to collect the items I had waiting around the fields. We made such quick work of it that Coylie insisted on driving over to show me the field where "our" space would be on Thursday morning.

That field is surrounded by chain-link fence, but today it was a simple matter to drive in. There were no guards, no paperwork to show, just a large empty grassy field with a few small outbuildings on it. He pointed out the spot where we would set up on Thursday. It was a great location, on a main path, not too far from the back gate, on the parking lot side.

We both admired the spot, and we agreed that if Thursday was a clear day, we wouldn't even bother putting up the tent until after the first rush was over. We'd just pull the stuff out of the truck and put it on the ground, maybe lay it out on his Navajo rugs.

"Okay, Coylie, let's go see Al Finn," I said.

9

Al Finn. She hated "Althea" and had us call her Alyssa, Athena, Tina, and who can remember what else. I've known her since grammar school. I can't remember the precise year we met, but I've known her longer than anyone who's not a member of my family.

"An old friend," I said.

Except that I hadn't felt too friendly toward her back then. As a matter of fact, if I were forced to tell the truth, I'd say that I was more than a little bit envious of her. But who's going to force me to tell the truth?

"I was a little envious of her when we were young," I said.

Coylie grinned, slammed the van door shut, and said, "You were young."

I nodded and eased the van out to the edge of the driveway, where I waited until he pulled up behind me. Then we drove toward Al's B&B, just over the town line. The van hummed, and as we turned off the highway I thought about Al.

By high school, she had become a willowy, honey-colored wisp, with huge liquid brown eyes. "Ethereal" would have described her had I felt comfortable using the word back then. Friends were enthralled, and adults were warmed by her sunny countenance. She was everything I was not. While she drifted here and there on a cloud, I thundered from place to place, a stampede of one.

I too had developed. But my metamorphosis came later and was more sudden than Al's. One morning I was still the family's little cannonball, the next I was the object of adolescent male references to a pair of bowling balls.

It was a stressful time for me, but soon after that I met Hamp. He bowled me over. He was a handsome college man serving as a teaching assistant while acquiring a graduate degree. Ten years older than me, he was a man among the boys that I knew. Our relationship calmed my postadolescent anxieties.

Coylie and I arrived at the road leading to Al's place and turned onto a narrow lane. Old maples formed a dappled canopy, the road climbed steeply, and then the maples gave way to a tall evergreen hedge. At a break in the hedge, a pea stone driveway tumbled out to meet us. A nondescript aluminum mailbox planted at the junction disclosed that we'd arrived at "Al's B&B."

We turned our overstuffed vehicles onto the driveway, and once past the thick hedge took in the full view of the house, a big old Victorian on the crest of the hill. When I first saw it, years ago, it was a nightmare of decayed ostentation. Chipped and peeling paint covered the old ornate gingerbread. Moss coated the north-facing clapboards.

Al had inherited the house and some farmland on a wonderful old country road. It came with a barn that was in far better shape than the house. Best of all, it came along with a healthy purse. To everyone's surprise, she chose to throw herself into the task of returning the house to its original beauty.

I think of Al's house as the first significant disagreement between Hamp and me. I loved the place. Hamp hated it.

"She might as well throw her money out the window," he said, often. "No matter how much time and energy she puts into that place, she'll still end up with a dump."

But when she was finished, he grudgingly admitted that she'd done a first-class job. I wonder now if he was fearful that I'd want such a grand place, too. But he did point out something I'd missed. He noted that during the renovations, which had taken almost two years, Al had changed. She, too, had gained substance as the house had taken on its rejuvenated form.

He was right. She'd handled the job skillfully, shaken off a mantle of inexperience, and taken on a more seasoned composure that's hers to this day. Then she'd turned her thoughts to the rest of the property and to creating the business that had taken shape in her mind.

She still calls it a bed-and-breakfast, but I'm not sure that's what it really is. It's open fewer than thirty weeks a year. The rest of the year is her own. During the three separate weeks each summer that the Brimfield Antiques Show is open, individuals who have made reservations a year in advance can stay in the guest rooms, or in the small dormitory housed in the old barn. At any other time, the entire B&B must be reserved.

Her idea was a success from the start. She had a new building constructed, designed to look like another barn and suiting the location perfectly, but it's not a barn at all. It's a mini conference center with meeting rooms, a communications room, and all of the show-and-tell space that businesspeople seem to need. That's the segment she went after: corporations.

Al's B&B is also a lovely place for a club or church group to rent while visiting nearby Old Sturbridge Village, or when leaf peeping in the fall. But it's become a haven for corporate leaders and their minions to escape their glass and steel towers. Al gives them shelter from their inbred, confined community. Shelter that allows a quiet look at new ideas. She calls that a corporate retreat.

I love to visit the place. Coylie and I drove up the driveway. Halfway to the house the driveway splits into two spurs. One part loops by the front door, then curves back again toward the road, in a giant horseshoe.

We took the road more traveled, cruising by the side of the house and beginning a gentle descent into the backyard, where I drove directly to the older barn. This is where Al lends me storage space.

I pulled the van out of the way. Coylie backed his truck up to the door and jumped out. The door was locked. I didn't have a key, but before I could walk up to the house and buzz myself in, Al emerged. She waved and called out from the porch, and I waved and helloed back to her. She stepped back inside, and in seconds we were buzzed in.

Soon everything was unpacked and stacked neatly in the storeroom. We'd emptied Coylie's truck back to his own things, and the van was down to a few packing blankets, a carton of odds and ends, and Supercart. The whole job took less than twenty minutes.

Coylie and I walked up the hill to the back of the house. When I climbed the few stairs to the back door, I turned and pointed toward the west. Coylie, following me, turned back to look. I heard the intake of breath as he caught the panorama now visible above the trees that had screened our view down at the barn. A stunner.

Inside, the kitchen smelled wonderful, and Al offered us coffee and warm gingerbread. I introduced her to Coylie, and while she puttered with the coffee things I showed him around the first floor of the house, which wowed him.

"I'm never comfortable with Victorian," he said. "But I've never seen it done like this. I could live with this."

I grinned. "She doesn't tolerate anything fussy. I think this is what you might call a minimalist's interpretation of Victorian," I said as we circled back into the kitchen.

"Enough about the Victorian furnishings," Al greeted us. "Have some gingerbread, and tell me about the murder."

"Bad news travels fast," Coylie said. "Did you know Monty?"

She knew neither Monty nor Billy, but she suspected that I would.

"You know everyone in antiques."

I rolled my eyes. "Not quite, but antiques is a small world, and a tight one. You probably know as many antiquers as I do, from your guests here."

"Not even close. I have the same guests year after year, and they've gotten quite clubby. They come from some distance for the antiques show. But I did hear that Monty is from your old stomping grounds nearby."

"True," I said. Worcester, where I'd opened my first shop. "I still belong to the Dealers Association there, though we've lived on the Cape for eight years."

"Well," she said, "I knew that if there was a murder, you'd somehow get yourself involved in it."

"I'm not involved," I said. She always jumps to conclusions. But Coylie and I did tell her what little we knew about the murder and Billy's arrest. I also explained that I had no intention of getting involved.

"There are people who might think that your trip to the police station was 'getting involved,'" she said.

"There are people who are beginning to sound a little prissy," I said.

Coylie was shoveling gingerbread into his face, but he was absorbing the conversation at the table, his eyes shifting back and forth between Al and me. Al had served the gingerbread warm, with warm applesauce over it, and a dollop of something that seemed like whipped cream on top of that. It was better than cream. Could anything be better than cream? It had a golden cast to it, and it melted on contact with the tongue, or the finger.

"What is this?" I said as I swiped my finger across the cream, and tasted it without the flavors of gingerbread or applesauce.

"It's Maya Angelou's recipe for Golden Whipped Cream," she said.

"Oh? Did she drop by and give it to you?" I said.

"It's in her cookbook. If you ever decide to read something, I'll lend it to you," she said.

"I read books," I said.

"I mean other than the annual antiques price lists," she said.

Coylie stood up, held his dish close to his face, and scraped the last of the gingerbread into his mouth.

"You ladies seem to have some issues, so I'll just be getting on back to Brimfield, and I thank you for the fine gingerbread," he said, nodding at Al.

Al and I looked at him. Often, people don't get our relationship. We have no issues.

I was saved from trying to explain when Al said,

"Lucy and I have always been as critical of each other as sisters, since neither of us has any real sisters to criticize."

It was a brilliant explanation, and truer than anything I'd have thought up. Coylie laughed and said that he had plenty of sisters, and that we hadn't even come close to sister-style criticism. Nevertheless, it was time for him to leave, and Al sent him back with a chunk of gingerbread for later.

Al and I visited through another cup of coffee.

"Do you ever come across rocking chairs that would suit the bedrooms here?" she asked.

"They're all over the place, almost any style you'd want. How many do you need?" Long before I opened my first shop, I helped Al furnish the place with suitable antique furniture. Through the years she has asked me to help her upgrade items that were showing wear and tear, or sometimes just to provide some visual change.

"Sooner or later, I'll probably want them in all of the rooms, but for now, two, or even three will do," she said.

"Have I missed something? Did rocking chairs suddenly become hot items when I blinked?" I asked.

"I don't think so," she said. "But a CEO who brings me lots of corporate business mentioned, in front of his subordinates, that the rocker I had in his room had helped him solve a problem that had been gnawing at him for some time."

"Did he say what the problem was?"

"No, but almost as soon as he turned his back, one

of his minions came to me and asked if he, too, could have a rocker in his room. And five minutes later another made the same request."

I rolled my eyes, and asked if she had any price guidelines in mind.

"Can I get anything nice for a couple of hundred dollars each?"

"Plenty. Do you want rockers that are ready to go, or will you take them if they need work?"

"Ready to go would be best, but I know where I can have minor repairs done," she said. "Spare me from anything needing reupholstering, though. I haven't met the upholsterer yet who understands what I'm requesting."

I nodded my understanding, gathered my purse, and readied myself to leave. The rocking chairs wouldn't be a problem, and I'd enjoy looking for them.

10

Back in Brimfield, I pulled up behind Coylie's truck. He was gone. Probably chasing the fellow who owed him a moving fee. Activity in most of the fields had quieted down. People were taking their time, looking things over, buying, selling, and moving. But the frenzy of opening, and even the second run-throughs, was over. At this time of day a few amateurs straggle in.

"Amateur" is a derogatory term used by a small and somewhat cliquish circle here. Brimfield is open to anyone: dealer, collector, or amateur. Who belongs in which category is a subject of debate, but anyone can buy, and anyone who's paid the town for a permit and rented a spot from a promoter can sell.

The amateurs buying at Brimfield drift in after finishing their real jobs. On weekdays their numbers are small, so they don't make too much difference. But from

Friday afternoon through the rest of the weekend they are an annoyance. They pour in and get in everyone's way. Well, they get in my way. They take precious time making their decisions. Then they want to *talk*.

Some dealers are amateurs, too, but they get educated fast, or they drop out of the game. Occasionally I help in their education, but I was in no mood for that today.

My van was organized for the trip back to Boston, but I hesitated. Maybe I'd take one last look around. Check out the rocking chair situation.

I got out and stretched my legs. I'd walked more today than I had in ages, but I couldn't sit still. I was full of nervous energy and needed to move. I strolled out to the roadside and turned toward the sun. Then I did exactly what I knew I shouldn't.

I walked to the field where Monty was murdered. I needed to look at the spot. I still believed I wouldn't get involved. I just wanted to stand there quietly and get a feeling for what had happened. The murder site was at the rear of the field, which had a very small, and rough, parking lot.

This one was newer and smaller than most, but it had attracted a full array of dealers. The tents were lined up tight. The field was squeezed in among the older fields, and the rough parking lot appeared to be an afterthought.

Behind the parking area, the land fell off steeply, then more gently toward the woods. It appeared that someone had intended to clear the area, probably to extend the field for more selling or parking. Trees had been cut, gravel had been dumped, and then the job had been abandoned.

Monty's body had been found on the open slope a short distance in front of the trees. There had been no attempt to hide him. I stood at the edge of the field and looked at the setting below. I had no need to root around at the exact spot, still festooned with the yellow plastic streamers left by the police. It was dark when he was killed. The dealers in this field would have been setting up their booths.

Both Monty and his killer must have walked down the rough ground toward the trees. They couldn't have driven into that terrain in the dark. It was an obstacle course of tree stumps, undergrowth, and mounds of gravel. Any attempt to drive in there would have drawn attention.

So why would he have walked down the dark hillside, where nothing was going on, with a stranger? Couldn't be to show an antique, or to look at one, because it was too dark. Someone up here would notice flashlights. He might go there with someone he knew, but why? That didn't add up.

He could have gone there alone and met someone he didn't know. But why didn't he yell when the situation got nasty? You could hear him a mile away when he was just talking. People up here would have heard him yelling.

It made no sense, none at all. Maybe he just went there to pee in the woods. He might have done that.

Then some nut got him and strangled him for his money, and Monty didn't make a sound.

I couldn't buy that, either. I just couldn't buy it.

While I stood there imagining scenarios, I'd been hardly aware that other people were coming and going nearby. Rubberneckers? Just as likely to be folks trying to make sense of a senseless act. It wasn't until I heard my name spoken that I came back into time.

Mr. Hogarth spoke again. We'd met several times today. I smiled, noting the garish outfit he'd assembled through the day. Some people don unconventional clothing while attending Brimfield. Often, young women look particularly fetching in vintage clothing. But sometimes the getups are just a peculiar reflection of the wearer's idiosyncrasies.

"Hey, Mr. Hogarth, you look like my favorite Doctor Who with that scarf draped around you."

He smiled and his face crinkled. "I think it may have done time as a sari," he said, patting the silky fabric. "You were looking pretty serious there, Lucy. Have you figured it out yet?"

"Not even close, Mr. H. But don't get the idea that I'm working on it. I'm just trying to understand. I can't get it through my head that Monty's gone."

"Get used to it, Lucy. No more hurricane roaring in to pester us with his pitch. He's gone. It's sad, but there were times, many times, that I cringed when I saw him coming."

"He could be insensitive. I think he came from a

hardscrabble life," I said. "But he always had fun stories to share, and he almost always brought me things that were perfect for my shop."

"Insensitive? He was obnoxious," Mr. Hogarth sputtered. "And yes, he sometimes brought me the right thing, too, but remember, he was just as insistent that you buy it when he'd picked the wrong thing."

I decided to ignore the truth in that statement.

"Well, I'll miss him, rough edges and all," I said.

"I'm not sure I will," he said, nodding. "I had to tell him to stay away. More than once I told him, 'Stay the hell away from my shop.' "

"Why?" I asked, then wished I hadn't. Mr. Hogarth was upset and my question was sure to irritate him further.

Mr. Hogarth looked down at me. "That boy was offensive. Didn't he ever offend you?"

"No." Well, maybe. Closies don't count for dead people.

Mr. Hogarth shook his head, slipped a thumb under his suspender and snapped it. Uh-oh. Monty mimicked this gesture when he told stories about Mr. Hogarth. His stories perfectly captured the old fellow, and they were often funny.

"He went over the line with a customer, too," Mr. Hogarth said.

"Oh?" This was news. Monty's irritating streak was familiar to me, but he had always been circumspect around customers. He had even, of late, picked up Bil-

ly's habit of tipping his hat and inquiring if he should
come back later when I appeared to be in the middle of
something with a customer. "What happened?"

Mr. Hogarth snapped his suspenders a few times
and told me about a deal with a woman who'd brought
a vase in to be converted into a lamp. She wanted him
to drill a hole in it to pull the wire through. "We'd already discussed the risk in drilling the vase, when
Monty broke in, uninvited, to tell her that she was a
fool to ruin a beautiful vase like that."

"He didn't!" I said, incredulous.

"He did. I apologized for him, and she left, ostensi-
bly to think it over. I called him down for his audacity,
and he had the gall to tell me that he had done me a
favor."

"What was the vase, anyway? Anything interesting?"

"It was an early Rookwood."

"Wow." Monty had certainly done the woman a favor. Early Rookwood is wonderful. It would be a tragedy if it broke while being drilled. But I tsked as best I
could. "I know he annoyed people. I guess he just had
to blurt whatever was on his mind. I think he meant
well, even though he left nothing unsaid."

"He left some things unsaid, but that kid was troublesome, just plain troublesome."

Monty was a few years younger than I. No one but
Mr. Hogarth could refer to him as a kid. I didn't mention how much I enjoyed the gossip Monty carried
down to the Cape after we moved.

Mr. Hogarth knows how much I love American art pottery, and I know how much he loves beautiful lamps, so we avoided further mention of the Rookwood vase. But our conversation was unsettling. There was no love lost between Monty and Mr. Hogarth. They both seemed willing to imagine the worst in each other. The whole thing was too much for me. I wanted to step back and let the proper authorities take care of it, but I didn't feel that the authorities were properly interested.

Mr. Hogarth quieted down as we walked away. I asked if he was ready for Captain Kirk's. Not hungry myself after the gingerbread at Al's, I knew that a nice visit, filled with the antiques gossip of the day, would lift me out of this mood. Maybe it would jog Mr. Hogarth, too.

"Captain Kirk's is just what I need. I hope they still have some creamed chipped beef on toast left. What could be more comforting?"

I looked at him. Was he speaking ironically? It appeared not. That was a quicker lift than I expected. So, Captain Kirk's it was. They start dinner at two in the afternoon there, and call it supper. The signature cuisine is comfort food. But better than the food, it's always filled with people I hadn't seen in a while. Buyers and sellers gather at Captain Kirk's.

We drove there in our own vehicles. Easier to continue in our separate directions after visiting. The buzz of chattering people could be heard from the parking lot. The place was warm and steamy, full of good smells. It's tiny, and most of the tables were full. We stood in the doorway a moment, and people from several tables called hello and waved us over. We headed in opposite directions. Mr. Hogarth works the room like a politician, and will visit every table in the place before he leaves.

I stopped for a few quick hellos myself as I meandered over to a table occupied by two women. The one I knew, Mildred, sold and collected cut glass of the brilliant period. Exquisite stuff. A dish heaped with hash and home fries steamed on the plate in front of her. Both the hash and the home fries are served crispy on the outside and creamy on the inside at the Captain's. It smelled wonderful.

Mildred's hair, currently maroon with pinkish roots, was exactly the same shade as the woman's sitting across from her. Maybe it was the lighting in there. She introduced her companion as Muriel, her sister. Well, of course. I didn't know Muriel, but as I took her in, I realized that I could have picked her out of a lineup. It was not just the matching hair and eyeglasses. The tilt of the head, the scarlet complexion, and the configuration of body mass also proclaimed their sisterhood.

They could be twins, though no one said so. Muriel had a grilled cheese sandwich in front of her. She smiled, mumbled a quiet hello, and cast her eyes back down to the plate in front of her when Mildred introduced us. That made them different.

Mildred, a retired schoolteacher, could have been

the activities director on a cruise ship. She could have been a Realtor, or a radio talk show host. Muriel, in contrast, seemed somewhat inward. Before she retired, Mildred sold her glass from various antiques co-ops. After retirement she opened her wondrous jewel of a shop. It's full of brilliant cut glass, which she accessorizes with a few unusual pieces of silver, and lights with sparkling crystal chandeliers. It's a tiny but exquisite place. She calls it the Ice Palace.

I said I'd had a poor day of buying, not up to my opening day standards, and that got us into a discussion of the day's happenings.

"The murder has us all off our feed," Mildred said.

She appeared to be having no trouble navigating heaping forkfuls of hash to her mouth as she spoke. I looked at her, puzzled. She looked back, rolled her eyes, and tilted her head toward Muriel. Muriel's head was down, still concentrating on her plate. She was using her knife to scrape the toasty crust from the top of her sandwich. I had no idea what Mildred meant.

"She's feeling snarky," Mildred said. "She's upset because she thinks that I was the last person to see Monty alive."

Wow. "How do you figure that?"

Muriel, still with her head down, was now cutting her sandwich into finger-sized strips. When she finished that, she turned her plate halfway around and began cutting the strips into cubes. She said nothing. So far she hadn't taken a bite.

"This morning at four o'clock, I had an appointment to look at a chandelier before anyone else," Mildred said.

"A hot prospect," I said.

She grinned. "I was on my tricycle wobbling my way toward Route 20, still half asleep in the dark, when I brushed by someone who said, 'Watch it, Toots.' The voice was unmistakable—it was Monty. We spoke briefly, and we both went our separate ways, and that was that."

"Did he say anything about where he was going, what he was doing?" I asked.

"No, we only spoke for seconds." She slapped her palms against the tabletop. "Nothing of substance. I wanted to be on time for that appointment. We said a quick hello, good-bye, and that's what Muriel is so moody about. She thinks I should report that meaningless meeting to the police."

Mildred picked up her fork again, and Muriel sniffed. I turned her way; her eyes looked dry, her nose, too—maybe it was an editorial sniff.

"That's not much to report," I said.

"It's nothing," Mildred replied. "But if I went over to tell the police about it, I'm sure they'd want to make something of it."

Maybe Mildred was right. "Was Monty with anyone?" I asked.

"No, and I'm sick to death of this discussion. We keep covering the same ground, but there's nothing new to add. My sister doesn't have enough to keep herself busy since she retired."

I stifled a question about who else she'd seen on that early run this morning. I figured that if I irritated her further she'd shut me out, so I changed the subject.

"Did you find the chandelier you were looking for?" I asked.

"Yes, I did," she said. "I knew exactly where to find it. I'd made arrangements days ago. It's just as wonderful as I was led to believe, and I bought it. It's a good one, small but elegant."

"So you got off to a good start," I said.

"It was a good start, but the rest of the day was hard work," she said. "There's plenty of glass here, but cut glass is scarce. Have you seen any today?" she asked.

"No, but I haven't looked for it. I don't collect glass except for Sandwich."

"You like Sandwich glass?" she asked.

"I do, but there's so much reproduction Sandwich around that I don't spend a lot of time sifting through it," I said.

"I ran into the real thing this morning, where I picked up the chandelier."

"Oh, rats," I said. "I imagine it's all gone by now. They've had a whole day of selling. I can move all of the Sandwich glass that I can get my hands on at the Cape. Do you think any of it could be left?"

"They can't have sold everything, because they're not opening until Thursday. They're here early because they want to get in some buying. I imagine they're doing some selling, too. I'm probably not the only buyer they had lined up."

It was surely an outside chance, but I had nothing to lose. And since I had nothing to lose, after getting directions and gathering my things, I asked the question that had been teasing me: "Who else did you see when you were out looking for that chandelier?"

Rather than having a hissy fit, she thought a moment and said, "I don't recall seeing anyone else. There were people around, but it was dark. I may not have even noticed Monty if I hadn't heard his voice." She gazed around the room, her eyes stopped, and she pointed. "I think I saw that fellow."

I turned toward where she pointed. It was Mr. Hogarth, who had approached someone at the counter. He was standing over the guy, speaking intensely. His expression was severe, and I wondered if he was still carrying on about Monty.

Mildred was having second thoughts. "I'm not really sure," she said. "Maybe it was later in the day when I saw him. I can't remember."

I'm sure that Mr. Hogarth was at Brimfield as early as I, but I wasn't about to get into another discussion with him about Monty. Mr. Hogarth shifted his weight, and I saw that he was speaking to John Wilson. Mr. Hogarth's complaints about Monty likely fell on fertile ground, but Wilson appeared to be shrinking away from Mr. Hogarth.

Good. There was no way I was going to go over and smooth-talk Mr. Hogarth. Let Wilson sweat out the old man's ire. He deserved it after spreading his "disgruntled employee" theory this morning. What on earth was Wilson doing here anyway? Had Captain Kirk's started serving creamed foie gras on toast? Truffle burgers?

I said good-bye to Mildred and Muriel and left without any further visiting. I was off to see her hot prospect, and I didn't want to miss another opportunity. I drove back toward Brimfield, following Mildred's directions. After a while I sensed that I had missed a turn. The drive was beginning to feel too long for someone who had been riding a tricycle. When I ended up at the wildlife sanctuary, I turned around and headed back to Brimfield.

I was sure that Mildred told me to turn left at the east end of the marketplace. It turns out that she meant the *other* left, the one that curves toward the right if you are coming from the Captain's. When I finally took a chance on the correct turn, I came almost immediately to a small cluster of campers parked in a flat spot on the hill. There I found the dealer without any trouble.

"Where have you been?" he called as I stepped out of the van.

He seemed to be waiting for me, and when I raised my eyebrows in question, he explained that he'd been waiting since Mildred called him from her cell phone.

"I've got some glass on the kitchen table for you to look at." He waved for me to follow him into the camper.

Glass? I wondered if I had wasted yet more time. But it really was Sandwich, mostly small pieces. A very old doorknob, some lacy salts, a matched pair of curtain tiebacks, and two lacy pattern plates that were about eight inches across. It was all clear glass, none colored, and his prices were fair, so I took it all.

"I have a customer who would like an early blue salt," I said when we finished our business.

"I have some colored glass, including blue salts, back at my shop," he said. He gave me his card, told me I could call him or give the card to my customer. I nodded. There are customers that I can send directly to another dealer, and there are some for whom I prefer to remain a middleman.

11

I drove back to Boston fending off thoughts of Monty's murder. I looked forward to relaxing. We keep a phone, but no answering machine, so no messages, and therefore, no complications. A long soak in the huge old bathtub and a good night's rest would bring me back to life.

Even as I pulled the van into what was surely the last parking space in Boston, I could remember nothing of the drive home. My body was heavy with fatigue. I hurt in several places where I long ago had muscles, and my left hip was stiff again. I let myself into the apartment.

The place looked cozy, furnished sparsely with cast-offs I had picked up for a song. Future antiques, we'd called them. The building, converted to apartments, then converted later to even smaller apartments, and then finally sliced into itty-bitty condos, was once a

single-family home. Our place was on the parlor level;
the entire apartment had once been the front parlor.

Now it's an oddly proportioned living-sleeping room,
a tiny kitchen, and an even tinier bathroom, where a
big old-fashioned bathtub takes up most of the space.
When we first leased the place for Nancy, I had rearranged the furniture a dozen times, but I've since
surrendered. It is what it is—a small apartment built
within a large room.

Two notes, I saw, had been slipped under the door:
"Lucy, call Matt when you get back, Sonny," and,
"Lucy, call Hamp when you get back, Sonny." So much
for no answering machines.

Sonny's door is across the hall; his apartment occu-
pies the back parlor, or sitting room. We see him rarely,
and might never have met, except that he had once interrupted an argument between Hamp and me at the
front door of the once elegant old brownstone.

We had arrived without warning because we—that
is, I—wanted to surprise Nancy with an antique desk
that she had greatly admired when she was last home
at the Cape. Hamp wanted to call and tell her we were
coming, but I knew she'd be here. She had the week off
from school, and she was determined to spend it study-
ing in Boston. Otherwise, of course, she would have
come home to the Cape and spent time with us.

Sonny heard Nancy's name mentioned and asked
who we were. Except that he was wearing a gigantic
cowboy hat, he looked like a pretty regular guy to me,
and I began explaining who we were. When I said we

were her parents delivering a desk that she wanted, he said, "No problem." He'd be happy to let us in.

"You have a key to Nancy's apartment?" we asked.

"Sure, I pick up her mail and bring it in for her."

"Huh?"

"Sure, she has a key to my place, and I have a key to her place, no problem."

And with that Sonny opened the heavy door, unlocked his mailbox and Nancy's mailbox, and took the mail. Then he dashed into his place, found Nancy's key, and ushered us in.

The apartment looked oddly neat. Sonny told us to knock on his door when we were through moving the desk. He'd lock up after us. No problem. Hamp and I were still gaping at each other after he closed the door.

No problem. No daughter. I noticed the absence of her high-tech sound system equipment, and the stack of unopened mail on the mantel in the little apartment. I sensed that I understood the rest of the story, but I said nothing to Hamp until later. I was just too tired for the scene that I thought would follow.

Sonny's messages stared back at me now. I'd have to return both calls. I should call Natalie, too, and explain why I hadn't met her this morning. I decided to put off calling Hamp until later, and jabbed Matt's number into the phone to get it out of the way. He answered on the first ring.

"Billy will have to spend the night in jail," Matt told me. "Under the right conditions I can get him released tomorrow. They're holding him on a fairly unsubstantial warrant. My best, and quickest, shot will be to show that he's being held without probable cause."

"Can you do that?" I asked.

"Well, unless they can come up with something more tangible than the premise that Billy collected lace, I can. I intend to show that the charges are too flimsy to hold up. So, what can you tell me?"

I could tell him little, except that I knew Billy hadn't done it.

"I'm looking for something a little more fundamental," he said. "You were there all day. I imagine you've been snooping. What have you learned?"

"Nothing!" I protested, ready to argue the snooping, but another thought occurred to me. "Since when has Billy collected lace?" I asked.

"He says he doesn't collect lace, but they found a box of old tablecloths in the truck. Most of which were lace, and that's what they're hanging the arrest on. Come on, Lucy, are you holding something back?"

"No!" I wished I knew something, so I could hold it back, at least for a little while, but I didn't, so I couldn't.

Wait a minute. Did I know something? Could that brief meeting between Monty and Mildred mean anything? It took less than a minute, seconds really, and nothing of substance was said. I decided to let it go.

"Are you going back there tomorrow?" he asked.

"Yes."

"Well, while you're there nosing around, let me know if anything about that lace comes up, or if there's something that just doesn't smell right to you."

He lost interest in me immediately, as I had nothing more to offer. As soon as we'd hung up I realized that I had forgotten to ask Billy's last name. My stomach begged for succor; I'd had enough chaos. Before I could make reparations, I called Natalie's number. No answer. I didn't bother leaving a message.

I gave up the idea of a soothing bath—I realized that I couldn't be soothed tonight—and took a quick shower instead. I wasn't really hungry, but I rifled through the tiny kitchen, looking for food to tranquilize me before I called Hamp.

Nothing in the fridge but a stick of margarine, a bag of Starbucks Kenya rolled so far down it'd barely make tomorrow morning's allotment, and a jar with about a tablespoon of salsa clinging to its sides. I scanned the cabinet shelves, but I don't know why I bothered. A large can of tomato juice, a jar of popping corn, and a half-full bottle of vodka. Hamp and I occasionally snack here, when he can get away from the Cape for a little rest and relaxation, but we rarely bother to cook. We love the wonderful restaurants in town.

I was too tired and it was too late to go out and get something. I opted for a pot of popcorn, and while it was popping I scraped the salsa jar clean, relishing every morsel the spoon could capture. I opened the tomato juice and nipped at it straight from the can. Mmmm, warm. I knew better than to look for an ice cube; the trays were cemented into the freezer, buried in frost. The small refrigerator that came with the apartment was so old it thought it was an icebox.

I took the pot of popcorn and the rest of the tomato juice over to the phone and called home. Maybe Hamp missed me; he'd seemed so troubled lately.

The phone rang eight times. I'd let it ring once more, then hang up. After that, the machine would answer, and I was too tired to understand whatever witty repartee it had in store for me tonight.

Only three of our five kids live at home just now; they come and they go, but mostly they keep coming back. We had been down to just two of them when Philip married Monica. But he gave up his little apartment in the shadow of the Bourne Bridge on the mainland side of the Canal so they could move in with us. That move would allow Monica to get her degree at Lyman, where Hamp teaches, almost without cost to any of us.

"Hello." It was Monica, Philip's bride. I didn't know what to make of her. She was very quiet, and I couldn't tell yet if she was reserved, or shy, or just a quiet person. I told her I was returning Hamp's call.

"I think he's asleep," she said. "Would you like me to wake him?"

Before I could respond there was a stirring at the other end of the line.

"'Lo?" It was Hamp, his voice full of sleep.

"I didn't mean to wake you," I said.

He cleared his throat. "There's some good news. I didn't want you to miss it." I could hear the mangled words through his hand, which, I knew, was rubbing the sleep out of his face.

"I can handle some good news."

"It's about the apartment," he said. "We may be able to get rid of it."

"Huh?" A cold feeling moved into my stomach. I love this apartment.

"Someone wants to sublet it until our lease is up," he said.

He went on about a foreign couple who would be in Boston for the summer, working at one of the universities. While he spoke, I thought about what objections I could legitimately offer to keep them out.

"If they do any damage to the place," I asked, "will we be liable for it?"

"I don't know," he said, "but as middle-aged, serious scholars, they're hardly apt to be destructive."

I wished I had put some vodka in the tomato juice. A pause in our conversation let me know that he was waiting for a response.

"When are you coming back?" he repeated. Did he miss me?

"I'll be here in Boston again tomorrow night, and then the next night, Thursday, I'll come back to the Cape. I'm not sure yet about Friday or Saturday night," I recited, repeating the schedule that I had announced again and again, and also posted on the refrigerator door at home.

"Good, good," he said quickly. "Do me a favor. Pick up some ingredients in Chinatown tomorrow when you get back to Boston. I need them before my next lesson."

He missed having someone to run his errands. "I'm not sure I'll be back here before the markets close," I said. Hamp was learning Chinese cooking from a colleague at the research center.

"If the markets are closed, Professor Chou says to go to the kitchen at the Happy Dragon and buy them there."

Oh, great. Much as I enjoyed the new cuisine at our house, and especially the fact that I didn't have to cook it, I didn't feature rushing back to Boston tomorrow to hunt for dried lily buds and fermented black beans. Even so, I read the rest of the list back to him, and we hung up. We have our ups and downs, Hamp and I, but most of the time we've been lucky enough to enjoy a rich and loving relationship. We give each other plenty of room to develop our interests, but lately Hamp needs even more time to himself, and I find myself missing the easy intimacy that's been ours for so long.

It was eleven o'clock. My day had begun more than twenty hours before. Not a standard day. I didn't even unfold the sofa bed. Something was chewing at the corner of my mind. I couldn't shake it, couldn't bring it forward. I leaned back on the pillow. I hoped the day's chaos wouldn't keep me awake.

12

At four thirty the next morning, I surged out of a sleep so deep that parts of it were still slipping away as I sat on the edge of the sofa bed. Five hours of sleep leaves me looking for a nap on an ordinary day, but on a Brimfield day it is enough to exhilarate me throughout the hunt.

Late in the week the lack of sleep catches up with me. Mostly I can just about match my energy with the number of days left. I promise myself a forty-eight-hour nap when Brimfield is over. The older I get, the truer that promise feels.

Today's drive was lovely. The dawn came up behind me soon after I was on the road. Forsythia and jonquils looking recently past their prime attracted the day's first sunlight and shimmered deceitfully in a flagrantly luminous dance, a final dazzling seduction before their botanical clocks ran out.

Everything was right for a great day of gathering treasure. Coylie waved me into a space next to his truck.

He danced around the door of my van as I parked. Something was up.

"Wait'll you hear this," he said. His eyes were round, and his pale face made the bright orange curls even more vivid. "I spent the night of the murder in the tent next to the killer."

"Wow." No wonder the kid was supercharged.

"And," he said, dragging the word out several syllables, "I talked to him, just before he went off and murdered your friend."

"Coylie, what are you talking about?" Why didn't he tell me this before?

"Look. Look at this," he said, and he dashed over to his spool table, grabbed a newspaper that he had put by for this moment, and showed me the front page.

"Holy shit," I said. I couldn't help it. There, plastered across the front page of the *Mid-State Chronicle*, for all the world to see, was Silent Billy's face, big as life, along with a story that appeared to accuse him of the murder. This was terrible.

I tried to concentrate on the story in the paper, but I wanted to know what in the world Coylie was talking about. It took a little sorting out before I understood.

"Frankie had to go home," Coylie said. "He was upset. We were pulling stuff out of his truck, tossing it into mine. It was a mess."

"So, where does Billy come in?" Enough about Frankie's bad luck.

"He was in the next tent, up at Jay Bean's. They only charge three bucks a night to camp up there," he said.

"Coylie, please, what happened with Billy?" I said.

"Okay, okay, I'm getting to it," he said.

I squashed a flash of sarcasm; I really needed him to get on with his story.

"I was yelling back at Frankie. Maybe we got into a tussle. I had to get to work at the parking lot, but Frankie wanted to pack more stuff onto my truck. That's when this guy, the murderer, stuck his head out of his tent and looked at us. He didn't say anything for a minute, just watched us."

I winced. Murderer. "Call him Billy. But, you said he spoke to you?"

"Yeah, sort of. I had to leave, and Frankie was tying down the stuff he had to take back to Scottsdale, both trucks were a mess. The kil— um, Billy saw something in the back of Frankie's truck, and said, 'Good stuff,' or something like that. Me and Frankie thought he meant a painting, but turns out he meant the frame. It looked like a damaged frame to me, but by the time we figured that out, I had to leave."

That was the story. All of it. Coylie had left Frankie and Billy talking about a broken picture frame. The end. So then Billy runs off and murders Monty. Okay. Or wait. Why was Frankie so worked up? Maybe *he* ran off and killed Monty. Thin, very thin.

"What time was that?" I asked.

"Just before I met you at the parking lot yesterday. Maybe ten minutes before we met."

We thought about it, before four a.m. Could the time be important? Monty was still alive at four o'clock, when Mildred saw him.

"Any other campers up there?"

"A couple."

"Are they still there?"

"Some. I'm staying until Thursday morning, myself."

"Maybe I should talk to them."

"I doubt they're there right now. They're probably standing in the six o'clock line. People have been heading that way for over an hour."

I'd see the campers later; right now I'd head for the six o'clock opening. Today's openings were staggered, and I had time for each, including second run-throughs.

I did my best to make up for yesterday's lost time. I pored over furniture; I looked over shelves and tables loaded with things that were offered up as antiques. Plenty of junk mixed in with the real stuff.

Junk is not daunting. My eye eliminates it, and any other object that doesn't fit my requirements. Today nothing slipped by me. I was methodical. I was determined. I executed a meticulous search. I was good, my mind completely engrossed in the hunt.

Time did its thing and I did mine. I filled Supercart and hurriedly emptied it into the van; I'd arrange things later. I'd have plenty of help today. Every time I dropped off a load of goodies I felt a wave of energy, my step lightened, and all was right with the world.

My second run-through was productive, too. The second time through is easier. Negotiations may become extended, but the buying and the selling is more relaxed. Here's where I can allow myself to shop for vintage costume jewelry. I can't do that on a first run, when time is of the essence. When jewelry shopping, I get so carried away that I forget about the time.

I unfolded Supercart's counter and studied this morning's collection. A fine assortment that nearly filled a gallon-sized plastic baggie. Antique and vintage costume jewelry is a relatively new avenue for me. I started collecting it a few years back, when I wanted a few pieces for myself. I meant to jazz up the black dresses I wear to camouflage my, ahem, fat. I'd been offended when the kids referred to the simple black dresses in my wardrobe as my vampire-wear.

When other women admired the jewelry I wore, I'd put a few pieces into the antiques shop, and the response had amazed me. Costume jewelry takes no room, it brings customers back, and it's far more profitable than other tiny items. Hamp had been dismayed when I sold a piece of it right off my dress to the dean's wife at a faculty party.

I still use jewelry to camouflage the black dresses that camouflage the fat, but now I also tuck it into little spaces around the shop; a pillow stuck with rhinestone pins, a cut glass bowl filled with pearls, an old brown velvet hat covered with cameos. Wine goblets full of amethyst, amber, or jet. Little surprises waiting to be discovered as one browses among the real antiques.

Today's search had gone so well that I'd finished fine-combing the field earlier than I'd expected. With a little free time before the nine o'clock opening, I trotted toward one of the fields that I'd missed yesterday. The crowd was thinner. The sun had ripened the morning, and the fickle New England spring was inspiring false hopes that it was here to stay. The sky was blue and cloudless, the air polluted only by the gossip about Silent Billy.

The murder, its early shock value defused, was now reduced to the status of small talk. Still, it was the first item mentioned in most conversations.

The news from those in the know, and this morning that seemed to be everyone, was that Silent Billy was guilty. People, on the basis of hearing about his quirky quietness, had overwhelmingly concluded that Billy was a "head case." Therefore, the reasoning went, he must be the killer, because, "Guys like that, they live on the edge, y'know. They snap."

Occasionally someone would pronounce Billy innocent, but risking a jury selected from the peers that were kicking around Brimfield today would be perilous indeed. I'd call Matt later today to see if he had been able to get Billy released. He hadn't sounded absolutely certain on the phone last night.

Billy's lack of conversational skills was no reason to hold him for murder. The police had to abide, to some degree, by the probable-cause restrictions. And collecting lace was a new one to me. I've always been interested in linens and lace myself, but I've only known Billy to be interested in restoring and refinishing furniture. I didn't think he collected anything. I suspect that he views furniture restoration as his work, not his hobby.

Billy's situation teased at my mind as I scanned the booths I passed. I didn't expect to see anything I wanted. Here, on the day after a field has opened, it's often items of lesser value that remain, or items more commonly found. Sometimes what looks genuine turns out to be flawed, or a repro, or to have some other problem, and that's why it remains.

This is common knowledge among experienced sellers, and many move out of tents opened the previous day into fields not yet opened, getting two or more opening rushes at their inventory. Most fields have a rule against moving "prematurely," and sellers sometimes have to guarantee that they'll stay open for the duration of the field's selling days.

But what's common knowledge is never one hundred percent true. A smattering of sellers handle *only* exceptional items. They attract buyers by always carrying the best, and I was headed for a booth that was exceptional, always. The Andersons would be in their usual spot. They transport a premier collection of American art pottery here year after year.

The pottery is sublime, chiefly from the old Ohio Valley potteries. Always beautiful, and of excellent quality; their prices are top of the line. They have been featured in all of the slick shelter magazines, and with good reason.

I approached their booth, happy to see that both Andersons were there. We greeted one another in the Old Home Week style popular in Brimfield. We hugged, we kissed, we declared how wonderful it was to see one another again after all this time. We probably all wondered why, if we were such good friends, we didn't ever get in touch with one another between antique shows.

"I'd like a Normandy jardinière, a large one, to place on a wonderful Roseville pedestal I bought yesterday," I said.

"I'd like one, too," Jane said. "But no can do. We don't have a single Normandy item, of any size."

"Rats." It had been a long shot.

"The only Normandy we opened with was a small pair of wall pockets, and they went in the opening rush yesterday," Jane said. "We have what's here in the booth, but there's also some stock you can look at in the truck. We hold some things back, so we can put out fresh items each day we're here."

"But," Dick added, "when a collector, or a serious buyer, rather than a browser, shows up, we offer them a look into the back of our truck."

I wondered how they could tell a browser from a serious buyer. I never can. "I will peek into the truck," I said. "But it's the jardinière that I'm really after."

"What'll you take for the pedestal?" Dick asked, as he gave me a hand up into the truck.

A good question. The pedestal had been an excellent buy. I'd paid three hundred dollars for all seven pieces of pottery. If I could show the pedestal with a matching jardinière, I could expect to turn a nice profit. I'd probably ask fifteen hundred dollars, which I'd discount for certain customers. But how long would it take me to find a jardinière, and how much would I sell him the pedestal for? I should have been ready for that question.

"I'm not sure I want to sell it without the jardinière," I said.

"I'll give you five hundred for the pedestal alone," he said.

"Not until I've given the search for a jardinière a whirl," I said. I may not find one at Brimfield this week, but sooner or later, I'd meet up with one. I hesitated, trying to figure out my chance of acquiring a matching jardinière.

"Six," he said. "But that's my best offer, and it has to be in good condition."

"Okay," I said. Better not to be too greedy. "But it's in storage. I can bring it back here tomorrow if you'd like. It's in perfect condition."

"I'll take it," he said, and I was on my way.

I made it to the next opening a little late and had to rush in behind the sharpest buyers. I zipped by several booths before finding one that drew me in. It specialized in decorative metal objects: brass, bronze, and some cloisonné. The display was a mix of styles and periods. There was an interesting collection of American Art Deco from the twenties and thirties, none earlier, and an exquisite display of old Oriental bronze and cloisonné objects. An odd combination, I thought, but nice.

I picked up an Oriental vase, bronze with a design of concentric rings. I was about to put it down because the asking price was so high, when I noticed the rim of another vase peeking out of a cardboard box on the tent floor. Despite what I thought I was seeing, I didn't lunge at it. I sauntered over and poked around a bit, with all of the indifference I could muster.

I took the vase out. It was cloisonné, enamel over bronze; the metalwork between the enamel design work was heavily tarnished; probably silver rather than the usual brass or bronze. The shape of the vase was classic: widely curved shoulders tapering down to a narrow rim at the base. It was dusty.

Usually dealers clean their wares before they drag them out to the shows, but this might have been a last-minute choice, thrown in, to be taken care of later. Then, too, sometimes dirt or dust is sprinkled over an object on purpose, to hide something. This dust looked standard, the kind I keep a collection of around the house.

The vase was at least a hundred years old, new by Oriental standards, antique by American. I was afraid to turn it over and look for the mark that I expected— afraid, because of a serious character flaw that does not allow me to maintain a poker face.

The enamel was in good condition, but the widest

part of the shoulder had a little ding in it where it must have fallen hard against something. The enamel showed no chipping around the dent. I didn't brush the dust off it. I knew what it looked like under there, and I didn't want the dealer to decide that I coveted it enough to pay the top price for it.

The design was exquisite, three goldfish with fanned tails, looking as if they were about to dart away from their deep blue enameled abode. It was Japanese rather than Chinese, I was sure. I asked the dealer if it was for sale.

"Hey, lady," he replied, "everything here is for sale." I looked at him for the first time. He was about twenty-five, maybe twenty-six, chewing whatever it was that had scented the air with the fragrance of grape. Young to have such a distinctive collection. I knew I had a real find in my hand, but the dealer didn't seem too interested.

"That's good stuff," his voice said, but his posture indicated boredom, and he stayed where he was, scanning a newspaper, leaning against the tent pole, chewing. Several thin wisps of hair on the underside of his chin waved with each roll of his chewing gum. He appeared to have little interest in the vase. Odd. Now is when he should tell me some little story about it, to reel me in. Something was wrong here.

"Pretty." My usual response whenever I'm interested, but don't want to seem too interested.

"Yeah," he said, "I just took it out of my uncle's cellar when I packed to come here."

His uncle's cellar? His uncle's cellar? Oh, my, my, my, my. Could he be the man of my dreams? I breathed as slowly and as deeply as I could. Quietly.

"Pretty," I repeated. Oh, for pity's sake, isn't it time for me to think up some other refrain? "Have you decided on a price yet?" My nonchalance was making my stomach hurt.

"A grand," he said. It was almost a question.

"A grand!" I said. I nearly dropped it. Doesn't he know what this is? I turned it over slowly, and sure enough, there was the mark on the bottom. I didn't want to peer at it. A grand. A gift!

"Maybe I can take something off it, if you're serious," he said, "but I'd want cash, and it's good stuff. My uncle was behind the times, but he only collected good stuff."

All dealers fantasize about finding someone selling treasures at rock-bottom prices. Stories abound where, because of some fluke, the seller has devalued the treasures and dumps them on the marketplace for a pittance.

I've never found one of these mythical dealers; the closest I've come to the legend is second wives. I love second wives. They dump the first wife's treasures as fast as they can, eradicating all signs of the previous possessor, and at the same time making space to display their own impeccable taste. So this guy had an uncle.

"Is he here?" I asked. I hoped he was not.

"He's dead, but he wouldn't have given you a discount, lady." He stroked the several hairs under his chin. Maybe he was counting them.

"My uncle was as hard-assed as they come. When he put a price on something, it stayed put. I'm getting rid of his stuff; look at the prices he asked. That vase isn't priced. It was in the cellar because of the dent, but he would have asked more than a grand, I'll tell you!"

He had that sheepish look kids get. It was a look that gave him away. I knew, as surely as if he had announced it, that he was the cause of the dent in the shoulder.

I looked around, and sure enough, all of the Oriental pieces wore stickers of the same old-fashioned style. Red-rimmed rectangles, with corners cut off at an angle. The brass and the Art Deco objects sported little white self-stick tags with rounded corners. The kind everyone uses now. The prices on the old, red-rimmed stickers were high indeed. The uncle was a lover.

Lovers are not unusual in the antiques trade. They're collectors masquerading as dealers. They select each piece lovingly or greedily, and they price them so high that they get to keep them. Most of the dealers I know have succumbed to this syndrome occasionally. Certain pieces are so thrilling that one wants to hang on to them. The uncle apparently made it a way of life. The nephew had his own agenda.

"I'll take eight fifty for it, because of the dent, but only if you take it off my hands right now for cash."

He was still negotiating price, while I was wondering if I could take anything else away from him.

"I think I'll take it," I said, forcing my voice to remain steady. The vase was signed with the chop mark of Nagoya Hayashi, which is not a person but a school of Japanese master artists who had worked in bronze and enamel. If perfect, the vase would sell quickly for twelve thousand dollars. Nice markup, and I could get an even better price, if I didn't mind waiting for exactly the right buyer to come along. I didn't even want to put it down to get my money out.

I had been speaking as quietly as I could in order to keep our conversation private. I knew that if we were overheard, others would catch on to my find, and that discovery could nix any further negotiations. I wrapped up the deal on the injured vase quickly, and then we began to discuss other pieces. Despite my efforts to keep the situation quiet, other dealers began to catch the scent of blood in the water, and several had assembled in the tent.

I was fearful that the gathering crowd might break the spell and that some inkling of common sense would slip into his skull, but I needn't have worried. For all that he was indifferent to me when I'd begun my inquiries, *now* he fixed his attention on me, and could see only me.

He was aware that some of the crowd was watching him wrap up a big sale; that they saw it as entertainment. He didn't seem to realize that some were here to buy. He ignored them as customers, and played to them as his audience.

Now I began to worry about the audience. They

wanted to get in on the action. I didn't want to step on toes. Didn't want anyone to start bidding against me. I knew I'd better not be greedy. I'd have to be quick. He wanted to appear the *master*, wrapping up a big deal. One slip and I'd be down the tubes.

We negotiated two more purchases. He was firmer on the stuff that his uncle had price-tagged, but now that I was taking the damaged vase off his hands, he was able to see his way clear to some interesting discounts. I'd probably only make about a 500 percent markup on those items. God, this guy was better than a second wife.

While the money changed hands, he took great pains to explain to me, and his audience, that his interest was limited to Art Deco, and once he cleaned out all of his uncle's stuff, he would carry only Art Deco. "It's the coming thing," he said sagely, and I nodded in agreement. Yes, Art Deco is fine stuff, and it's making more headway all the time, but *this* was like throwing out your Leonardo da Vincis because Erté is the coming thing.

I left the tent. One dealer patted my shoulder on my way past, and another winked, quiet acknowledgment of a job well done. This tent would probably be specializing in Art Deco before the next hour was over.

Oh, God, I hope Hamp doesn't become a widower before I sell off all of my inventory.

13

I searched the rest of the field, but didn't find another prize to equal the injured cloisonné vase. There was plenty that pleased me, though, and I filled Supercart several times. I transferred things into the van, admiring them again as I repacked. The cloisonné vase was the cream, its eminence undisputed, but there was plenty of tutti-frutti to keep it company.

I'd picked up a Boston rocker for only thirty-five dollars, all it was worth in my opinion, a copy of a copy. But it was nice and sturdy, with an unmarred finish, and Al would be happy with the bargain. The back of the van was filling up.

I took a minute to call Natalie from a phone-on-a-stick. I was in a perfect mood to cheer her. When her machine answered I was able to chat with it without antagonizing myself, and I left an extensive message outlining my plans for the next few days.

TJ, my regular Sherpa, would be here for the final field opening today. I'd been preparing him, and didn't want him to miss out. I hadn't yet figured out how to tell him about Monty's murder; I didn't want to shock the kid.

I drifted into another of yesterday's fields; most would remain open for several days, some for the whole show. When I came upon a tent selling old hand tools, not usually of interest to me but perhaps to TJ, I stopped. I use simple tools. My feeling for them is strictly utilitarian, and I'm always surprised that so many people find them interesting as collectibles.

TJ's interest in vintage musical instruments seems natural enough to me, but his interest in old hand tools is a bit of a surprise. I scanned them, making a mental note to bring him back later. I wanted to pack his visit with as many of the pleasures of this place as I could find. In fact, I hoped the kid would love the place.

The tools were attractive, in their way. They were laid out on shelves of scaffolding. Old burlap bags on the ground under the shelves also held displays of larger, heavier tools. They seemed to be sorted by kind, and also by size. I rattled around a bit, not knowing why, nor quite what I was looking for. The dealer was busy with customers and didn't approach.

I looked at an assortment of picks. Some had curved ends, some straight; some were longer, some shorter. There were one-sided picks, but most were two-sided. Some had a different sized pick on each side; others had entirely different tools opposite one another. Who used these picks? Did each user have a special pick that suited him perfectly? Or did he prefer a variety? Different picks for different jobs? Would a woman choose a different pick for the same job?

I leaned over a burlap bag where some steel objects rested. They were a variety of interesting shapes. I picked one up. It was heavy for its size. Oily, too. I didn't know what it was, but I dallied over the display. The steel had a certain sculpted quality. I picked up another piece. I thought I could use an object such as this.

The dealer approached. "Whataya lookin' for?"

I put the oily tool back where I'd found it, and wiped my hand with a tissue. How should I explain? "I'd like to buy a gift for someone," I said.

He squinted, scratched his head, and focused on me. I may have lost my cloak of invisibility.

I picked up another piece of steel, also oily. "What is this thing?" I asked. It had a nice heft to it. It was bigger than my fist, maybe five inches thick, had round sides, and flat sides, and curves and angles. There was a kind of beauty to it.

"It's a whatcha-may-callit," he said, grinning.

Good enough. "Do you know what it's used for?" It was shaped like the head of an oversized hammer, with no place indicating where the handle belonged. There was a bulge where the flat part, that hits the nails, should be.

"Nah, it came out of an old machine tool place in Worcester. Went out of business years ago."

"Worcester?" I said. Serendipity. "My first shop was in Worcester. Was it made there, or just used there?"

"I can't say, I demolished the place last year. Made way for an empty lot. I'm a scrap metal freelancer," he explained.

"What was the name of the place it came from?"

"Iduhknow, lady. I got no pedigrees here. Place stood empty for years. You want it? Fi' bucks, it's yours."

I took it. I'd return it to Worcester later this afternoon. I strolled away satisfied. It was almost time to meet TJ.

I looked up from the path and spotted Mr. Hogarth ahead talking with John Wilson. I was in no mood for either of them or their opinions about Billy's guilt, or Monty's character. But I didn't see how I could avoid them, and just then Mr. Hogarth noticed me and waved me over. I was hard to miss, wheeling Supercart along the narrow path.

"John has been telling me"—Mr. Hogarth hesitated as a quick look passed between them—"that he hasn't seen much fresh merch here today, Lucy."

"Fresh merch," I repeated. "Are you looking for something specific?"

I'd bet he was tracking a treasure. Fresh merch is what draws us all here. It's the stuff that dealers bring from elsewhere. Stuff that's been hoarded away in attics and cellars, stuff that's been scouted for, that's recently been estated back into circulation. Fresh merch. How had he missed it? Brimfield is loaded with my favorite oxymoron: new antiques.

"I'm looking for things that will suit the museum, but not for specific objects, Lucy," he said.

"I don't remember ever seeing much old jade here," I said.

"There never has been, except for the occasional odd piece of jewelry. And the jewelry that does show up here is apt not to be museum quality," he said. "Today I'm looking for the kind of object that I can use to set off our existing collection. Furniture, or accessories that will compliment the jade that we already own."

"I just saw some nice Oriental cloisonné that a young fellow is selling back there, mostly vases. Excellent work, good prices," I said.

"We have more vases than we can use in a lifetime," he said.

Not interested. Should I show him my acquisitions? Jade would show well with the Oriental pieces from that booth. But something was off here. I just offered Wilson a lead, and he showed no interest in even hearing about it. He was here on a treasure hunt just like the rest of us. But he wasn't listening to any leads from me.

He was probably hot on the trail of a certain treasure, and he didn't want to say for fear that someone would grab it first. If he thought that someone was me, he was right. But I wished him luck anyway.

"There's only one more opening today. Then you can go home and relax."

"I can't stand the chaos here," he said. "It leaves me exhausted."

"I know what you mean," I said. "But the chaos seems to energize me."

Mr. Hogarth nodded his agreement.

But Wilson had had a poor day's hunting, and he told us that he'd gone home empty-handed yesterday, too. I sympathized, thinking about my own poor day's pickings yesterday, and kept quiet about my great day today.

Wilson shook hands with Mr. Hogarth, and turned to me. "I'm sorry I upset you yesterday," he said and walked away.

"Upset you?" Mr. Hogarth said.

"Not really, but he was so certain of Billy's guilt yesterday, I guess I did get a little touchy."

"He's got a lot on his mind," Mr. Hogarth said.

"Yes," I agreed. "So what's the big secret? What were you and Wilson really talking about when I arrived?"

Mr. Hogarth laughed. "There's no secret, Lucy. I just had a feeling that he wasn't in a mood to discuss it. He's thinking of quitting the Jade Museum."

"That's the secret? Wilson leaves all of his museums as soon as he finds one with a better offer," I said. No big deal there.

"It's hard to find anything wrong with improving one's situation," Mr. Hogarth reminded me, looking nettled. "And in this case he's not looking at another museum—he's considering opening a consulting business, fund-raising."

"That is news. I understand he's good at it," I said.

"He's been enormously successful," Mr. Hogarth said. "He's thinking that he might be better off making a career of it."

I agreed. There are plenty of organizations that need that kind of help, and that's probably a more suitable milieu for Wilson than tramping around the fields here looking for a needle in a haystack.

I walked along Route 20 to the other end of the market-place, checking for a good spot to catch TJ before he passed the entrance to our parking lot. It would be easier for me to spot him driving along in the big rental truck than it would be for him to see me in the crowd. I pulled Supercart as far off the road as I could and leaned back against a low split-rail fence. I turned my face into the sun and felt it wash over my skin. It felt good. I let it flow through me. Sunblock be damned.

My bones, still rigid with winter's compression, gratefully absorbed the spring warmth and became flexible. My mind couldn't be too far behind. I could hear the traffic inching by me, moving slowly along Route 20.

Sherpas come and Sherpas go. They're almost always short-term helpers. It's the nature of the job, which fea-tures irregular hours, low pay, and plenty of heavy lift-ing and moving. I used to feel that dependability was a necessary qualification for a Sherpa, but brute strength is what's really needed most of the time, so I've adjusted my sights to that, and anything over that is gravy. Some of them turn out fine.

This year I have TJ, a young rock musician. He uses the job for sustenance while he develops his band, the Ravings. I pay him slightly more than minimum wage and I use him twenty-five to fifty hours a week. I have no regular schedule for him, and I keep him busy moving and delivering antiques, and doing other odd jobs. He and I are both surprised that he loves it! He's a great Sherpa.

My skin cooled, and I opened my eyes. A big yellow truck had pulled up to the split-rail fence, inches from my outstretched legs, blocking my delicious sun. I hadn't heard it. Was it possible that I had fallen asleep while resting my buns on the fence? Naaah!

I looked up and was surprised to see TJ, grinning his huge, silly smile. He was already midsentence before I tuned in to what he was saying. He was explaining that it wasn't really my snoring that had led him to me. It was Supercart's blobs of red paint that he had noticed.

14

"I was just resting my eyes," I said, and TJ agreed, but his silly grin belied his words. His hair, tied in a ponytail at the nape of his neck, was combed straight back and looked wet. A new style for him.

Tall and slim, his outfit du jour made him look more gangling than usual. Narrow, ragged jeans flared into a pool of black denim over his enormous sneakers. He sported a black T-shirt featuring a skeleton wearing a shroud, and over that he wore a black leather vest trimmed with chrome objects.

The huge hands and feet attached to his long narrow limbs are usually balanced by a massive head full of flying chestnut curls. Puppy-like. Today the slicked-back ponytail gave him a different look, older maybe, and those huge hands and feet looked false, like something he picked up at a joke store.

"Man, oh man," he said. "The traffic is backed up all the way to Sturbridge."

"Did that surprise you?" I asked. My Brimfield stories, recounted at great length over the past months, usually included some variant of the traffic jam theme.

He rolled his eyes and grinned; my attempts at sarcasm never faze him. "I just couldn't believe that an antiques event could rival summer traffic back at the Cape."

He had pulled the rental truck as far off the road as pedestrian traffic would allow, but its back end projected a little way out into the street. At first the cars on Route 20 drove around him and moved on, but before long a few timid drivers pulled up to his left bumper rather than steer around the truck, and traffic stopped behind them. The first driver, apparently unable to use his steering wheel, had been able to master the art of horn honking, so it was time to move along before one of the traffic cops made trouble for us.

TJ offered to put Supercart in the truck and drive me to the van, but I pointed out our lot, diagonally across Route 20, and told him that it would be simpler for me to walk across and meet him there. He moved the truck carefully through the people ambling around on foot, and had it backed up, nice and cozy to the back of the van, just as I arrived pushing Supercart.

He burst from the truck, his face alive with excitement. As it turned out, Brimfield was not the foremost cause of his excitement.

"We're on, Lucy. We did it," he said. "We're at the Rat's Patootie, this weekend, for money. This is majorly huge." His face glowed with joy, and his outsized hands fluttered above an air keyboard visible to his eye only.

Coylie drifted our way, arriving in time to hear about TJ's gig. Fascinated, he asked about the band, and they were off. TJ was effusive when the subject was music. They fell into a discussion that continued as Coylie, unasked, joined him in unloading the van and packing the rental truck. I tuned their chatter out, and concerned myself with packing individual items for the trip.

TJ had brought cardboard boxes, lots of newspaper, and stacks of blankets with him. I always carried a few blankets in the van, but didn't fill the van's space with boxes and packing stuff.

We worked smoothly, until startled, I realized that the conversation between the boys had lurched into trouble.

"Sorry, dude," Coylie was saying. "I didn't mean to rattle you. Was he a good friend of yours?"

Coylie had blurted the news of Monty's murder to a stunned TJ. Damn. I'd avoided the issue when TJ was floating in the good news of his upcoming gig. I'd resolved to tell him when we could spend a quiet moment together.

"No," TJ responded. "I didn't like him. In fact, I couldn't stand him, really."

"Why?" Coylie asked. "Was he a bad dude?"

"Not really," TJ said, and he thought for a moment. "He was just such a pain in the ass. The guy could never come into the shop and just say hello. He always called me Rich Kid, as if I, personally, had two coins to rub together. And he always asked who I'd taken advantage of today. He went on and on about my advantages, wouldn't quit, and at the top of his lungs, too. He just couldn't leave it alone."

"He teased everyone, TJ," I said. I didn't feel the need to remind him that Monty had frequently referred to me as Double Wide.

"Maybe so, Lucy," he said.

He winced at the news that Monty had been strangled, and seemed startled by the fact that the murder weapon was a piece of lace.

"Lace? The killer used lace?"

"Yeah," Coylie said. "Watch out for those dangerous tablecloths, man."

I shot Coylie a warning look, and TJ shook his head and settled into the realization that someone in his life had been murdered. He quieted down, brooding as we packed the stuff I'd gathered, engrossed in his own thoughts.

TJ turned to me, his eyes wide, his mouth serious.

"What if they think I did it, Lucy?"

I looked at him, and squashed the automatic response that springs to mind, the response my kids can't stand. I've really tried to quit saying, "Don't be silly." When they hear those words, my kids say it's a sure thing that I'm about to point out how silly they are.

"What would make anyone think such a thing, TJ?"

"Well," he said and hesitated, "I had it out with Monty recently."

"Had it out?"

"Those stupid names he always called me. I told him to quit it." He hesitated again. "In no uncertain terms."

"When was that?"

"That day at the auction, when he—"

"Oh, TJ, I was there—no one in their right mind would think you were threatening him." But I snickered, recalling the scene. "I think I remember you calling him an asshole that day."

"I said, 'perfect asshole,'" he said.

Coylie and I laughed. But TJ, who was quite pallid, looked wounded. His face crumpled, his lips turned inward, and a burst of sound came from deep inside him. Oh, God, the kid was going to cry.

"TJ, no one could possibly think of you as a killer," I said.

"That's right, dude," Coylie affirmed, having known him for at least twenty minutes.

I reached up to throw my arm around his shoulder, but could only reach far enough to pat it awkwardly. He grimaced, trying to smother the coming sob. I felt helpless to head off his pain. And then it erupted, an explosion of laughter. He shook with it. Gales of convulsive laughter burst from him.

Coylie and I caught each other's eye, and shrugged.

"I know it's not fun-fun-funny," TJ said, trying to

speak as more laughter burst from him. He lurched forward, bent at the waist, and sputtered out another surge of laughter.

Coylie rubbed his other shoulder. "It's okay, man," he said, and he giggled a bit. I looked at him, and he returned my look, straight-faced and guilty. Then he snorted, hummed a bit, and touched off a torrent of laughter that he, too, tried to suppress.

This was not good. Coylie's strangled laughter morphed into a broken series of high-pitched barks. TJ looked at him, started to speak, and burst into maniacal laughter. They were behaving like overwrought six-year-olds.

"Okay, boys, put a lid on it," I said. People were beginning to stop and look. "Come on, the party's over." I don't know why I said that; such a cliché never stopped my kids when they were in the midst of hysteria. I felt silly and laughed, though I didn't mean to. Both boys looked at me and disgorged further rushes of laughter.

Then it was all over for me. I was in it now, too. I became consumed by the laughter. I tried for a while to control it. When I could keep my eyes open, I saw people looking our way. Some were laughing, and this elicited yet more laughter. Some looked on with disapproval clearly showing on their faces, and this, too, incited me to wild laughter. It was going to have to wear itself out. And after a while it did, with irregular outbursts, at longer and longer intervals.

Our audience broke up and strolled off toward the last opening of the day. We straightened up, avoiding eye contact, and calmed down. TJ still wanted to explain that he didn't find Monty's murder a bit funny, but I shushed him. "Later," I said. I didn't want to provoke another wild breakout, and I didn't think it was too far beneath the surface.

With our packing done we walked, all three of us, toward the final field opening for the day. Our conversation was stilted and extremely polite. When we got to the gate, the line was forming rapidly, as people came from every direction and joined it.

We hurried into the pack without ruffling any feathers. The boys stood awkwardly for a minute while I poked at Supercart, making unneeded adjustments and dusting its corners with my fingertip.

But the line was lively with anticipation. Our topsy-turvy introspection about Monty and thoughts of our laughing jag fell away as we involved ourselves in the present. Everyone nearby expected to acquire treasure shortly, and the conversation and visiting was spirited. Both boys were naturally affable, and before long we all relaxed and joined in the buzz of chatter ricocheting around us.

I had exactly nothing on my mind, and I stood in the warm sun, catching bits of conversation around me. A good-natured argument about the year of the eclipse was in progress.

"That was a total eclipse."

"No, it was an annular eclipse. A ring of sunlight showed around the edges. It was my best year ever."

I almost broke into that conversation to announce that it was my best year, too. I think it was my first year here as a dealer. I had been here before, but that year was different. It was wonderful and terrible at the same time. The eclipse surpassed all of the superstitions I had ever entertained about opening a business. I was convinced that it had brought me good luck. But before I could add my two cents' worth, that conversation had swerved from good luck symbols to bad.

"The worst year was the time they dragged it out for ten days in order to catch two weekends' worth of business."

A chorus of groans went up. I had forgotten. What a mess. Sellers and buyers alike had been torn between deciding which days to close their shops and come here to buy or sell. It was a total washout, and it created some bad feelings.

"That's how the Connecticut show got such a toehold on the antiques market."

Maybe, maybe not, but other antiques markets have been growing rapidly since about that time. The television shows have also spurred people on in the race to make a killing in the search for treasure.

I had expected to accompany TJ through the first rush, but when Coylie offered to "show him the ropes," he looked interested. He turned to me, as if for permission. Piece of cake. It would be much easier for me to dash through the field without stopping to explain things.

I wished them luck and suggested that we meet at two at the Patio. "Remember, don't buy anything unless you love it, and if you love it, don't wait until later to buy it, because it's not going to be there."

TJ, who had heard these words a number of times, rolled his eyes and said he'd be at the Patio at two.

We crossed paths a couple of times in the next hour. Lucky for me, they were as involved in their search as I was in mine, and we barely exchanged nodded greetings before ducking back into the fray. The newly opened field was particularly productive from my point of view, and it yielded up a number of those very special furnishings that give the shop an edge and bring in a different sort of shopper.

I'm careful about buying stock in this category. High-end items do pop up at Brimfield, but the search gets dicey. There are fewer pieces to be found, the risks are higher, and there are no returns. This afternoon I acquired three outstanding prizes: a cherrywood Biedermeier bookcase, a secretary that I'll feature prominently, and a mahogany desk that will show itself off with distinction.

I introduced antiques in the high-end category when I finally opened St. Elmo Fine Antiques, about a year after we moved to the Cape. It broke my heart to close Olde Stuff, but the move to the Cape was unavoidable. Hamp was offered the perfect job: more research and less teaching.

I never dreamed of living in two different locations at that time, and had no plans for myself other than to get settled into our new home and then figure out what to do. Hamp and the kids were, at first, happy to have me running the house again and taking care of things. Before long, the cottage at the Cape looked comfy and cozy, the family had settled into their lives, and I was bored silly.

On my second run-through I looked up a wicker platform rocker that I had noticed on my first dash. It was still there. It had a woven motif, the likeness of a sailing ship on the back of the rocker. It would look wonderful on a porch that overlooked the ocean. It would look wonderful anywhere. I suspected it would be a little pricier than I wanted to pay. I took a closer look.

Someone, or several someones, had applied many coats of paint to the rocker. The paint was chipped in places, and glints of a variety of colors showed through the final coat of yellow. A few of its curlicues had broken off and were missing. No price tag.

"What are you asking for the rocker?" I asked.

"Five hundred," he said.

"A little high for me," I said.

"It's a Heywood-Wakefield," he said.

Good stuff. "I'm not sure I can find someone to do the work it needs," I said.

"I thought I had it sold to a guy who can do the work himself, but he never showed up."

Yeah, right. "It's heavy for wicker," I said.

"That's because the rocking mechanism that connects the rocker to the platform has heavy old steel springs," he said. "Sit in it. See, it doesn't squeak, and it's well built. That rocker will never hop around the floor."

I rocked in it. It felt right, good and solid, but the grass floor of the tent was not a good place to test for hopping.

"Would you take four hundred for it?" I asked.

His face reddened, and he looked irritated. "This rocker is a fine piece of American craftsmanship, even with its surface imperfections. It's worth every cent I'm asking, and probably more," he said.

"I'm sorry," I said. "Truly, I'm picking it up for a friend and this is over the limit she gave me."

He thought about it. "I'm only here until tomorrow morning, and I'd hate to drag it back home. I can knock off fifty dollars."

It was more than I should pay, but it was a fine-looking rocker. As I stood there looking at it, my appreciation grew. After all, I had only paid $35 for the other rocker. That would still only average out to $242 each. Not too much more than Al's guidelines.

"I'll take it," I said.

The boys were chatting with Mr. Hogarth at the Patio when I arrived at two o'clock. They were enjoying their success. Coylie had found some railroad ephemera that pleased him, and TJ was happy with a small wooden dulcimer.

"I don't think it's antique," he said. "But it's older than I am, and I'm sure it's handmade."

"Is it a toy?" I asked. It was very small.

"I don't think so," he said. "I'll bet it was made by a father for his child. I just tuned it. Listen."

His huge hands plucked the strings of the little instrument. He can play anything. The soft, sweet sounds of an old song came to life. What was that song? A fellow nearby held up his hand, pointed at TJ, dove into his wagon, came up with a fiddle, and joined in.

I couldn't remember what the song was, but I loved the gentle sound. Mr. Hogarth began clapping his hands in time with the music, and soon people around us joined in, and then with a flourish the song ended. The crowd applauded. Someone said the song was "Red River Valley." Of course!

This kind of impromptu happening was not unusual at Brimfield, but there had been fewer light communal moments this time around than there usually were. TJ and Coylie were delighted with the feeling that had suffused the event. Mr. Hogarth, too, had lightened up. He'd had some mood swings lately, was not his usual self.

Before we collected the furniture that I had waiting for me around the field, I took TJ to the tool dealer I had visited earlier. He and the dealer made instant friends of each other when TJ said that he was in the metal business, too, and the dealer caught on that he meant metal music.

"I almost called my scrap metal business Metallica, but my son's an attorney, and he told me that could be troublesome," the dealer said.

While we waited for TJ, Coylie told me that he'd

been thinking about lace. "If it's as strong as you say, it's a perfect weapon."

"Why so?"

"It's silent, no big bang. No blood splash-back as with a gun, or especially with a knife. And best of all it's easily available, and probably not traceable."

I couldn't come up with a way to trace the lace. Maybe it was the perfect weapon.

TJ finished up with the tool dealer, and he and Coylie got into the big rental truck and followed me to fields where I had furniture waiting. Then we drove to Al's, where they made quick work of loading my stuff from the van and the barn into the rental truck.

With that job finished, Coylie took TJ into Al's. I tidied up my almost empty van, and when I got to the kitchen they were already at the table tearing into Al's treat for this afternoon, lemon squares. We visited, and I told Al that I had found another rocking chair for her, and that it was a little pricier than she had been looking for.

She shrugged. "It must be special," she said.

Good. I nodded agreement, and before we could discuss it any further, I got up, announcing that we had to get TJ back on the road to the Cape. Our leaving created enough of a flurry that I never did mention exactly how much I had paid for the rocker.

Al packed lemon squares for both boys, and we all said good-bye to TJ at the end of her driveway. I drove Coylie back to his campsite. Not much going on there.

"Where are the campers who were here yesterday when Billy was here?" I asked.

Coylie pointed to two tents nearby. I called "Hello" in front of the tents, but there was no answer.

"Do you know their names?" I asked.

"Nope."

"I'll try to catch them early tomorrow," I said.

15

I had an errand in Worcester. I avoided the Mass Pike in favor of a shortcut over Dead Horse Hill. The road crested, dipped, and crested again, unveiling, at every level, a woodsy New England that is fast disappearing. I coaxed the van up a series of climbs. Spring greens exploded out onto the road. Crystal pools mirrored the vegetation. Streams rushed by, bashing and bubbling against stony beds.

Dead Horse Hill still shelters a few small orchards, one-man farms, and picturesque woodlands—a patchwork bound together by mossy old stone walls.

The carton with the vase and hammer rested snugly on the passenger seat next to me. With a little luck the vase would revert back to "museum quality" before the day was over. I'd begun to feel uneasy about the hammer. I worried that I'd made a mistake buying the silly thing.

I crested the last hill and caught a fine view of the city below. When we'd lived in this area it was the first time that a place had provided me with a sense of contentment. Thinking about that made me feel good. I reached the last bump before the final steep grade and treated the van to a splendid plunge down the hill. It screamed "Whee!" in delight as we descended.

I drove toward Webster Square, which may have actually been a square at one time. It's been a sprawling, busy neighborhood for as long as I've known it. The emissaries of franchise-land are more fully represented now than when Hamp and I settled in the area. The fast-food chains and gas stations have been joined by hardware outlets, lube joints, nail salons, convenience stores, and video emporiums.

None of this competition seems to have choked off the zeal of the local entrepreneurs, who still offer an innumerable variety of goods and services. The area is busy with cars, pedestrians, baby carriages, dogs, and bicycles. It teems with color and noise and movement. The three-deckers that are still abundant throughout the city are packed together tightly here, and the smattering of elegant but shabby old Victorians still give testimony to the fact that the neighborhood began with higher aspirations.

Hamp and I moved to Worcester the day after he finished graduate school. We, and our rapidly hatching flock, settled at first into a three-decker in the heart of Webster Square. It was low rent then and it's low rent now. It was great fun.

*   *   *

I eased into Edgar-the-auto-body-guy's driveway and parked the van as far out of the way as I could manage. The yard was busy with activity. Cars were being worked on in the mild spring sunshine, and more cars waited their turns. The garage doors were open across the front of the building. The hammering and clanging of the work blended nicely with the eruptions of music coming from several radios, each playing full blast and tuned to a different station, inside and outside of the building. The squawk of a police scanner clawed the air for its share of the melee.

There was a busy feeling at Edgar's Auto Body Shop. Things were chugging right along for Edgar. But no Edgar in sight. I wondered if he'd seen me coming and ducked. I took the carton with the cloisonné vase and the hammer out of the van and headed for the small office in the corner of the building just as Edgar stepped out of the door.

"Hey, Loose Lady, how-ah-yuh?" he said and smiled, which is something he does with his whole face. Then he noticed the box I was carrying and his smile froze.

"Oh, no, Loose Lady, you ain't gonna con me into another one of them antique projects." It began as a statement, but ended as a question.

"Of course not, Edgar. I don't *do* conning, but I do have this vase, and you did tell me yourself that you're one of the few left who can do this sort of work. That you were trained when cars were made of steel, not plastic."

"Aww, Loose Lady, that's what I get for bragging. I never shoulda done it," he said. "Lookit the business I got here. Lookit the jobs I got waiting for me. I got work here. Real work. Respectable work. I ain't no vase repair guy. Jeez, Loose . . ." His words hung there.

Edgar was sorry he had, long ago, while repairing one of my early fender benders, shown off his metalworking skill. He was proud of his work. He had done it to cheer me up. And it had. Immeasurably.

I didn't learn how to drive until we moved to Worcester. Prior to that we lived in the cocoon provided by graduate school, and I didn't mind trotting around for anything I needed, or waiting for Hamp to chauffeur me on my errands. That changed, of course, when we moved out into the *real world*, where I quickly learned how to drive well enough to acquire a driver's license, but not well enough to stay out of trouble.

I engaged in a number of minor accidents, fender benders really. Some were my fault, but several took place when the car wasn't even moving. I happened to be behind the wheel, though, so I was given credit for them. Hamp, at first sympathetic, began to be irritated by the situation.

Edgar took pity on me. He stopped replacing the old car's parts with new ones, and began hammering out my various bumps and dents. That made it a little less expensive. He joked that I was one of his "preferred customers," and assured me that I was lucky I didn't drive a new plastic car. Edgar is a good person. I'm sympathetic that he feels a lesser man when he repairs a vase, but his attitude makes no sense to me.

"Just take a look at it," I said, and pulled the cloisonné vase from its newspaper swaddling in the box, holding it up for him to see.

He looked away from the vase and contemplated the garage walls. He took a sidelong peek at the vase, tried to avoid another look, but couldn't. He finally let his eyes rest on it.

"It's that enamel stuff, huh?"

"Cloisonné."

"Yeah, cloisonné," he said, and he looked at me. "Why do you do this to me, Loose Lady?" He approached the vase but didn't touch it. His eyes were drawn again to its lines. "Enamel over bronze, a little silver in there, too," he mused. "Old bronze can be brittle, you know, and when that old brittle stuff busts, not even *I* can fix it."

As he lifted the vase from my hand, he made a cooing sound. Calming the vase? Himself? With both hands, he turned it, caressing its surface with his palms. Warming it, weighing it, imprinting its design against his palms.

Then he nodded. He had made an agreement with himself. He held the vase by the neck with both hands and slid his thumbs down inside. I watched. He pressed his thumbs against the inside of the bronze. We stood, still as statues, me watching Edgar, he watching some distant place. Seconds passed quietly; then the vase made a hollow popping sound. We looked at it. Fixed. Edgar-the-auto-body-guy smiled.

He handed the vase back to me and he said, "There. Now don't come back here again unless you need your car fixed. I don't repair antiques, and someday I'm gonna break one-a them things. Then all hell will break loose, Loose Lady."

"Edgar, it's beautiful," I said, and it was. "What do I owe you?"

"The same as always, Loose Lady: nothing for vases. But I'm warning you, if you break your car again, you had better bring it here to be fixed. Or I'm calling in my markers." He was smiling again.

I wondered if he would accept my gift in the right frame of mind. Maybe it would antagonize him. If he didn't like it I'd plead insanity.

"Edgar, I have something here for you. . . ."

I gave him the hammer.

"Here, Edgar, it's a . . ."

"I know what it is. It's a dolly."

". . . hammer of some sort."

"It's not a hammer, unless you see an anvil as a hammer. It's a dolly. It's beautiful, Lucy. This is hand-forged, you know." He held it gently and looked at it.

"Yes, I know." I didn't know. But if he liked it, he might as well think that I was aware of something special about it.

"It's beautiful," he repeated. "Where did you get this?"

"At Brimfield, where I got the vase."

"Brimfield? That's where the guy up the street was murdered," he said.

Not exactly up the street, but by neighborhood standards, Monty's Contents was in the vicinity.

"Did you know him, Edgar?"

"Not really. I knew who he was. I seen him around, him and his helper. But I can't say I knew him."

"They come in here?"

"Uh-uh, not here. Last time I seen 'em was in the Viet restaurant across the avenue. I like their seventy-sevens."

"Me too. They call them summer rolls where I live now."

"Yut, well, just before the murder, I saw Monty giving the quiet guy a bad case of grief," he said, nodding.

"Oh?"

"Yut, then when I heard about the murder, I goes, that was brewing the day I seen 'em."

"What happened?"

"Well, the quiet guy just sat there, taking the dressing-down Monty was giving. But Monty wouldn't quit; he just kept nagging. You couldn't help but hear him. Everyone in the place heard him. He kept bitching about a table or something. He goes, you shoulda never done that. That's the worst thing you coulda done, and on and on. Never do that again, he goes, unless I tell you it's okay."

"It was about a table? What about it? Anything else?"

"Nah, he was rankin' on the guy, but it was the same thing all over again. He really trampled the guy. I felt like punching his lights out myself."

"Was there any actual punching, Edgar?"

"Nah, like I said, the quiet guy just sat there, brow-beaten."

"And that was the day before the murder?"

"I think it was two days before. Yeah, two days. The whole neighborhood is talking about the murder, and that ain't gonna change quick. His place was just broken into."

"Monty's Contents was broken into?"

Edgar, who didn't know that appellation, explained that he had, less than an hour ago, heard his police scanner say that Warehouse Used Furniture had been B&E'd. "The police are probably still over there right now," he said.

Wow.

I left Edgar's. My plan had been to then zip over to Coney Island, but, with the slightest of detours, I drove by Monty's Contents for a bit of a gawk. I didn't intend to go into the place, only to notice if the police were still there. Approaching the building, I saw Matt's BMW parked by the side door. Other than that, the lot was empty. No police cars, nor was Billy's truck there.

I pulled up next to Matt's car and went into the place. It turned out that Silent Billy was there. He must have been chauffeured by his attorney, Matt. I would have loved to have seen the meticulous Matt driving the scruffy Silent Billy anywhere, but I missed it. Billy nodded hello, and Matt said, "You missed the excitement, Lucy."

16

"The burglar didn't get what he came for," Matt said. Billy stood nearby, nodding silently.

"How do you know?" I asked.

"Billy says nothing is missing," Matt said. He seemed to be taking his role as mouthpiece literally. "The police were here for a few minutes; they didn't look for fingerprints. They thought we might have scared the perp away when we arrived."

I turned to Billy. "I'm glad you're free," I said.

"He's not exactly free," Matt said. "The police would like this to be temporary. They're working overtime to put him back inside."

Bad news. I wondered if the police knew about the rift at the restaurant, but didn't bring it up. "How did the perp get in?" I asked.

"The outside door was easy," Matt said. "It has a simple lock. It was jimmied. Monty recently got concerned about the lock and bought a new one, as well as an alarm system, but he hadn't had time to install it."

"The inner doors were forced, too. The office door and the antique room door took more effort," he said.

Billy motioned for us to follow him through the huge dusty warehouse. Used furniture was lined up in long unbroken rows of tables with tables, sofas with sofas, lamps with lamps. No attempt at decor had been made. We passed the workshop and the antiques room; neither looked any different from usual. Next we passed the tiny room with a cot in it; then we were at Monty's office.

What was left of the office door hung open. The door and the wooden frame were splintered. We looked into the tiny office. It was a sight to behold. Small and overcrowded, with papers and stuff everywhere. A large battered walnut desk and chair took up a lot of the space. A file cabinet and an old-fashioned Coke machine were squeezed tight to each other against the wall to the right of the desk.

Stacks of papers, miscellaneous objects, and boxes filled with oddments covered every space, including the floor. Billy tiptoed quickly around the stuff to the file cabinet. There, he picked up a shoe box that had been set on top of some magazines. He riffled through it and pulled out a lock and several components of an alarm system. He held the pieces out for me to examine.

Everything looked the way it should. I wondered if I was expected to tinker with the parts. I flicked the lock back and forth. It opened and closed just as it would if it were installed in a door. I wasn't sure how to tinker with an alarm system, so I didn't.

"Do you suppose it was the murderer, after the rest of Monty's cash?" I asked.

"What do you mean 'the rest'?" Matt asked.

"Well, whatever he took when he killed Monty probably didn't satisfy him, so he came back here and—"

"The murderer didn't take any money from Monty. He had a roll of bills in his pocket when they found his body, Lucy. It came to almost seven thousand dollars."

How could that be? I was sure the motive had been robbery. "You mean he wasn't robbed?" I said.

Matt cocked an eyebrow and stretched his mouth wide in a tight line. "Isn't that what I just said?" He murmured impatiently.

Well, of course it was, but I was having a little trouble assimilating that information. I handed the lock and alarm assembly back to Billy. That made everything different. Very different. Monty had *not* been killed in a robbery that went bad.

Billy put the lock and alarm back in the shoe box. He turned to us from inside the office. "Cokes?" he asked. On hearing his scratchy voice, I noticed that my own mouth was dry, and I accepted immediately. Matt said nothing.

Billy sidestepped along the narrow space to the old Coke machine. It was more compact than a new one, a little shorter than Billy and half again as wide. Its sturdy metal shell had rounded edges and Airstream corners. It could have used a little attention from Edgar-the-auto-body-guy, but I held my tongue. It was made to dispense Coke. Not Diet Coke, not Classic Coke, not flavored Coke, and certainly not any other kind of soda. It was a *Coke* machine.

Billy took a dime from an ashtray atop a stack of papers nearby and turned back to the machine.

"Dimes?" Matt, who had appeared not to be watching, said. He was suddenly interested. "That machine takes dimes?" And, without waiting for a response, he said he'd like a Coke, too.

The Cokes dropped into the well and Billy took them out of the machine. His drawn face cracked into a grin, and he nodded and handed one to each of us.

The Cokes were in fluted glass bottles with tapered waistlines. Mine was icy cold; it didn't have the crimped metal cap that needed to be opened with an old-fashioned church key. It had a screw top cap. I knew that Billy's Cokes had been produced by some standard bottler only a few short days before, but the one I was drinking tasted so special it took me back to a different time.

"I heard they were a nickel in the good old days," I said.

"Couldn't find a mechanism for nickels," Billy said.

Matt tipped his bottle, drank deeply, and then turned to me. "Billy and I are going to have a long talk." That was my cue to get lost. Just when it would have been interesting to be invisible.

"One question before I leave, Matt. What was the situation when you defended Monty all those years ago?"

"I've been thinking about it," he said. "There's not much there. Monty was just a kid at the time, maybe eighteen, old enough to be called an adult. He was one of my earliest clients when I was fresh out of law school.

"He had a pickup truck and a rented garage where he kept a continuous garage sale going. All he handled was junk back then. Strictly junk. I think he even came by his garage sale stuff by way of hauling people's junk."

"He called himself a junk dealer to the end," I said, recalling Monty's frequent declarations. "But how'd he get into trouble? Surely he didn't mistake a stolen treasure for a pile of junk?"

"No, he didn't. It was a silver teapot that did it. He never told me how he came by that piece. I'm sure he was covering for a pal. I was too green at the time to realize how common that ploy is among the equally green."

"What do you mean?" I asked.

"It's a tired old story, Lucy, and I'm sure you've heard variants of it over time. Some sly fox with a lot to lose convinces a pigeon with a clean slate that *he* should take the blame."

"Oh, sure," I replied. "Protectors of the underdog or something. But I'd have guessed that Monty might be a fairly wily fellow himself by the time he was that age."

"He was street-smart, all right." Matt frowned and hesitated, then went on. "But there's a certain type of slick-trick sophistication among the street smart that Monty lacked. At any rate, he was a young fellow who covered for a friend. He felt, I'm sure, some sort of misplaced loyalty. He may have felt he owed the friend, or the friend may have put pressure on him. Something caused him to cover for someone else.

"It was the first time he'd ever been in trouble, and the whole thing might have been dismissed, except that this particular teapot was so special. It happened to be part of a larger heist of truly fine stolen objects. The teapot was the first item to surface, and Monty was caught with it red-handed.

"Over time it became clear to the cops that Monty'd been a dupe who may have had no real involvement, no knowledge of the crime, and no further stolen merchandise. But they did feel that he knew *something*. What they wanted was for him to hand over whoever connected him with that teapot. He never did.

"Had he given them the friend, he might have got off clean. As it was, because he'd had no priors, he was sentenced to a few months, reduced to a year's probation. But, because he was just a little too old to be tried as a kid, his record was never expunged," Matt said.

"How about the rest of the stuff?" I asked. "Did it ever surface? That could leave a trail to the real culprits."

"It showed up long after," Matt said. "When it did, there was no hint of where it came from, and no visible connection to Monty. That was a long time ago, and Monty had put it behind him."

I drove away. At Coney Island, filling my face with hot dogs, savoring the sauce that makes them Coney's own, I ruminated over the situation. Monty had not been murdered for the cash he carried. Then why? No matter which way I looked at it, a motive eluded me.

Nor could I see a way to connect that early incident with his murder. Matt had pointed out that handling stolen antiques was not the same thing as stealing antiques. But Monty was caught with the goods and was mixed up in that mess somehow. I agreed that he had put it behind him. I had seen him operate for years.

His sudden interest in an alarm system was interesting, though. It was as if he was expecting today's break-in. I turned it over in my mind as I drove away.

17

When I got back to Boston I drove directly to Chinatown. The streets were crowded with people strolling in the mild weather. I circled the area for twenty minutes before finding a semi-legal parking space, and made it into Run Run just as they were locking the door for their seven thirty closing time. A young Chinese woman let me in. She smiled sweetly, and locked the door when I was inside. I was happy that I didn't have to search out Hamp's second choice, and relieved that she didn't turn surly at my late arrival. She noticed my dithering and helped me find everything on Hamp's list. When she let me out of the place, fifteen minutes later, she was still smiling. Ah, the harmony of the Eastern spirit.

I had eaten enough food throughout the day to keep several families nourished, but the aromas from a neighborhood full of Chinese restaurants overcame me, and I stopped at the Imperial Pearl for an order of steamed dumplings. The sky was dark but the streets were brightly lighted, still full of people, when I waddled back to the car.

When I got there I found that some idiot had double-parked, blocking my car, so that I couldn't get out of my space. I banged on the horn for twenty minutes before two young Asian men came bounding out of a building across the street. They were laughing and talking to each other and pointedly ignoring me as they headed for the vehicle that had trapped me.

They were identically dressed in glossy silk suits sporting unnaturally wide shoulders, long jackets, and tapering pants reminiscent of old-time zoot suiters. I muttered at them to get a move on, and they both flipped me the bird as their car rolled away, but it was too late—I had already waffled regarding the harmony of the Eastern spirit.

When I got into the apartment there were no messages under the door. Splendid. I buzzed around the place for a short while, gathering my things for the next day. A small gym bag would do for my trip back to the Cape tomorrow night. I placed the vase on the marble mantel. It was so striking that I was inspired to get some cleaning things out. I gave the vase, the mantel, and the outside of the fireplace a better cleaning than they'd ever had during our time there.

It didn't take me long. I don't waste much time on housework at home, or in the little apartment. For some reason, though, I never mind cleaning and polishing my inventory at the shop. Since I've opened my own business, I've become acquainted with cleaning products that I never dreamed existed. I made a note to myself to bring the little can of marble polish from the shop back here so I could give the fireplace a real treat.

I called Natalie again, but when her answering machine came on I didn't bother leaving another message. I thought about calling Hamp, but he had something on his mind, and had little to talk about lately, so the rest of the evening was mine.

The opened can of tomato juice was chilled tonight, but it tasted a little tinny after sitting overnight in the fridge. I added a charge of vodka, and with the drink in hand I treated myself to a nice long soak in the tub. Comforting. Then, wrapped in the shabby terry-cloth robe that I keep at the apartment, I burrowed into the ancient wingback chair, feeling splendidly relaxed.

I pulled a bunch of receipts from the past few days out of my purse, and sorted through them in an attempt to do some bookkeeping. This is the part of owning a small business that I like least: the paperwork. Maintaining and updating lists of inventory, of buying and selling prices, of expenses while hunting, all of this is bothersome and I see little point in it. I buy stuff. Then I sell it. Isn't that enough to keep track of?

Dealers frequently "forget" to give receipts, especially in receipt of cash. This is against IRS rules, and accounting rules, and against the rules at Brimfield. It's another thing that's almost impossible to enforce, however, and I have yet to see or hear of anyone doing something about it.

When a dealer forgets, I make a little self-sticking note for my own record keeping. Our accountant has told me that as long as these receipts do not constitute an unreasonable portion of my record keeping, it's okay. I've agreed with him, but I'm not sure we define "reasonable" the same way.

I went through the slips, occasionally scribbling a more detailed description of the object. I also asterisked a few receipts to remind myself to photograph them later. Decorators often want me to mail photos before they drive out to the Cape.

My mind drifted away from the task at hand, however, and I thought instead about Monty. Not a robbery victim after all. Someone had murdered him for reasons even more odious than good old impersonal money. I thought about other motives: anger, fear, revenge. Soon the thinking stopped, and my own anger took over.

Whatever the killer's motive, there in the dark, taking Monty's life, he should be exposed. He should be examined in the daylight. He should have to "explain" to his peers, and to the rest of his world, the arrogance that allowed him to take another man's life. The evil that now allows him to let another man stand accused of his crime.

My anger warmed my skin, but deep inside me, ice began to crystallize, and I realized that I needed to take part in the process that flushed Monty's killer out into the daylight. I guess I'd known it all along, but I hadn't wanted to deal with the problems it would create for me. I resolved to help solve Monty's murder without putting myself, or anyone else, in danger.

It was eleven thirty when I realized that Baker may not know about the money in Monty's pocket. I also wanted to ask if he knew about Monty's old trouble. Baker writes a crime column in the *LIAR*. If he knew about that old situation, maybe he could enlighten me. I called his office rather than his home, and readied myself to leave a message, but he answered the phone.

"All of this is news to me," he said. "I'll see if I can find out more, but that's a long time ago, and I didn't start writing the crime column until the big heist at the Gardner Museum, so I missed out on Monty by a couple of years."

"I'm sure we're overlooking something that's right under our noses," I said.

"Maybe it has something to do with this candlestand," he said. "I've just been looking at it. I've looked over every inch of it. It's an excellent piece of workmanship. Butternut and cherrywood. Truly elegant in its simplicity. One of the drawers has been repaired, a fine job, glides open and closed smoothly. But there's not a speck inside, or under, or between the drawers that tells me anything. I find nothing. Nothing except that it's an exquisitely made piece of furniture."

"Who knows what he was up to, Baker. Maybe the candlestand itself is the message."

"I can't think of what it might be saying, except that

if he meant to interest me in Shaker furniture, he succeeded."

But if Monty didn't want to *sell* it to Baker, and if he only wanted Baker to hold it for him, was he hiding it? He had to be. So, was that what the burglar at Monty's Contents was looking for?

18

Ordinarily on a Brimfield Thursday I can sleep a civilized six hours, because the first opening is at nine. This time, helping Coylie, and tracking down Billy's campsite neighbors, I'd make four hours do. But for the first time since Monty's murder, I was sure I knew something.

The murder had, at first, seemed more complicated by the fact that Monty was not killed for his cash. This morning I realized that the actual motive, whatever it was, was personal. Had it been money, the killer might have been any stranger hiding in the crowd of thousands. This morning, after a brief but deep sleep, I could eliminate anyone who was a stranger.

Monty's killer knew him. I was sure of it. That still left a large pool of suspects, but now the motive would tell the story. As soon as I figured out why, I'd know

who, and I could do that without endangering myself
or anyone else.

It also meant that I could avoid mentioning the murder to Hamp. After all, finding out a few facts, and
then thinking about them, is hardly meddling in police
business. I don't like to worry him.

Before I left the apartment I phoned Natalie. It was
early for social calls, but I figured it was a good time to
catch her in. Wrong. Her machine answered again, but
again I left no message. If she was on her way to Brimfield from the Berkshires, chances were that I'd run
into her before the day was over.

I gathered my things for the Cape tonight. The small
bag of clothes, Hamp's ingredients, and a few other
odds and ends took up very little room. I considered
taking the cloisonné vase with me but decided to leave
it on the mantel in the apartment, where I'd enjoy admiring it when I returned. I caught myself fantasizing
about the vase, a "museum piece." The phrase had become a joke between Monty and me.

"New museums should be opened hourly to house
all of the objects spun into that category," he said.

"I *like* believing that I'll find a museum piece out
there," I'd said. "That's half the fun of the treasure
hunt."

"But does it have to be a museum piece for you to
enjoy it?" he asked. "Can't you just enjoy an item because it is what it is? The phrase has become value-
less."

"Probably."

"I myself keep a room full of museum pieces down at the museum—oops, I mean warehouse. And I invite you to come and select a few museum pieces for yourself."

That was the first time he'd mentioned his antiques room at the used furniture warehouse. I'd already heard about it by then, and correctly sensed that he was about to allow me in.

"So what would you call an actual museum piece?" I'd asked, not willing to let the matter go.

"At a minimum, the object in question has to be in good shape for its age, or of the finest quality, or if that doesn't apply, then it should be a very rare example of its kind."

I'd never seen him so serious, but it didn't last. He began naming things that had lately been called museum pieces. "Lava lamps, cabbage patch dolls, cutesy whiskey bottles, and while I'm at it, odd beer cans," he said.

I caught the spirit and joined in.

"Plaster Elvis statues."

"Franklin Mint coins."

"Hummel figurines."

"Commemorative Christmas plates."

"TV show memorabilia."

"Movie posters."

"Hey, wait a minute," I said. "People pay plenty of money for those old movie posters."

"Sure they do, and they pay plenty for new ones,

too, and all that other stuff. Then they squawk about the price of gas. Gas is what belongs in a museum," he said.

"Museum piece" had become a code word between us. We laughed whenever it came up. He'd used it whenever he got the chance. Which was often.

"What about actual museums?" I'd asked.

"They're full of phonies, including the geniuses running them," he said.

But after that he usually announced himself with, "I'm here with a few museum pieces for you," when he came into the shop.

Real museum pieces are as scarce at Brimfield as anywhere, and after the first opening rush has passed they're almost nonexistent, at least for a dealer expecting to resell. Collectors with big budgets can still find treasure, but not at a killing. Nevertheless, I still harbored the thought, more of a wish, that the cloisonné vase was suitable for a museum.

I arrived at Brimfield as daylight broke, excited by my new outlook. I'd look at Monty's murder from a new point of view, and I'd see the antiques marketplace from the other side.

I hadn't really sold antiques here. On occasion, as I intended to do with the pedestal, I'd sold an item I'd just purchased. People here call that flipping. But I'd never rented a space and sold antiques from it.

I picked up the Normandy pedestal at Al's barn, then drove to Coylie's camping spot. I transferred the pedestal from the van to his truck, and he packed his tent and camping gear. While his booth was open today, he would camp there. I looked around the campsite.

I knew which tents I was interested in, tiptoed over to the closest, and stood listening to the low rumble of snoring. Not good. I didn't have time to hang around this morning. I leaned forward and helloed a few times softly. I didn't want to startle the guy, only to wake him. The snoring inside the tent stopped. I stood back and waited a few minutes. Nothing, then the soft buzz of easy snoring again.

Okay. I cleared my throat, tuned my voice, and then yoo-hooed my at-home-with-the-family wake-up call. The snoring stopped abruptly with a snort. I waited again. I was wondering if I should give it another shot when someone tapped me on the shoulder. I hadn't heard him creep up behind me.

"It's five o'fuckin' clock, lady. What in hell are you tryna do? Run a train station out here?"

Startled, I swung around. He was huge, wearing baggy shorts and a T-shirt, and carrying an aluminum cane with a big rubber stopper on the bottom. I stepped back. The cane didn't appear to be a weapon, but his mood was nasty.

"I just need some simple information."

"You couldn't wait for a decent hour to get this information?" he said, glowering.

I knew it was best not to offend him further. If he

actually knew something, I wanted him to share it with me. I was about to begin some quick fence mending when the tent flap in front of me opened, and a fellow wearing striped pajamas and huge furry slippers appeared.

"Talk nice to the lady, Bertie," he said.

"She's here screaming her head off at five o'clock in the morning," Bertie said. "Why should I talk nice?"

"So she'll know what a nice guy you are," he said. He looked familiar.

"You the guy who sells baseball cards?" I asked.

"Mostly I buy them," he said. "But you've got me. I'm the baseball card guy. So what is it that you want?"

I told him, and he filled me in on what he remembered about that morning, encouraging Bertie to add his thoughts.

"The ruckus started a little after three thirty," he said, and Bertie agreed.

Bertie was still put out about the noise. "Sleep is at a premium around here this week," he growled.

He drew his eyebrows together and swung his thumb in Coylie's direction. "The redhead and the guy from Scottsdale were throwing things around out here. The yelling and crashing around was enough to wake the dead." Bertie was courting a blood pressure problem.

Both campers agreed that they left the campgrounds at about ten past four, which only got me about twenty minutes further along the clock than Coylie had left me. They remembered that Billy and Frankie were still talking when they left, but of course neither knew how long Billy and Frankie stayed there.

I got in the van and followed Coylie down to the marketplace. The campers didn't know enough to help Billy. I needed more information. I parked the van. We would ride into the field in Coylie's truck.

We were only allowed one vehicle in the field, and it was ready. We had organized his truck and worked out our display and selling tactics yesterday. Coylie knew how he wanted to handle the unpacking and setting up of the inventory. This morning all we had to do was double-check that everything was exactly as we planned, which we did four hundred times.

I found it hard to believe that I was so nervous. I'd been in this business for fifteen years, and before that I was a collector for as far back as I could remember. How could Coylie's little booth cause such a panic in me? But he was jumpy and I was snappish.

When the clock approached six a.m., the earliest we were allowed into the field, we still hadn't decided what time we should move in. We knew that earlier gave us a better chance to make preopening deals, but a long wait inside the field might become unbearable. They have monitors patrolling the aisles, checking that no one unpacks, or sets up, or does any buying or selling before the official word goes out.

We finally decided not to head for May's until quarter to eight. That would get us through the traffic and into the field an hour early, which would give us time to quietly check out the nearby dealers. We swung into the truck's high seats and waited. I leaned back and closed my eyes; maybe I could grab a little sleep.

I may have dozed for a moment, but I soon became aware of Coylie whistling through his teeth. After a while I recognized the song, "The Yellow Rose of Texas." He whistled the same few bars, over and over, faster and faster. I was about to scream that it was giving me a nervous breakdown, but when I looked over, he was looking back at me, grinning.

"Boy, you can stand it much longer than my mother can," he said.

"Shut up," I said, and closed my eyes again. But there would be no sleeping. I was wide-awake now.

"Lucy," he said.

"What?" I rasped through clenched teeth.

"Can we revise our plan?" he asked.

I looked at my watch. We'd been there for almost twenty minutes.

"What do you want to do?"

"I'd like to go over there now," he said.

"What took you so long?" I said.

Coylie started the truck, and we were off. Lines of buyers were already forming at the front gate when we drove up. Some people stand in line for three or more hours.

My own habit here has been to arrive about a half hour before opening. The two lines that form along the chain-link fence wait for hours in relative order. I usually choose to join the group across Route 20 because it's always unruly, which makes it easier to end up in front.

"Have you got our paperwork?" Coylie said as we reached the gatekeeper.

I handed it over, he showed our papers, got our passes, and we were waved in.

Some of the dealers who would be setting up were already in place. Some sat in their vehicles, some stood around, all careful to give the appearance of playing by the rules. No unloading, no setting up, no obvious selling. Coylie drove directly to his assigned spot.

When he parked, we got out, and several of the neighboring dealers drifted our way. Some were familiar-looking. Right on their heels was a field monitor.

"Everything okay here?" the monitor said. A subtle reminder that there was no deal making allowed.

One of the dealers looked at the monitor, opened his eyes wide, spread his palms, and whined. "I was just going to ask how old Frankie is doing," he said.

"He's got troubles; he had to go home," Coylie said.

Frankie again. There was a guy I didn't want to think about, but now he required some attention. Coylie explained Frankie's situation to the dealers, and a discussion ensued about Frankie's bad luck, with the dealers showing extreme concern while the monitor hung around. But when he finally moved off toward the back gate, the Frankie report was over.

A Humpty Dumpty–looking dealer said, "Frankie was bringing a painting here for me. A Georgia O'Keeffe–style landscape—large, an over-the-sofa piece, lotta pinks and purples in it, Frankie told me." He looked at Coylie. Coylie blinked. "Oh, yeah, I know the one you mean," he said. "It's in the truck, but Frankie went back home with a lot of the stuff he'd hauled out here."

Humpty nodded. "Well, when we open here, I'd appreciate it if you'd hold off displaying that one. I'm pretty sure I want it."

Coylie thought about that and another dealer spoke. "Maybe he wants it, and maybe he don't. But you hold it too long, you'll be cartin' it back home again."

Humpty looked irritated. "Don't listen to Bozo," he said, clamping his hand onto Bozo's shoulder. "I dragged something here for Frankie, too. We'd have made our deal long before this field opened, except the poor slob got called back."

Coylie, swiftly understanding, said, "Did you bring the Hoosier cabinet?"

"No, that's probably the guy down the field. See the guy wearing the red cap?" He gestured with his chin. Coylie nodded. "Him. I brought a pair of painted bookcases. Blue, with kind of Dutchy designs."

"Frankie mentioned those bookcases," Coylie said. "He wondered if they might be Swedish rather than Pennsylvania Dutch."

"Naa," Humpty said. "The Swedish stuff is rosemailing. These are more like the painted barn signs in Pee Aye."

The little group went on, with Humpty holding forth, and the others kibitzing, advising, meddling.

Coylie looked like he was paying attention. He was being indoctrinated, and he knew it. Knew he'd learn the drill despite the fact that some of his "mentors" were offering imperfect advice.

But Frankie, what about Frankie? What about his visit with Billy? He had Coylie's cell phone, so calling him should be easy enough.

I looked around, didn't find much promise within sight. It was mildly disappointing. People talked to one another in nervous little groups of two or three. Others paced back and forth within invisible boundaries. I felt constrained. Couldn't quite get myself up for pacing, but I needed to move.

I wandered off toward the front of the field. No one stopped me. I'd say the Porta-Potties were my excuse if anyone asked why I was wandering around, as long as I didn't have to actually use them. I nodded and waved to a few dealers along my path, and they returned my gestures, but no one motioned me over to offer a special deal, or to ask what I might have to offer.

Frankie, Frankie, Frankie. He left Brimfield in a rickety truck on Tuesday morning, probably no later than four thirty a.m. If he drove for fourteen hours, maybe more, before he stopped, that would bring him into, say, Tennessee. Some rest, a few more hours on the road, and by then he's got to sleep. That's twenty-four hours, and if he pushed on as far the next day, he's still on the road right now, probably somewhere in Texas.

By the time I got close to the front gate I had convinced

myself that nothing was going to happen here, no one was going to pop up and offer me a treasure. Furthermore, I was going to have to get in touch with Frankie. I noticed my tiredness again. I had been so wound up for this experience. Now the idea that today was going to be a washout began to trickle into my thoughts.

I turned to head back to Coylie's spot and saw a fellow heading toward me. Not a field monitor; a dealer, I guessed, with curly hair. He looked familiar. What now?

"Are you the one who bought the wicker platform rocker yesterday?" he asked.

"I bought one," I said. What was his interest in it?

"I thought I recognized you from the description I was given. You're the one with the huge cart that folds up, aren't you?" he said.

I laughed. "Supercart." A lot of people recognize me from Supercart. "Yeah, I'm the one. So, what's up?" I asked.

"Would you be interested in selling the rocker?"

"I don't think so. I bought it for a friend."

"A wicker collector?"

"Not really," I said. "But she asked me to pick up a couple of rockers, and that's one of them."

He hesitated, looking quite serious, and thought for a moment. "Okay, how about this. I know the price you paid for it yesterday, because I intended to buy it myself, but I got hung up elsewhere and I couldn't get here until this morning."

I nodded and made sympathetic noises. I knew where we were going.

"How about if I offer to double what you paid for it?" he said.

Good offer, very good offer. It must be special in spite of the condition it was in. Still, I hesitated. I had already told Al it was hers. How could I take it back from her? He must have realized I had a problem.

"Okay," he said. "How about if I throw in another rocker, wicker but not a platform rocker, in addition to doubling the price?"

Does he know what this rocker is? It's nice, but it needs work. "Have you seen this rocker?" I said.

"Yes," he said. "The dealer sent me an e-mail."

E-mail? I'll never be able to learn how to use a computer. "Does an e-mail show you what condition it's in?"

"The dealer made no secret of its condition," he said.

"Okay, I'll take your offer," I said. "But I have a problem: I don't have it with me. It's in storage about twenty minutes away, and I can't get there until late this afternoon." Not to mention that I really didn't own it anymore.

"I don't need it this minute," he said. "I need it before this week is over. I was so sure that it was mine that I sold it to a decorator, who, it seems, has already sold it to a client of his."

Wow. None of us owned the damned thing when we were selling it. No wonder he looked relieved when

I agreed to sell it to him. I don't want to antagonize the decorators I work with, either. They're an excellent source of sales.

We quickly worked out how we would trade the cash for the rocker. Our whole exchange took less than a minute. I headed back to Coylie. The field had filled in behind me; people and vehicles added color and motion and buzz to the field.

On my way back I spotted Mildred and Muriel standing by their oversized van. They waved, and I joined them. One of the field monitors must have noticed the wave, and headed over, too. No matter. I didn't need any cut glass, and I had nothing to sell the two Ms, so let him come.

We said hello, nodded to the monitor, and Mildred and I talked about the week so far. When we'd bored the monitor enough for him to move off, we had a laugh over it, and I was about to leave when Muriel spoke.

"Thank you for the invitation to the picnic," she said.

I was startled to hear her voice, and even more startled to hear that I'd invited her to the picnic. But I was quick enough to respond that I'd been looking forward to visiting with her. What began as a glib lie was rewarded by her smile, and the realization that I was in fact looking forward to knowing her better.

"I'm leaving my sister here alone tomorrow, so that I can share a tent with some old friends," she said.

"Sounds like fun. Is this a new interest for you?"

"No, I've been a collector for a long time, but now I'd like to deaccession some of my holdings," she said, laughing.

"Trying to simplify your retirement?" I asked.

"Yes. My retirement is finally beginning to come together after a year of hits and misses. When I left the museum I couldn't imagine what I'd do with my time. I was sure I'd stay connected with the people there, but for the most part they've lost interest in me." She didn't appear to be upset by that.

"What museum were you with?" I asked.

"The Meadows in upstate New York."

"That's a beautiful place. I slip over there when I need to have my priorities realigned. What did you do there?"

"I was assistant curator for a dozen years before I retired, but I came up through the secretarial ranks rather than from school with an MFA."

There was more substance to her than I'd realized. "That's quite an accomplishment. The Meadows has become a world-class museum during your tenure."

"Yes, but like so many other museums, it's really hurting for funds," she said.

"I can sympathize," I said. "These are tough economic times for museums. Fund-raising is becoming a major function in their survival. So, tell me, what will be offered in your tent tomorrow?"

"Well, one friend features glass, another has pottery, another has Shaker pieces, and I have flow blue. Actually, there are six more of us, each with a different interest."

"How about the guy selling Shaker? I'm interested in a Shaker candlestand."

"I'm not sure what he's selling, but he collects fine examples."

Maybe I'd get a line on that candlestand from the friend.

19

The field was now swarming with dealers and their vehicles. This created enough bustle to keep the monitors busy, and I managed to do a little business on my way back.

On my return, Coylie agreed to take a turn around the field. "But I'm leery about buying something I've never seen, from someone I don't know," he said.

"I feel the same, except that I haven't paid for anything yet."

"Why does it have to be surreptitious? I hate this cloak-and-dagger business."

"Because the best stuff of its kind will be sold so fast that unless you're the very first one to see it, you'll never see it."

"So why do the field owners insist on these rules? We're paying a fixed rent here—we're not promising a percentage of our sales. They're getting the same rent for the space whatever way we sell it."

"Coylie, in this particular field, the owner felt he was guaranteeing an even playing field, giving everyone the same chance at the goods. Those of us who figure out how to shop the fields before they open get the best prizes. The rest don't get a chance at the stuff we buy."

"It's not fair either way," he said.

But he soon left to see what was happening around the field, and returned grinning like a Cheshire cat, explaining that he'd had fun buying things he hoped would be wonderful.

Shortly before nine we congratulated ourselves on our preopening luck. We had done well. No cash had changed hands, but we had both done some buying, and some selling, too. We had dibs on a good many items we hoped were special. Additionally, there were several items in the truck that would be held for other dealers.

We were once again going over our plan for unpacking when we heard a rumble in the distance.

"Thunder?" The sky was clear and sunny.

"What, then?" And with a few minutes to go, the sound became clearer. Oh, yes, I had forgotten.

"Moo, mooooo, moooo!" And louder, "*Mooooo!*"

The crowd here sometimes shows its impatience during the last few minutes of waiting by mooing. After waiting in line for many hours, with just a few minutes to go, someone will start mooing. The mooing grows as the crowd picks it up and joins in.

I've been in the crowd when this has happened. Mooing's not my thing, but as part of the impatiently waiting crowd, I recognize it as a signal to get ready to move fast. Now, standing here with Coylie, listening, I was intrigued with the sound. Then it broke into a roar, and I woke up. This field opens punctually.

"Coylie, that's it. They've opened the gate, the buyers are on their way."

"Holy shit," he said, and his eyes went blank. "What should I do?"

"We have a few seconds," I said. "They have to stop inside the gate to pay. That bottleneck gives us time."

This field charges five dollars on opening day, usually nothing the rest of the week. One learns quickly not to get behind someone with a twenty-dollar bill. Worse luck is when some idiot pulls out a checkbook upon arriving at the gatekeeper. Save me from those people. As a buyer, if I can't be first, I scan the crowd and get behind some large fellow with a fiver grasped in his hand.

But finally, Coylie and I jumped up into the truck. Then the next three or four hours were a blur, and I have trouble putting things in order. I was out of the truck in a flash with as many cartons as I could carry, which I quickly piled onto our space.

Coylie stayed in the truck, moving things to the edge, where I could grab them, swing around, and place them in our space. Dealers around us scurried to set up. No one attempted to raise a tent; the fine weather had saved us from that struggle.

I noticed some dealers defining the edges of their space with inventory as they unloaded it from their vehicles. I copied this method; it made movement easier, and would make arranging the inventory simpler later. Before we had a dozen items out, the first of the crowd approached.

"Civil War, Civil War items, Civil War." He's always among the first to cover the ground. The sellers expect him, the experienced ones anyway, and he didn't disappoint them. If they had anything they could even remotely call a Civil War item, they waved it at him or pointed to it.

Often, he just nodded, with maybe an "I'll be back." He didn't always have to stop and pay in advance; he was such a fixture and so dependable that it was no gamble for the dealer. He'd be back for his booty, for sure. It, whatever it was, would very likely be the first sale the dealer made in the newly opened field. I knew that we had nothing for him. I shook my head to let him know, and he was off in a flash.

Now the rest of the crowd flowed our way, a tidal wave of hunters. We saw everyone during that early rush. It was almost fun. People we knew said quick hellos. Some rushed by, some stopped briefly to look or buy, then moved on. Within what seemed like seconds, Mr. Hogarth was in front of us. He scanned our space, bought a pair of hammered tin lanterns, and asked if he could leave them in the booth. We set them aside.

That's when we noticed that we had forgotten to bring the red "sold" tickets that everyone uses. We piled our sold stuff in a corner of our space and covered it with an old packing blanket from the back of the truck. We had trouble keeping people away from that blanket; they were sure that it hid exactly the treasure they needed.

Coylie emptied the truck quickly and I did the selling. I didn't bother to arrange things. There was no time. Soon both Coylie and I were both busy selling.

Frankie's paintings surprised me. They were the kind of pictures I thought of as wallpaper. Large over-the-sofa pieces, in a Southwestern but hackneyed style. And people were snapping them up like they were Old Masters. Without quibbling over price.

In addition to selling an amazing percentage of our inventory, for amazing prices, we also took turns running out to the places where we had prepurchased stuff. Then rushing back, to sell yet more inventory.

When that first rush ended, Coylie began setting up the tent while I organized the inventory. People now arrived one or two at a time for the second run-through. When the tent went up without a hitch, he appeared to be as astonished as I. With all of my assurances that everything would be fine, I had no idea that it would go this well.

We had managed to gather enough good stuff to

create quite a heap under the blanket. I had a half dozen pieces of furniture, too heavy to bring back, which I would collect later. When it really quieted down we began sorting through the pile under the blanket, and stashing our own purchases deep inside Coylie's nearly empty truck.

With that out of the way we were able to arrange the rest of our inventory attractively, and make it easier for people to see. I looked for my Normandy pedestal so that I could bring it to the Andersons later, but I didn't see it. Perhaps Coylie stored it in the front of the truck. Not there. I asked him about it.

"Oh, yeah," he said. "I sold it."

I looked at him; he was serious. "I promised that to someone."

"I know, but the guy offered me eight hundred dollars, and you said you were only going to get six hundred for it."

"Coylie, aren't you the guy who was outraged because a dealer could sell something out from under the person he promised it to?"

"I didn't see it that way. And didn't you tell me that you sold the rocking chair that you'd promised to Al," he said.

"That's different." But was it?

He just smiled his goofy smile, and waved at me over his shoulder as he set off on another foray into the field.

While I was there alone, Wilson stopped by.

"Looking for anything special?" I asked.

"No, just browsing." He looked around with raised eyebrows. "This can't be yours," he said, and swept his hand around, indicating what was left of Frankie's Southwestern art. "These paintings look like carnival prizes."

I held back a smile of agreement and attempted to rise to Frankie's defense. I can be a snob when I'm in the mood, but I didn't want to cozy up to Wilson if he was going to be condescending about my friend's friend.

"The seller is a beginner." Pretty weak defense, and also untrue, since only Coylie was a beginner. Frankie had been at this for some time.

But Wilson had already moved on. He hovered over Coylie's jewelry case.

"Interesting," he said.

Well, okay, that changes everything.

"I'm just beginning to appreciate it," I admitted.

"I'm not quite there myself," he said. "I always feel that jewelry should add elegance, but Indian jewelry doesn't strike me as elegant."

Oh, he meant *that* kind of "interesting."

"Elegance isn't the same thing for everyone," I said. "This particular jewelry is well designed, and wearing a work of art can create its own elegance." Coylie had been telling me that many of the Indian jewelers were true artists, and I was coming to appreciate their work.

"Still, some of it is too bulky to be attractive," he said.

"That's probably because so much of it was made to

be worn by men. It's larger—some pieces are huge—but notice the graceful lines."

"This stuff would overwhelm someone like you," Wilson said, measuring my stature with his eye.

I wondered who someone like me could be. "Some women can carry off big jewelry," I said. "I'm not one of them, but I can enjoy looking at it. And I have been admiring this little brooch with the birds on it."

"That piece is small enough," he said. "But it's the only piece in the case that's not made by the Indians."

"Really?" I was surprised. The brooch looked rustic and sophisticated at the same time. It was worked in silver, and had tiny turquoise orbs and a large emerald-cut amethyst worked into the design. The amethyst was flawed, but the brooch was very pretty and the design suited me.

In matters of taste, I'll put my opinion up against Wilson, or anyone else. In matters of attribution, if I haven't done my own research, I'm willing to defer to the specialist. Wilson, though not an authority on jewelry, had such broad experience within the museums that I deferred to his background.

"I've been thinking about buying it. But you say it's not Indian? Is it a fake?"

"It's not Indian," he said. He shook his head, looking irritated. "It's Mexican, the work of a peasant called Matilde. Notice the flaw in the large stone; she used anything that came along in her work. I wouldn't call it a fake—it's just inferior."

We looked at it. I still found the brooch striking. If it

doesn't go, maybe I'll buy it. I'll do a little research, but even if it's not fine stuff, I think I'll enjoy wearing it. So there.

We didn't have much to say after that, and Wilson was able to tear himself away without much effort. As he walked away, I spotted Coylie coming back with his arms full. Wilson carried nothing. I hadn't seen him carry anything all week. What was he after?

Coylie enjoyed showing me his finds. We were both satisfied with the day. There was now plenty of space in our tent. Customers were few and far between, so Coylie unfolded his lawn chairs. We threw ourselves into them and laughed about getting through the day.

My part in the opening had long been over, but I had enjoyed myself so much that I stayed. We had stockpiled bags of junk food to encourage us throughout the opening, but we had been too busy to open any of them. Now I got into a bag of cheese popcorn, and Coylie a bag of M&M's. Coylie wet his finger with his tongue, slid the pointed finger into the bag, and extracted a blue M&M on the end of his finger. He captured many blue M&M's this way.

While we were thusly engaged, Baker came by, flushed and out of breath. He looked upset.

"RAM wants to close down the whole kit and caboodle here," he said.

"Who's Ram?"

"RAM is Residents Against Murder, as if the rest of the world approves of the dirty deed. They formalized after Monty's murder, but I understand they're the same folks who have been trying to get the antiques extravaganza out of here for years. Now they want to close it up permanently."

"Why?"

"Well." He paused and looked at me over his glasses. His voice took on a higher pitch, he sputtered, and he picked at the empty tote bags slung over his shoulders as he said, "Think about how irritating we must be to the townies. The traffic, the parking, the crowds."

"I know that. It's the usual pain in the neck here, but what's RAM up to, Baker? If they're trying to make the case that this is a crime spree . . ." I sounded whiny myself.

Baker reached into Coylie's bag and took a handful of M&M's. "Lucy," he said, munching, "today their claim is that it's dangerous here. Especially now that Billy's been released from jail."

"Do you think they can close the place down?" I asked.

"In the long run Brimfield, I'm sure, will continue," he said. He looked convinced.

"But in the short run?"

"That's harder to say. It's possible that they could close down the rest of this week's festivities, or just as bad, they could create enough bad press to keep buyers away. I can't predict what will happen. RAM has called for a meeting with the promoters and the town officials."

Coylie continued selecting blue M&M's. Baker's hand was halfway to the bag again when he noticed Coylie's method. He stopped reaching, and held his hand, frozen, toward the bag. Coylie saw him and held the bag out. Baker politely resumed his movement, reached into the bag, and removed one red M&M.

"That's not the worst of it," he said. "While I was checking out Monty's old trouble with the law, I came up with another problem. A serious one."

"What now?"

"Monty's situation was pretty much as Matt told you, but what he didn't mention was that it became Monty's habit to hire helpers who were convicted felons."

Not good, not good at all. "Does that mean . . . ?"

"Billy was one of them," he said.

"What did he do? Do the police know about this? Will it make him look guilty?" I couldn't even form all of the questions I wanted to ask.

"Slow down, Lucy. Of course the police know about it. It can't be used as evidence of Monty's murder, but they believe it's an indication that Billy is violent."

"So what happened?" I asked.

"About ten years ago he was involved in a bar brawl that left one of the participants barely alive. He spent a year in prison, then on parole. I spoke to his parole officer, who was Monty's old parole officer, and also the connection between Monty and the helpers he hired. He told me that Billy never drank again after that, and that he was never sure that Billy was responsible for the original violence, but he was caught, found guilty, and served time."

"That surely looks bad for Billy," I said.

"It is bad," Baker agreed. He shook his head, looking ready to crash, and turning the red M&M around and around in his fingers. He examined his fingertips; they were rosy.

I had no idea how to lift Baker out of his mood. Keeping him busy might take his mind off of today's troubles.

"Baker, after you go through this field, can you do me a favor?"

He responded as I knew he would. "Of course I can," he said without hesitation. His manners are courtly and old-fashioned.

Sellers bring their goods in allotted vehicles. When the selling starts, no further vehicles are permitted until three o'clock. I asked if he would bring my van in for me at three. I wanted to start packing and storing my stuff as soon as possible so that I could get an early start on my trip home to the Cape tonight.

"As a matter of fact," he said, "if you want me to get the van here before three, I'll be happy to try."

I hesitated. If he tried to bring the van in now, and they stopped him until the posted time, he'd have to sit and fret for an hour. I started explaining, but he interrupted me.

"They consider me the press around here, so they let me dispense with some of the rules," he said.

We decided to try it. I gave him the keys to the van,

and he trotted toward the front gate. Maybe keeping him busy was the right thing, but things had surely taken a turn for the worse.

When I asked Coylie for Frankie's cell phone number, he said, "That's *my* cell phone. I hated to give it up, but it was the right thing to do. I showed him how to use it, but I know he'll botch it up."

I stood up. "I'll try to get him right now."

"If you reach him, tell him we had good sales today."

I left the tent, stood in the line for the phone, then had to leave a message.

20

When I came back we resumed munching. I told Coylie that I'd decided to buy the Mexican brooch.

"Great, that's a beautiful piece."

"I heard that it's made by Matilde, and that it's not Indian jewelry."

"You heard wrong. Matilde didn't make that brooch," he said. "And while I'm at it, let me tell you that, contrary to popular opinion, Indians live in Mexico, too."

I looked at him. "I heard it from an expert."

"The expert was wrong. Did he pick it up?"

"No, he didn't seem to need to."

Coylie raised an eyebrow, got up, lifted the glass on his display case, and picked up the brooch. He turned it over and pointed to the inscription stamped on the back. I turned it slightly toward the sun, and didn't even need my eyeglasses: "MATL Mexico 925 Salas."

I knew that 925 meant sterling. "Looks like the MATL could stand for 'Matilde,'" I said.

"That's what it stands for," Coylie said. "Her name was Matilde Poulat, and this was made in her studio. Salas stands for Ricardo Salas, her nephew. Her name went on everything, but his name only went on his own work. They both made wonderful jewelry and ornamental objects. Artists are still copying their work today."

"Should I have the amethyst replaced?" I asked.

"Hell, no. Don't let the flawed amethyst bother you. That's what she used. When you see a perfect amethyst that large, in old Indian or Mexican work, it's apt to be made of glass. This is good vintage. Google it and see how many jewelers are still copying their work," he said.

Someday I may Google something. In the meantime the brooch was mine, m-i-n-e, mine. The longer I looked at it, the more I found to admire in it.

We were just wrapping up the sale, when something at the back gate caught my eye. It was Baker coming through in the van. I guess they do make exceptions for the press.

We transferred my purchases from Coylie's truck to the van. I also had furniture held around the field, but we were almost an hour early, and if we drove around picking it up, our flagrant flouting of the rules would create trouble. A stroll through one of the other fields would be good. Neither of us had expectations of buying anything.

We stopped while I looked over a mahogany low-boy. Nice. Refinished, but well done. Made in the Queen Anne style, a style that keeps returning; it was about ninety years old. A reproduction, but a nice representation of the style, and old enough to be interesting.

"That's a very special piece," the dealer said, and he patted it. Everyone is into marketing.

He used the "dealer-discount" pricing system. In an upper corner a circled number indicated that the piece would be discounted by so much to a dealer. I don't care for this system, as it often means that the dealer is rigid about his discounts. I like a more flexible discount system. As long as the flexibility is downward.

Still, it was a nice piece, and heavy; it wouldn't be much fun for the dealer to pack up and drag back home again.

"Is that the best you can do?" I asked.

The dealer hesitated, a good sign; he was figuring his chances that I'd take it at a further discount.

"That piece will double in value before the summer is over," he said, grinning.

"It's a repro," I said, glancing around at the rest of his stuff. Nice; not the big-time treasures that I craved, but good solid pieces nonetheless.

Baker moved his glasses to the tip of his nose, looked over them at the lowboy, and said, "Nothing is going to double in value over *this* summer, and especially not repros."

"This one will." The dealer's smile said aces. "It was

refinished by Silent Billy, the murderer, and you know what a juicy story does for an antique."

Baker and I looked at each other, dangling jaws and slumped faces mirroring our dismay. Then we turned away. I knew that he was as floored as I, though neither of us uttered a word. We took a step or two back toward the path.

"Hey," the dealer called after us, and he named an attractive price. Ordinarily I would have taken it, but I was so dumbfounded by the thought of what he had just said that I couldn't consider it.

Baker hesitated, and returned to the lowboy. What on earth? He stopped, dug around in one of his bags, and placed something on the lowboy. When he turned back to me I saw the watermarked red M&M.

Baker spoke quietly. "It's true—a good story can improve the value of an antique." His mouth was set in a grim line.

Numbed by the thought of the lie that was taking hold around the marketplace, my thoughts spun. Many people, it seemed, had no trouble at all believing that Silent Billy had murdered Monty. My mind shut down and I decided that I had done enough shopping for the day.

Finished or not, my eye scanned the offerings as we plodded back to the van. A flicker of silver and mother-of-pearl glinted in the sun. Natalie's pickle castor! Well, I'd have to tell her that no one else had taken it home, either. She'd be glad to hear it when I finally caught up with her.

It was still a few minutes before three when we returned to the booth, but close enough to get started picking up my stuff from around the field. I offered to drop Baker off wherever he wanted; then I'd go pick up my stuff. But he needed company, so he got into the van with me. This created another problem. Most dealers are willing to lend a hand with the lifting and packing when the buyer arrives alone. However, with Baker by my side, they let us do the moving and packing ourselves, and Baker was becoming more useless by the minute.

After struggling with a couple of pickups, I gave up and decided to move along to Al's. Baker couldn't hear my gentle suggestions that he follow me in his own car. He rode in the van with me. I'd come back later for the furniture, and I hoped that Baker would quit helping me so I could get the job done quickly and drive back to the Cape while it was still daylight.

He sunk into the seat beside me; his explanations faltered, then finally halted. He'd slipped into a quiet mood of despair.

Unloading at Al's barn was the same. Baker was gentle with my treasures, but so slow and awkward that I found myself wishing he would just get out of the way and let me do it alone. I racked my brain trying to think of ways to get out of having him help me, but it was useless. Baker clung like a fearful two-year-old.

When I shut the barn door and heard the lock snap, we headed for the house, where Al was dashing around the kitchen, which smelled wonderful.

"Coffee's fresh," she said when I finished the introductions, "I put it on when I buzzed you in." She took a long look at Baker and said, "Sit down. I have something for you."

The kitchen table was set for coffee. Al placed the coffeepot on the scrubbed oak table, returned to the counter near the stove, and fiddled with a bowl of batter. Within minutes she had a plate full of golden nuggets that smelled like apple pie and looked like heaven. She placed the plate on the table next to two huge aluminum shakers.

"Apple fritters," she said to Baker. "Try them and decide whether I should serve them at breakfast tomorrow." She pointed to the shakers. "Cinnamon sugar and powdered sugar—choose your weapon." She nodded at me to dig in also.

The fritters were so hot we could hardly handle them. I tossed one from hand to hand with scorching fingers. The smell emanating from it teased my nose and made my mouth water. Baker took a bite. "Ambrosia!" he said, and blinked his eyes.

I sampled mine. It dissolved in my mouth. I tried another. A toasty crisp coating surrounded the sweet apple slices. The edges of the apple slices had melted during the cooking, but the centers retained enough body to allow the warm cocoon of batter to cling intimately. Bliss.

Baker, delighting in each mouthful, threw himself into the task. "Cinnamon for sure," he announced. He was convinced. "Or, maybe powdered."

Al beamed at him. "How about the batter?" she asked. "It's an egg batter, but maybe beer batter will stick to the fruit better."

I realized that this was my chance, grabbed up a handful of toasty fritters, and announced that I was going to go back to the barn to organize my things a little better for the next load. Baker and Al nodded. Al brought another plate of fritters to the table. Baker's eyes liquefied as he gazed at the plate.

"Some people like maple syrup on them," she said.

In another minute tears would flow. I slipped out the door. I spent about a minute "organizing" my things, and then I made a break for it. I'd think of something to tell them when I came back. In the meantime, I headed back to Brimfield for another load.

I picked up my furniture, and heard the news that the RAM meeting was in progress right across the street. I headed over and saw that people were already leaving.

"It was over before it started," someone said. "The fools from RAM never considered what the fees generated by this event mean to the town."

Good news to bring back to Baker. There was little enough of that lately. The coffee stand was quiet as people drifted toward the field I had just left. I sipped on a latte and enjoyed a moment's solitude. Bad news and unanswered questions prevailed. I tried to reach Frankie again, to find out how long he had talked to Billy the morning of the murder, but I had to leave another message.

No good news for Billy yet, but I hoped to learn something about the Shaker candlestand tomorrow at Mildred's tent. That was another piece of the puzzle that didn't fit. What was Monty's interest in that candlestand?

It was almost two hours later when I returned to Al's barn. I couldn't decide what excuse to offer Baker and Al when I came back. I went up to the house to see if they were upset with me. Baker was still at the table, still plucking fritters from a tray in front of him. He had slowed down since I left. He looked up and grinned at me.

"I'm sorry, Lucy. I've eaten most of them. I've never had anything quite like this before. Althea needed to save some apples for breakfast tomorrow, so she made some blackberry fritters. She's going to try cheese fritters sometime, too." His voice hummed with satisfaction.

Althea?

At that moment Al came into the kitchen from the pantry and set out a fresh cup for me. Neither of them seemed to notice that I had been missing.

Baker rejoiced at the news about RAM. "Of course," he said. "I should have put two and two together, Lucy. The town would never give up that income without a fight."

"What does the town get?" Al asked.

"Each vendor, whether antiques dealer, collector, or amateur, has to pay the town thirty dollars for a permit to sell. Since there are between five and six thousand dealers at each show, the fees have been a windfall for the town."

"If they sell at the spring, summer, and fall shows, do they pay ninety dollars?"

"Yes, and there have been rumblings that the state is eyeing all that income and wants to get in on the action."

I poured coffee and enjoyed a fritter; blackberries burst in my mouth, warm and sweet. Life was good.

"And a tidbit I forgot to mention," Baker said. "When I checked my crime sources, I found that the Shaker candlestand is clean. It's not reported as stolen."

Small blessings, I thought. Baker made the trip back to Brimfield with me. On the way he wanted to talk about Althea. He explained that she was an amazing woman.

I explained that I was seeing a Shaker specialist to-morrow, and it would be great to have a photo of the candlestand. "I'll e-mail it to you when I get back to the office," he said.

Oops. I reminded him that I was computer de-prived, and he promised to get a print to me tomorrow. I pulled up to the parking lot, where he retrieved his car. I drove off. I had plenty to think about on the long drive back to the Cape. I wondered if a computer would help me figure things out better.

21

When I got home, there was only one other car in the driveway. Unusual. This afternoon our driveway, generally an elephant graveyard, looked spacious.

I gathered my bundles together. Monica, the new addition to my family, came out to meet me. She helped bring my things in. I wasn't ready yet for this girl, this woman, my daughter-in-law. Philip had asked me to stop referring to his wife as "whatsername." I love Philip. I'll try.

"Hamp will be back in half an hour," she said. "I sent everyone else away for the rest of the evening, and I'll be leaving shortly to pick up Philip. You and Hamp can have the evening alone."

I looked up at her. A pretty face framed by copper ringlets. An evening alone with Hamp? Rare indeed. Could it be he missed me?

"Did Hamp suggest that?" I asked. Wow! He'd been so reserved lately.

"No. Sorry if it's the wrong thing, but you haven't seen each other for a while, so I thought you'd have lots to talk about."

"Oh." I wondered what.

I sorted through my stuff and busied myself putting things away. Chinese ingredients on the counter for Hamp, laundry from my few days away in the washer, plastic baggie full of antique costume jewelry on the dining room table. Monica fiddled around in the kitchen and I pulled my thoughts together.

"I saved some of tonight's dinner for you, in case you didn't get a chance to eat," she said.

"I ate all day long. What did you have?" I only asked to make small talk. I knew that if Hamp didn't make Chinese food, and Philip didn't make sandwiches while I was gone, they probably brought in pizzas.

"I cooked," she said. "Macaroni and cheese—it came out good."

The poor kid. Should I try some? My family detests macaroni and cheese. She'd need encouragement. I could probably give her some hints about what Philip enjoys.

"I would like a little taste of that," I said. I actually like macaroni and cheese, but we never have it because no one will eat it. Monica busied herself at the microwave while I got the laundry going.

When I finished, I settled at the table with the bag of jewelry I had collected over the past few days. I wanted to go through it and check the markings and findings with a loupe. Later I'd clean it, my way, and decide which pieces I should keep for myself and which would go into the shop.

"Ready," she said. She came to the table, where she placed in front of me a dish with a heaping portion of something that looked suspiciously like packaged macaroni and cheese. My God, I'll bet they broke her heart.

Monica sat down across from me; her gaze never left my fork as I speared it into the pale orange and white mass and brought it to my mouth. "Mmmmm, wonderful." I smiled and nodded. Cheese-flavored glue—the poor kid. I remember how hard it was learning to cook for Hamp; he had such odd tastes, and I had no feeling for cooking back then. Maybe I'd just take Philip aside and tell him to humor his bride; she was really looking for approval.

"What are the little red things in here?"

"I chopped up some pickled peppers. That's how to make packaged foods taste homemade," she said. "You just add something wonderful, and voilà, you're a cook." She smiled.

"Thanks for the tip." She noticed no irony.

I enjoyed the rest of the trembling mound on my plate, savoring, I felt, the peppers, as well as the flavor of the cardboard box that had contained the macaroni. When Monica finally tired of watching me and listening to me say how good it was, she asked me about the jewelry baggie. I emptied it onto the table. She oohed and aahed over the jewelry. She picked out several pieces for special compliments. I wondered if she were turning the tables on me. Had she noticed that I'd overacted a bit about the macaroni and cheese?

But, sure as Shinola, she showed a good eye for period costume jewelry. When I told her so, her response floored me. Could she come with me sometime when she had a day off? Like tomorrow, maybe? Startled, I told her I'd be on my way at four a.m. A whole extra hour of sleep. She was welcome, but I wouldn't wait for her, or anyone. When I'm ready, I'm off like a prom dress.

No one else in this family has ever been interested in the business of antiques. Some of them might enjoy the antiques, some not, but none of them has a speck of interest in the *search* for antiques.

I found myself warming toward her. She interrupted my cozy thoughts by asking what she should call me. I'd known her less than two weeks. Philip had brought her home, his bride, after knowing her only a few days. How about Your Dowagership? "Well," I said, "I answer to Lucy."

So in the next five minutes she called me Lucy twenty times, explaining between "Lucys" that she had made a double batch of macaroni, but the family had plowed into it with such abandon that she had opened yet another package in order to set some aside for me.

Huh? And she wasn't even embarrassed about the package.

She soon left to pick up Philip. I walked around the house I had left on Monday. Streaks of light still glowed on the horizon, but it had become dark enough indoors to turn the lights on. I was alone in the house for the first time in months. How had she done it? Should I be irritated that she had arranged for the rest of my family to be missing when I arrived?

Come on now, really? The answer was still no. Not on your life. When I'd left here on Monday, I'd seen most of them daily, except for occasional brief intervals, throughout the past thirty years. I wondered how she'd been able to extract the whole bunch of them at the same time. The house sighed in sudden comfort.

Hamp came in. We said hello. He hesitated at the kitchen door, his hand still on the knob. I had a feeling that he might turn around and leave. Maybe I should ask what'd been bothering him lately. Maybe I should tell him I missed him.

"How about that macaroni and cheese," I said.

"How about that Brimfield murder," he said.

Uh-oh. "Well," I stalled a bit, "you remember Monty?" If he hadn't, the murder had certainly reminded him.

"Don't get yourself in the middle of it, Lucy."

He calls that coming to the point. He thinks that's talking things over.

"I'm not in it, Hamp. I'm nowhere near it." But was I?

He looked at me. His eyes fixed on my face. God, he was still terrific-looking. Silver now fanned away from

his temples and blended with his tawny hair. It hadn't
aged him a single second. It only framed and softened
his features. I don't lie to Hamp. Sooner or later I tell
him everything.

Sooner would be my preference. But that's impossible. I've tried enough times. I start explaining something to him. He listens for a while. I dredge up every
aspect of the issue. He blinks. I provide him with facts.
Soon, his eyes glaze over; then he starts jiggling his
foot. I back up a little, tell him about events that led up
to the problem. He interrupts, and starts announcing
solutions I don't want, to problems I don't have. Finally, he tunes out. He's gone.

"You're up to your neck in this murder," he said.

"Why do you say that?" That wasn't true.

"Your big-time lawyer friend called here Tuesday
night. He grilled me for a phone number where he
could reach you." His glare bored straight into my
eyes. "You never said a word to me about the murder
when we spoke that night. Nor the next night."

"I didn't want you to worry." I looked away.

"Not worry?" he shouted.

That's it. We were off and bickering.

Today's bickering had nothing to do with the real
problem I saw here, which was his recent withdrawn
moodiness. You'd think that a man responsible for rigorous research at a university like Lyman would relish
solving a problem at home. But no, not him. At the first
sign of a problem he becomes quietly aloof. Inaccessi-
ble. He answers my attempts at communication with

one-syllable answers. He keeps to himself. After I've blown up, I respond in kind.

I've learned, through the years, to lead him into certain truths slowly. A bit at a time. With plenty of time for reflection and adjustment in between revelations. This, of course, can be done without lying. I have nothing against lying. I have no trouble lying to people outside of the family.

It's just that, in order to foil his outbreaks of stand-offishness, I've mastered the art of telling my own version of the truth in a way that makes lying unnecessary. A lie would be so much simpler, and quicker. Still, I feel better telling him the truth.

So I told him about it. Most of it. I told him about Silent Billy's arrest, and I told him about getting Matt involved. I mentioned the police station, and I told him that when that was done, I'd backed off. Well, I had backed off. Yes. That was only yesterday, before I'd learned that Monty hadn't been robbed.

"Lucy, that bullet . . ."

"Ummm." That bullet, that bullet. Will I never hear the end of that bullet? I still have a painful reminder on my left buttock, which I've finally convinced everyone is my hip. Do I have to listen to reminders of that incident until the end of my days?

". . . could've killed you."

"Hamp, that's over, long past. I stumbled into that mess with no idea how serious it had become. I'd never let myself get maneuvered into that kind of jeopardy again." And that was the whole truth, by anyone's most scrupulous standards. And I mean it. "That was so long ago." Why doesn't he just forget it?

"Not so long. Hardly seven years, Lucy. You're so mulish. You think the whole world needs you to fix their lives for them. To take care of them. Well, people don't need you running their lives. Give them a little room to work things out. Sometimes they're better at it than you are."

His shoulders slumped. He turned away from me.

He can't believe that I like carrying this load! Sometimes I get tired of taking care of people. Truly tired. Sometimes, everyone I know needs help from me. And then most of them want me to tell them that it's not putting me out of my way! That it's nothing. What is the matter with him? Oh, Lord, what's the matter with me? I do like getting into people's lives. I like getting involved. I tuned him back in again.

"Take care of yourself, Lucy. Let the rest of the world go," he said, over his shoulder.

Like who, Hamp? You? Is that what's really on your mind? Do you want me to let you go? Is that what you need? Is that why you've been so standoffish lately? Something's wrong around here, and I'm aggressive enough, finally, to go after it.

"What about you, Hamp? You're a master at letting go. What are you up to? You've been keeping to yourself lately. What's going on?"

There, I'd asked. That was the real issue here. Now it was out. Let the chips fall where they may. I could take it.

"Well," he turned and said.

No. Wait a minute. Wait. Don't tell me. No. Not yet. I don't need to know just yet. We can wait another little while.

"It's school, Lucy."

"School?"

"They want me to retire."

"Retire?"

"They want to dump me."

"Dump you?" Is that what he'd been chewing on? "You're not even sixty, Hamp. Never mind retirement age. You won't be sixty till . . ."

"I know how old I am, Lucy. Age isn't the issue. Getting dumped is the issue."

"I don't understand."

"They want to dump us. Get rid of us old guys. Bring in some new blood. Pay them less, and feature the trendy stuff the new PhDs are bringing into the academic marketplace. They want style, Lucy. Forget substance, forget scientific research. Bring on the flash. Bring on the dancing girls." His whole body slumped.

Well I'll be damned. It was only comforting that he needed. I put my arm around his shoulder. He rested his hand on my old combat wound, his chin on the top of my head.

Retirement? What the hell's the matter with those people? "We can work this out together, Hamp. You'll love to be retired. You've been telling me for years all the things you're going to do when you retire. You're not old. You're still young enough to do what you really want, and now you'll have time to do the things you'd like to do for a change." God, I wondered if we could handle it.

We stood like that a moment. He patted that old bullet wound. Then he began kneading gently, massaging the soreness away. Retirement? I must have sighed.

"Hurt?" he asked.

"No, just tired."

"How tired are you?" he asked. He wiggled his eyebrows, in his bad impersonation of Groucho Marx. He's so fair, and his movements so subtle, that his gestures resemble nothing so much as a man being surprised, very slowly, three times in a row. It does, however, send me a signal that he's moved into a different mood.

"What did you have in mind, sailor?" My impersonation of a naughty lady.

"Nothing specific," he said, dipping his chin down onto my shoulder and skimming his face along my throat. "We both need a rest. Why don't we lie down and see what happens?"

I looked at him. Well, well, well. What have we here? Quite a recovery from moaning about being dumped. And then, as the next thought struck me, I could read the same realization dawning in his face. The house is empty! While we'd been standing there wasting time, reviewing the error of each other's ways, the house was empty.

Without further conversation, we moved toward the bedroom. God, we could undress right here, and make a dash for it. We could even leave the bedroom door open if we wanted. Wow! Better not, though; someone might come back for a sweater or something. But, hey, we were alone.

Hamp closed the door behind us, and we both hurried out of our own clothes. Sensuously undressing each other is a fantasy of mine, but we'd never been able to work it into our repertoire. Never seemed to have time.

"Hamp, we don't have to rush."

"That's right, Lucy-love. We don't."

God, he hadn't called me that in ages. We dove into the bed and tried cuddling for a while. It turned out to be a short while. The past two, nearly three weeks had been tough. Though we hadn't ceased all communications, there'd been a reserve between us, an artificial politeness.

Now, as the reserve crumbled, the cuddling was left behind, and we plunged into communicating with an intensity approaching frenzy. With the house empty, we didn't even have to be carefully quiet. But maybe we were, from habit. I don't remember. What I do remember is that we both seemed starved for contact with each other, and when we connected, our congress was profound. When sated, we sprawled back side-by-side. Silent. I was incapable of thought.

I soon drifted into the sweet downy oblivion between waking dreams and sleeping dreams. Weightlessness tantalized my body. An indistinct web wrapped me in readiness for the dreams ahead, for sleep.

The body beside me rolled over, lifted its head, and mumbled, "Lucy?"

"What?" I was instantly awake.

"Don't teach her how to make real macaroni and cheese, huh?"

I'd have killed him, but I was already slipping back into that wonderful place.

22

Friday's four a.m. reveille found my energy level somewhat reduced, but within seconds my DNA reminded the rest of me that I had promises to keep. Minutes later I was behind the wheel, mildly surprised to see Monica tucking herself in beside me. First stop, St. Elmo Fine Antiques.

The shop looked great. It's one of my favorite places. Here, I'm the master of all I survey, I rule the roost, I'm in charge, my word is law, my decisions are final. God, I love it here.

This was Monica's first visit to the shop, so I took a minute to show her around. The front door, flanked by two narrow bay windows, opens into a long, narrow showroom, my main selling space. I flicked the switch that lit about two dozen lovely vintage lamps. They're part of my inventory, and they cast a warm glow over the place. I like it better than the spooky overhead fluorescent lights that came with the lease.

"It's beautiful," she said. Her gaze swept the room. "It's so elegant."

I could see that she was impressed, and it truly pleased me. "It helps that I have free rein with the decorating here," I explained. "No worries over whose chair has to be placed next to a thousand-watt lightbulb." She nodded, and encouraged, I elaborated, "On the other hand, no one can insist that dark rooms, featuring shadowy corners, make a cozy atmosphere." I escorted her along the narrow center aisle that leads to the back of the shop.

"I usually keep my premium inventory in this aisle," I said. "There are a few things here that I couldn't afford to keep in our house."

Mahogany and cherrywood stood radiant, glowing from within; no speck of dust violated the eye. Each piece of furniture presented itself on its best behavior. I'm exacting regarding the shop's appearance.

"Dusting and polishing here is a different story than at home," I said. A sore spot with me. My family finds it grand entertainment, this discrepancy in my standards. I braced myself for her comment.

"I can see why," she said.

"What?" I looked at her.

"I'm sure it's a pleasure polishing furniture like this." She gestured toward a set of mahogany library steps, each stair glossy. "It's beautiful. Even the corners gleam."

She was serious. More of this and I'd begin twinkling myself. "I usually keep a folded piece of chamois in my pocket when I'm here," I confided.

She nodded, and drifted down the aisle, mouth agape. She stopped in front of an arrangement of furniture. Her eyes swept the lines of a mahogany bowfront chest upon which I had placed a lap desk, an ink pot, and a quill pen. Next to the desk was a chair, the focal point. A simple mahogany Chippendale, made in Boston around 1770.

She looked at the price tag and raised her eyebrows. "Who can afford eight thousand dollars for a single dining room chair?"

I knew who could, but I had yet to tell him that I had acquired it. I wanted to enjoy looking at it for a few days. Instead, I told her who couldn't. "Someone who doesn't have Philip sitting on it, leaning backward, balancing on its hind legs."

She giggled. "He warned me not to do that when he brought me home to meet you."

"And you didn't, but you'll have to think twice before you begin furnishing a place that gets that kind of heavy-duty use," I said. "That's why I have that nice sturdy oak furniture at home." I could see her absorbing that information. I've tried everything to get my kids to sit with all four chair legs on the floor. No luck.

"But why is a simple dining room chair worth so much more than everything else in this group?"

"Because this is an arrangement of Federal-*style* furniture. All of it is old, most pieces more than a hundred years old, making them officially antique. But the chair is the only piece that was actually built during the late Colonial–early Federal era."

She hesitated, and then asked if the value of the more expensive piece would be devalued by its proximity to the less expensive pieces.

"Wow! Very perceptive question for a novice." Now, I was truly impressed.

"It's possible," I said, pulling my thoughts together. "In this case, I think it works the other way. I have a specific buyer in mind for that chair. When he arrives, he'll consider everything around it merely props for the chair. He's one of the few buyers who come here looking exclusively for top-of-the-line antiques."

"I thought the shop would look more like the house," she said.

"My first shop was like that," I told her. "Heavy oak furniture, some pine, mostly country furniture. Mission. I really snapped up the Mission back when it was more affordable. Arts and Crafts, too. My prices were cheaper, and my budget was smaller. I carried what I could afford on a tight purse, and I needed to sell it quickly. I sold the kind of things I could, and often did, use in furnishing our home.

"I still carry a lot of reasonably priced wares here." I gestured around. "Though I notice that my definition of reasonable has changed a bit."

She nodded, her eyes sweeping the place, still soaking up the ambience. She hadn't stopped nodding affirmatively since we'd come in the door. I enjoyed her admiration. I was showing off and she was easy.

"Since I opened this shop, I've moved on a bit. I've upgraded. But still, you'll notice that there's only a smattering of the really fine furnishings, at the very highest end."

"And that's what you'll be buying at Brimfield?" she asked.

I hesitated. "Sort of." I didn't want her to misunderstand our trip today. "Generally, the really high-end items come from fine auctions, estate sales, and an assortment of more obscure places," I said. "But, just often enough, Brimfield offers up a fine Duncan Phyfe table, or an exquisite set of Meissen porcelain.

"More often it's the bread-and-butter antiques that I bring home from Brimfield."

She looked at me. "Maybe there'll even be something that I can afford there," she said.

"There will be plenty you can afford there," I assured her. "But my advice to any novice, in addition to staying within your budget, is to only buy something if you love it."

We drifted to the back wall of the shop and peeked inside the small storage room for a minute. TJ had it stacked full. He knows how to keep it packed and still maintain a narrow pathway through it so that I, and certain customers, can scout around in there.

"Wow." Monica was wide-eyed.

"I rent a nearby garage for storage, too," I told her, tickled at her reaction. "It should be packed to the rafters before the week is over," I added. "I need even more space for storage, but good dry space is hard to come by here at the Cape."

Some lumpy pillowcases, piled just inside the storage room door, caught her eye. They were stuffed with linens that I wanted to sift through before deciding which would end up in the shop and which would go on eBay. Monica poked inside one, and it interested her. Before she got too involved, I steered her away, turning again toward the front of the shop via the farthest wall.

Two large alcoves open off that wall, one step up to each. They were originally rooms in the building next door, which is attached to the shop. This little cluster of shops goes back to when the owners lived in the back rooms, or upstairs, or next door to their shops.

Today, even those living spaces have been converted to businesses. Mostly boutiques. The buildings have survived hurricanes, blizzards, and ocean breezes approaching cyclone force. They've become quaint. Thus, they attract more shoppers, making the area attractive to even more upscale businesses.

My business doesn't depend on tourists—the inventory is hardly of the souvenir variety—but the neighborhood has become just right for the type of person who engages in a restful day of shopping for baubles: for the self, the family, or the home.

I'd enjoyed showing off, but I realized that I had to get moving. I told Monica to browse around while I took care of a few things. I needn't have bothered. She was everywhere, a hummingbird in a new garden.

TJ had placed some of the new stock from Brimfield around the shop. His treatments were complementary. They freshened up my little arrangements. I keep the shop loaded with treasures. More than the eye can absorb in one visit. That's how I want it. Elegant little vignettes at every turn, always drawing the eye, never the same scene twice. It's the kind of place you know you have to return to even as you're taking your first glance.

There were a few sales slips and notes under the brass inkstand by the phone. A note from TJ said that he'd see me at the early opening this morning. Great. He must have enjoyed the treasure hunt at Brimfield, because I had told him that I wouldn't need him until noontime today. The note also said: *Lucy, You need a computer and a cell phone.* That's how he ends every note.

He'd also left a sales receipt for the bisque hat pin holder. Great! It'd been around too long. I'd been thinking I'd have to send it to auction. It was so elegant that I'd been dejected when someone had called it a salt shaker. I chalked that up to unfamiliarity with turn-of-the-century customs, but I'd been dashed again when a most sophisticated customer asked me where the matching shaker was. And that, with a few hat pins stuck into it. TJ's sale was proof at last that someone understood. I know I shouldn't take these things personally.

While I was by the phone, I decided to call Natalie. There were no messages from her under the inkstand, or anywhere else. I fought the urge. Not quite four twenty in the morning. Might be a problem. But I resolved to reach her sometime today no matter what. I hadn't seen her at Brimfield since that first morning. Like many dealers she closes her shop during Brimfield Week, but no one I'd met had seen her there, or anywhere.

Why? Could she have been so distraught about the murder that she was sitting out Brimfield? Monty'd been a good friend to her. He'd done a lot to get her business rolling. But that didn't feel right. Murder was not what was keeping her away. It was probably not her love life, either. Though she gets skittish whenever the possibility of romance raises its lovely head, she calms herself by turning analytically abstract. So strike that.

She'd been so close to the spot where the murder took place that terrible morning. At that pickle castor booth, before his body had even been discovered. As I thought about that, it dawned on me that she could have seen something. If she did, maybe she was frightened?

That was it! I stood there figuring it out, so when Natalie said "Hello," she startled me.

"Where on earth have you been?"

"Do you know what time it is, Lucy?" That old refrain.

"It's time for you to greet the day," I chirped. "Especially if you're heading for Brimfield this morning." I poured as much cheer as I could muster into my voice.

Monica, now tearing through the pillowcases full of linens, looked up at me with raised eyebrows. She couldn't help hearing me; the shop was dead silent. I wiggled my fingers at her, nodding and smiling as I did, and she dove back into the linens.

I wished I had thought about what I'd say to Natalie. I could hear myself babbling, but I couldn't stop. I didn't want Monica to catch the drift of what I was talking about. The less she knew about murder and mayhem, and my part in it, the better.

"You are going today, aren't you? I mean, Brimfield's half over. This is your last chance to get the goods before the amateurs show up. And don't forget the picnic."

Nothing. I knew she didn't hang up, though; I could hear her breathing. I had little interest in the picnic myself, but I clutched at straws. If it could get me off the hook here, I'd give it a shot.

"I give up," she said. "What do you really want?"

"Nothing," I lied. "I've been calling you, and looking for you. I'm sorry I missed you earlier this week, so I've been calling." It sounded a little weak, even to my ears, but hey, what are friends for?

"I was in retreat."

"From who?" She *did* know something.

"The world, Lucy. I needed to think."

"About what?"

"About optimizing my alternatives."

"What do you need optimized?"

I heard a breath of air escape. "My life, Lucy."

Oh, that. "Well . . ." This was not the time for one of my little pep talks. She sounded aggrieved. The right platitude might be useful, but despite my firm commitment to platitudeanarianism, I couldn't bring the right one to mind. Still, maybe she knew something. What the devil could I say? "Well, I miss you and I want you to come to the picnic."

I listened for the line to go dead. It didn't.

"You called me at four o'clock in the morning to tell me you missed me, and to invite me to the picnic?"

It was at least four twenty now, but this was no time to correct her. "Well, sure, pretty much."

"Lucy, thanks. I've been grappling with issues that are beyond me. I needed to get away from the pressure."

"That's right, Natalie. Pressure's no good for anyone. You need to get it out of your system." Tell me what you know.

"Life's so short, Lucy. I've been so wrapped up in my own circumstances. Then there was the Monty thing, and I went away for a few days to think."

"What Monty thing, Natalie?"

"He was murdered, Lucy," she said. "Surely you must know that."

Jesus Aitch Christ. "Of course I do, Natalie." I took some deep breaths. "Where did you go for this retreat?"

She sighed. "A lovely place, near Barre. Peaceful and gentle feeling. They have a code of silence. A kind of Eastern harmony." Another sigh.

Oh, Natalie, get off the stick. I gathered my wits together and said, "It's good to get away and examine your problems. It makes the picture clearer, brings solutions into focus." God, I was starting to sound like her. My own picture was clearly muddy.

"Yes, I've been addressing my fear."

"Your fear?" Finally. Now, let's get down to cases.

"Yes, I've been fearful of the implications of collaboration."

"Collaboration? What do you mean, Natalie?"

"I'm contemplating effectuating the domestic context."

"Oh." This is all wrong. She's speaking Natalieze. She only does that when . . . "Natalie, are you speaking of a relationship?"

"Of course," she said. "You're inquiring after the reason for my retreat, aren't you?"

"Yes, of course," I said. This was going to drag on forever. It was going exactly nowhere, and it was time for me to leave. "But since I have you on the line, let me ask if you know anything specific about Monty's murder."

The line went dead.

Shit.

I grabbed the can of marble polish, stuffed it in my purse, and signaled Monica that it was time to leave. As we got settled, I mentioned that she'd have to ride back home in the truck with TJ, and this was her last chance to change her mind about going to Brimfield.

"No way," she said.

A few miles beyond the Bourne Bridge we stopped at a diner that might have pleased Edward Hopper. In minutes we were back on the empty road, with the smell of coffee and breakfast sandwiches filling the van. We nibbled and sipped in quiet comfort, and neither of us reached for the radio. The van hummed, happy to have the road to itself.

Monica understood that there was something peculiar about my phone call to Natalie. I had a feeling that she was turning it over in her mind, and that she wanted to bring up the subject. I was not about to volunteer any information about the murder, and plotted what I should say if she inquired.

After a while she asked, "Is Natalie an antiques dealer, too?"

Piece of cake. I have enough Natalie stories to fill every minute of the rest of our trip, and then some.

23

"Before I ever met Natalie, I knew her as 'Sacrifice,'" I said. "She wasn't quite an antiques dealer, but she was on her way."

"Sacrifice?"

"Yes," I said. "At that time, I always scanned the classified ads—still do. I never want to miss a treasure returning to the market. Once in a while I hit pay dirt. But at that time, I noticed an ad that had been showing up almost weekly, and it always began with the word 'Sacrifice.'"

"What did that mean, sacrifice?"

"Oh, it went something like, 'Sacrifice. Leaving area. Must get rid of,' and then it would list some items, usually things I had no interest in, such as kitchen tools, or secondhand maple furniture, or kids' toys. Or sometimes the ad would say, 'Sacrifice. Moving to smaller quarters,' and so forth. And then one day it said, 'Sacrifice. Tiffany lamp, must sell.'"

"And you bought the lamp!" Monica guessed.

I looked at her, snorted, and turned back to the road. "No way. Don't forget, I'd been reading those ads regularly. As green as I was, I knew that anyone who'd been selling that tag-sale junk was never going to have a real Tiffany lamp. But, as a matter of fact, it wasn't until much later that I came to realize that about ninety percent of the 'Tiffany lamps' in antique shops aren't Tiffanys, either."

I could see that Monica didn't know where I was going with this tale, but I was just getting my second wind, and I continued with my story.

"Well, it was a quiet day—probably a quiet month, back then—and to amuse myself, I called, asked a few questions, and I began to feel bad for the poor soul who answered the phone. She was confused, she had kids screaming in the background, and it was clear that she wasn't trying to put something over on someone looking for a Tiffany lamp."

"How did you know that?"

"For starters, she was asking something like twenty-five dollars for the lamp."

"A dead giveaway," Monica said, rolling her eyes.

"Right, and wait until you hear the rest. When I asked where I could see the lamp—I had always wondered where Sacrifice was located—she gave me an address in my building. The building where I had my antique shop."

"And you hadn't noticed?"

"Yes and no. When I rented that first shop, in Worcester, I picked a run-down building where the rent was cheap. There were a few struggling businesses in addition to mine on the street floor, and there were apartments on the two floors above us.

"I'd been there a short while when Natalie rented a little apartment upstairs. I used to see her arrive. She'd gather up her two tots, and her bags, and bundles, and get them upstairs. Then she'd rush back down and drag up several pieces of furniture, or cartons of stuff. She had a big old-fashioned station wagon, and there was always something in the back for her to drag upstairs."

"So she lived there, above your shop?"

"No. I thought that she was slowly moving herself in. But it turns out that she didn't want to actually live there, she just wanted it to look as if she lived there."

Monica looked at me, and I smirked. I had time to tell her about Natalie's business. We had almost two hours left before we reached Brimfield.

So I told her about Natalie selling used furniture because she didn't think she had the skills to do anything else, and she didn't think she could afford good child care, and furthermore she didn't want a bunch of strangers trampling through the tiny dream house that they had bought just before she was widowed.

Monica listened quietly, asking an occasional question, and before long, though I'd intended not to bring Monty into the picture, I found myself telling her how

Monty had found us, helped us, and had encouraged Natalie to develop an antiques business, which left the secondhand business to him. And then, of course, I blabbed everything I knew about Monty's murder.

We pulled into a parking lot not too far from today's action.

"I need to run over to May's before we get in line. I have to talk to Coylie," I said.

"I have a cell phone, if that would be easier," she said.

"You do?"

"Everyone has one, Lucy. Philip told me that you're technophobic, but they're easy, I'll show you."

"I'm not anything phobic," I said, bristling. "I just don't want to be on call twenty-four seven."

"That's sensible, but you can turn it off when you want to be 'out of range.' Mine is turned off right now. I'm saving the battery. When I get home tonight, I'll plug it in and recharge it."

"Didn't I read somewhere that you could be tracked down no matter where you were through your cell phone?"

She laughed. "Yes, if you have the FBI and the CIA after you. But if it's only the family, or almost anyone else, I guarantee you that if you turn it off, they can't get to you."

I didn't know that, but I had no wish to say so. Instead, I explained that we couldn't call Coylie because he had lent his phone to someone—in fact, the very same someone that I'd been trying to reach. I steered us over, introduced the two, and told Coylie that I hadn't been able to reach Frankie so far, but that I'd left messages.

"I tried him, too, and got no answer, but when I called his home phone they said that he was still on the road, but that he should be arriving home by mid-morning today."

I took his home number and said I'd try him there, later. Monica again volunteered the use of her cell phone. I took the information I needed, and both Monica and Coylie gave me a lesson in cell phone use, using short declarative sentences, and giving me extremely simple directions. I sensed some condescension, but decided that it was better for me to learn how to use the phone than to get upset about their patronizing tone.

That done, Coylie gave me an envelope Baker had dropped off earlier. It held several excellent photos of the candlestand. So, we were on our way. Coylie couldn't join us. He would keep his booth open until just before the picnic. On the way over, I spotted Mr. Hogarth. He was, of course, headed the same way we were going, and I maneuvered us right into his pathway.

Except for the black silk top hat, Mr. Hogarth was dressed rather staidly for him. His wide black suspenders clamped a plaid shirt in place and kept his voluminous khaki pants at full mast. A tall man, he claims he's shrinking, but he still reaches more than six feet. The top hat added another foot to his height.

He doffed his hat and bowed deeply to Monica

when I introduced them. Monica looked over at me, checked my reaction, and was satisfied that we were in the presence of a friend. Mr. Hogarth stepped between us, put a hand on each of our shoulders, and steered us in the direction of the only opening for Friday, J & J Productions. I basked in our high degree of reflected visibility.

"This place is often called the Girls' Field," he told Monica.

"That has the ring of political incorrectness."

"The girls referred to are the daughters of the original founder of the whole Brimfield shebang," he said. "Fifty years ago they were 'the girls' to him, and they became the Girls to the regulars here."

"The term seems to be less an issue than the fact that they changed the opening hour today to celebrate the fiftieth anniversary," I said. "That's why we got to sleep until four this morning."

"I guess I should be grateful for that," Monica said.

When we reached the entrance we saw TJ near the front of the line. He waved at us with the rolling motion that is an invitation to come on over, but I knew better. Line jumping is a subtle art at Brimfield and has to be done with sly cunning. This is one of those fields that has a well-organized opening procedure that excels at keeping things evenhanded. But, just in case we were inclined toward disputing that convention, there came from the crowd a rumble of warnings and comments, reminding us that cheating would not be tolerated in broad daylight.

TJ grinned at his faux pas, and seemed to be for-
given by the crowd since he showed an acceptable
level of embarrassment, nicely matched with his obvious youth. He was all in black again today: jeans,
T-shirt, and vest. Black does make people look tall and
slim, I thought, before I caught myself. He's at least ten
inches taller than I, and probably thirty or more pounds
lighter. His tallness and slimness weren't merely an illusion because he was wearing black.

Mr. Hogarth led our little group to the end of the
line, where he and I engaged in our Alphonse-and-
Gaston act—"You go first." "No, you first." "No, ladies
first." "No, age before beauty"—until Mr. Hogarth
humbly accepted the spot ahead of me in the line. As
he always does.

We nodded hello to several people around us, and
the line got longer immediately after we were in place.
With about an hour to go, the numbers get serious.
Multitudes of buyers gather.

"Several years ago, I watched a young couple get
married in this line," Mr. Hogarth said.

"Really?" Monica asked.

Someone nearby in the crowd answered, "I remember that. It was another great moment at Brimfield."

"That couple met in this very line the year before
they married."

Monica looked at me with a huge grin. "I wonder
what'll happen this year," she said.

"All I want to happen today is some good shopping," I said. I was happy she had come along; the lack

of sleep was getting to me, and her exuberance perked me up, made it easy to kill an hour in the line visiting.

The clock worked its way around to eight a.m., and we were off. Mr. Hogarth disappeared without a trace. We'd planned to meet again at the Patio. I told Monica that I always turned right when I entered a field, then scanned every booth, some quicker than others, then up and down every aisle. Not complicated, but consistent. "That's Mr. Hogarth's method, except that he always turns left," I said.

We stopped almost immediately so I could look at a small table. A leaf-shaped dish caught Monica's eye, and she picked it up and looked it over. She hesitated. It was pretty.

"Do you love it?" I asked.

"I don't know if I love it," she said. "I like it, and I can afford it. But I don't know if I love it."

"Visualize it doing something," I said.

"Doing something?"

"Yeah, like holding macaroni and cheese, or bonbons, or . . ."

She laughed. "I'm not sure," she said.

"If you're shopping for yourself, there'll be plenty here that you'll have no doubt about."

"I think this one's not for me," she said, and she put it down.

"Nor this table for me, so let's move on."

She looked at several things along our way. It slowed me down, but it was interesting to watch her getting into it. When we reached Muriel's tent, we looked around. It was a large tent where several sellers had joined together to sell their wares. Muriel had organized the group, and she had picked her sellers carefully; the tent was loaded with superb objects.

The friend with the glass had an assortment of fine cameo glass, including a stunning piece of Galle. Monica stopped when she saw a little glass figurine.

"My grandmother had a piece of glass something like this," she said. "She called it end-of-the-day glass, because her father made it with leftover material when his work was finished, back at the Pairpoint factory in New Bedford."

"Wow! Pairpoint was one of the fine glass producers. Their pieces are very collectible now. Does your family still have that piece?" I asked.

"I may have it," she said. "No one in our family wanted it after my grandmother was gone. I have a couple of cartons of her stuff. But I've never had a place to put it."

"This is an excellent example."

"I think I'll take it," Monica said.

"Now you have a collection," the dealer said.

We laughed. Monica would soon learn how true that was. She looked the rest of the tent over, and I purchased a small flow blue pitcher from Muriel, who introduced me to her friend Jake, who was selling a Shaker accumulation.

I told him of my interest in the candlestand. He admired the photos, said the candlestand was a fine example, but that he didn't recognize it. "Do you suppose your friend was hiding it because it fell off the back of a truck?" he asked.

"Stolen? No, it's not reported as stolen." And Baker is the last person anyone would bring a stolen object to.

"Some stolen stuff doesn't get reported," he said. "Some places don't keep track of things. A gallery would have to, but there are museums that might not even notice it's missing for several years. A lot of those places are lax about storage, and very slow to do inventory audits."

That certainly complicated matters, and when we finished our first round of shopping, I was glad that Monica felt ready to do the second run-through alone.

She moved off to shop. Nice. I wouldn't have to fumble through my call in front of her. I found Frankie's home phone number and punched it in. Finally, pay dirt. I gave him some background, said I was interested in Billy, and was surprised to find him unwilling to talk to me.

Remembering that he had been called home for an emergency, I attempted some sympathy, which he rejected with the comment, "My problem, not yours." Well, excuuuse me. I tried to get back on message, but Frankie was adamant about it being none of my damned business what Billy did on his own time.

Aha. Billy must have actually fixed the frame, then told Frankie not to mention it to anyone because his boss didn't want him working for anyone else. Rather than try to explain Monty's quirks to Frankie, I tried a different approach.

When I said I was a friend of Coylie's, and that I had helped him open the booth yesterday, he loosened up. But he was more interested in hearing about the opening sales than in describing his interaction with Billy. I finally pulled the information I wanted out of him. Billy *had* fixed the frame, and it had taken about a half an hour after they gathered the tools and equipment needed for the job.

"He was still packing his camping gear when I was ready to leave," Frankie said.

"What time was that?" I asked.

"I can tell you that exactly," he said. "It was four thirty. I called home just before I left. That stupid phone gives you the time, it tells you where you're located, and it tells you everything except how to operate it." I could understand, but I found that I just didn't like the guy, and said good-bye quickly. Okay, Billy was accounted for until four thirty that morning. That's better, and he was still packing his gear at that time.

I gave the phone a few seconds to disconnect from Frankie and quickly punched in Matt's number. I didn't want this to get away from me. I got a ringing signal.

"What time did Monty die?" I asked when he picked up.

Matt, who can ask plenty of questions, is not quick to answer them. "Why do you need to know?" he asked.

"Someone talked to Billy near the time of the murder."

"The campers," he said. "Billy told me about them, and I talked to them, but they knew nothing."

"How about the guy who drove back to Scottsdale?" I asked.

Silence, before I heard Matt clear his throat. "Billy didn't know his name or how to get in touch with him. How did you find him?"

"I used my little gray cells," I said. That could have backfired, but it didn't.

Matt laughed. "Okay, but understand this, Lucy: If I share information, I want what you know."

"Only fair, Matt."

"They're calling the official time 'between four and five a.m.,'" Matt said. "Monty's body was found at daybreak, which was five that morning. He could have been dead for an hour. But it's possible that it was earlier."

"Then I do have news for you. Monty was seen, alive and kicking, just before four, and I can account for Billy until four thirty," I said.

"Why didn't you tell me about that?"

"I just did." Matt, who doesn't get that kind of response often, at least from me, backed off. I'm brazen when I'm wrong, and I knew I should have mentioned Mildred's meeting earlier.

I said I'd have Mildred get in touch with him, and gave him Frankie's phone number.

"How can they figure the time, Matt?"

"Monty had clear eyes, the right body temperature, no lividity, no rigor."

"Can they fine-tune it any better?" I asked.

"The pathologist's report will pin it down by the condition of the stomach contents, but that's what they have right now."

It was time to hang up. I didn't want to think about lividity or stomach contents.

I decided to ease my squeamishness by beginning my own second run-through, and started on the other side of the field. That would keep me from following Monica; I didn't want to be in her hair as she tried to figure out what she wanted.

24

I decided to see that pickle castor again. The dealer, a woman I've seen at auctions and antiques gathering places, specializes in old containers. Mason jars, enameled soda bottles, tin boxes that once held tobacco, spice, or tea. Containers of almost any sort. She sells regularly here. I've looked at perfume bottles in her booth from time to time.

I couldn't bring her name to mind, though I was sure I knew it. She has a few years on me, and she's a woman who usually looks comfortable with herself. This morning she seemed somewhat frazzled. She rearranged her stock a bit, and tidied her booth in the quiet that usually precedes the arrival of the amateurs.

I looked at a lovely old hatbox. It was covered in pink silk and had a thick gold cord handle. Clusters of tiny silk roses adorned it. Except for some fading, the

silk was in excellent condition. I was about to ask the
price when my eye settled on the pickle castor.

I headed straight for it and gave it a closer look. I
wondered if I should show some interest in it. A pickle
castor is not my type of thing ordinarily. But if I could
grab it for the right price, I'd be able to kill two birds
with one stone. The negotiations could become my en-
trée into a conversation with this woman about the
morning of the murder. Then I could bring it to Natalie
as a peace offering. I stood hesitating, not sure how to
approach her.

"I wondered how long it would take you to get to
that pickle castor," she said.

"What?" So much for a good approach.

"The pickle castor," she said, and she pointed to it,
right there under my fingertips. Duh. "You're Lucy St.
Elmo, aren't you? You got yourself shot in the keister a
few years ago, outing some murderer down at the
Cape, didn't you?"

Shirley. Her name is Shirley, I finally remembered.
Now, how the devil does she equate that stupid incident with her silly pickle castor? I pulled my thoughts
together and nodded to confirm her question. I wondered if I should feign injured dignity.

"Well, I'm doggone glad you're here," she said.

She squinted, and peered at my face with such intensity that I wondered if I remembered my moistur-
izer this morning. A grin began at the center of her
mouth, then spread outward as she took a deep breath
and went on. "Now you can get cracking on this one.

Between the cops pestering me about the murder and the dealers pestering me about the pickle castor, I've had enough of this doggone foolishness to last me a lifetime.

"The minute I saw you I knew good and well that you didn't come here about any doggone hatboxes." She gripped my arm just above the elbow and jabbed her free hand into my shoulder as she spoke, the grin nearly reaching her ears.

Shirley thinks I'm going to solve Monty's murder!

"Why are the cops pestering you?" I asked when I realized this.

"They've been after all of us in this little corner near the slope. They've convinced themselves that we have a view of the spot where Monty was killed. Except that no matter how often we point out that you can't see that doggone spot from here even in the daylight, that it was dark, that we were rushing around unpacking our stuff, shouting back and forth to one another, and scuffling around moving things into our booths, they ask the same stupid questions. Did we see Monty? Did we see anyone near the spot? Did we notice anything suspicious?"

"So they've been questioning all of you?" That seemed natural enough, given the location.

"Yes, but when they get to someone who knows something, like me, they back off."

"And you, of course, know . . . ?" I still had no idea what she thought she knew.

She nodded vigorously. "I tell 'em about the doggone pickle castor." With that my shoulder took another pounding.

"The pickle castor?"

"Yes, every time they come here, I mention that doggone pickle castor, and they don't give a flying fart about the doggone thing." She took a breath, pulled her shoulders up to her ears, and spread her hands out palms up.

I backed away quickly and turned that shoulder away from her. She stepped toward me. The doggone pickle castor? As she closed in on me, I threw my arm over her shoulder and patted her on the back. Damned if she didn't burrow her face into my shoulder and sigh deeply. I could feel her shoulders tremble briefly. Then she backed away again, squared her shoulders, and took another deep breath.

"Well, Shirley, why don't you tell me about the dog"—I almost slipped "pickle castor?"

Shirley didn't bat an eyelash. She looked up at me. It felt good to be taller than someone. She's one of the dozen people on earth that I'm taller than. There, there, Shirley, it's gonna be all better. I placed a hand on her shoulder. That stabilized her. She didn't move. She certainly seemed to connect the pickle castor with the murder.

"Well, as you can see," she said, "I'm stuck with the doggone thing. After Monty's murder I was still sure a collector, or a museum, would pick it up. The doggone thing will drive me nuts."

I looked close. It was an excellent piece. Delicately

wrought silver vines dripping with wisteria surrounded the mother-of-pearl container in a sinuous embrace. A tiny set of tongs in the same vinous pattern hung from its blossom-clustered hook. It was meant to serve pickle at an elegant Victorian table.

The pickle was, of course, just as likely to be tart preserved fruit, or colorful crisp vegetables, as it was to be cucumbers or gherkins. Pickle was served in counterpoint to rich Victorian meals. Heavy, gravy-laden meat dishes. Salads, not unknown, being thought of as kitchen food, or even worse, French peasant food.

But how the devil did Monty's murder fit in?

"Monty came into my shop about a month ago," she said, answering my thoughts. "He got up that way maybe a couple of times a year."

"He made the rounds, didn't he?" I said. Her shop is in northern Vermont. I do some hunting in Vermont, but I seldom venture north of Quechee, and have never been as far north as her place.

She nodded her agreement. "He pounced on the dog-gone thing as soon as he spotted it. At first I thought he was angry, but he wasn't. He just wanted to know everything there was to know about it. He wanted to know where it came from and how I got it. He even asked if it had a provenance. Can you beat that? A provenance. Wanted to know if I had a written provenance." Her eyes were wide.

Curiouser and curiouser. A written provenance. Americans are very casual about what we call an antique, and even more casual about proof that an an-

tique is precisely what it claims to be. This is particularly
true in the under-a-million-dollars category, but even
in the big time, written provenances are scarce and
sketchy. The European antiques community claims to
look askance at this and other American practices. But
plenty of them were here today, and plenty of them
were buying and selling without papers.

I couldn't imagine Monty having an interest in a
written provenance, and I was as perplexed as Shirley
was over his behavior. His claim was always that he
was in the junk trade, but he had a rich understanding
of antiques, and I'm sure he loved them.

"And did you remember where it came from?"

"Are you kidding?" she said. "Of course I remembered where it came from. I can tell you where every
piece in my shop came from. Can't you?"

In fact, I can. I forget all kinds of things, but I can
always remember where I bought a fine antique. A
name might stump me for a while, but usually it comes
back to me. Even when it doesn't, I can describe the
person, or the shop, or the way I got to the place. That
nudges my memory. I'm able to do that for years after
an event.

"I got this before an estate sale," Shirley said. "The
woman who's lived across the street from me for years
had an oddball uncle who died. She had to dispose of
his estate, and she invited me to take anything I wanted
if I'd help her sell off what I didn't want. She wanted
nothing for herself. My understanding is that the uncle
was nasty, and you know how those things go."

"Indeed I do." That kind of estate sale is a dream come true.

"I made a killing on that one. I was, of course, the first dealer to see the stuff. What a day that was. . . ." Shirley gazed into the distance. She seemed lost in remembering the estate sale. She named items offered in that sale. She lingered over the triumphs of the day. Her hands were up by her own shoulders, beating at the air. I took both of them and held them, patty-cakes, nudging her back to me. We stood like that while she returned her mind to Monty's visit.

"Monty wanted that pickle castor, but he didn't want to buy the doggone thing. He asked me to lend it to him. I hesitated, but before I could make up my mind, he'd reconsidered. He said it would be better if I'd put it aside, then bring it here to Brimfield for the spring event. He said he'd bring me a buyer, and he'd guarantee its sale at my top asking price. The whole thing was odd.

"Monty usually came around to sell me something, not to buy something. I asked why he didn't just send the buyer up to the shop. He told me he had to witness this sale, and he kept assuring me that his buyer would pay a premium for it. I hate to hold anything for a month, but it's my off season at the shop right now. I do some business in this mild weather, but my big sales come during the ski season, when the skiers come up from New York City. New Yorkers have a different attitude about money than summer tourists do."

Shirley again strayed from the story I wanted. I began to see why the police had backed off. Her story is so convoluted that it's hard to separate the nuggets from the fruitcake. Hard to know if she really knows something.

Then Shirley told me that Monty was supposed to bring that very same buyer to her booth *before* the official opening of the Brimfield marketplace on Tuesday morning.

"Oh, my God." Now, I saw. She's right. Monty's buyer . . . is the killer. No. No, maybe not. But, if not the killer, then he may have seen the killer. He.

"Did he say if the buyer was a man?" I asked.

"I don't think so," she said. "I've been trying to remember exactly what he said, but I only recall him saying 'this buyer' when he was at the shop. Then, the day before Brimfield opened, he called to confirm. He definitely only referred to 'my buyer' on the phone."

"Did you tell the police Monty was bringing an early buyer on opening day?"

"In so many words," she said.

I'll bet.

When I asked the price of the pickle castor, it was easy to see why Shirley was still stuck with the doggone thing. Dealers and collectors had been interested in it, but Shirley's wildly inflated price had driven them away. I asked why she was so rigid, and she told me that it was a museum piece. I grinned and kept my mouth shut. Perhaps she would run into someone who had a museum with just the right spot for it.

I ended up buying the silk hatbox. I could visualize

it brimming with freshly laundered linens and laces. A bar of lavender soap in the bottom would fill the box with fragrance and permeate the linens, and its old-fashioned scent would burst into the air whenever the box was opened. People love to open a box and find wonderful things inside. I swaddled the hatbox in an old sheet and tucked it into Supercart. Then I rushed off to see Shirley's neighbors, none of whom had seen or heard anything unusual around the time of the murder. A variety of theories were offered, but they were the type based on *Law and Order*, rather than on fact or observation.

25

TJ and Monica were at the Patio regaling Mr. Hogarth with tales of their triumphs. They gloated over their success. When I arrived, Monica dug around in the tote bag she carried and came up with an amber brooch. A beauty, set in gold filigree. The amount of actual gold in the setting was likely to be minimal, but it was a finely worked and well-crafted piece of costume jewelry. And she'd acquired it for a song.

I was impressed and told her she had a good eye.

Mr. Hogarth inclined his hat toward her and explained that I'd just given her one of my highest compliments.

TJ, no longer able to stand all the praise going in Monica's direction, unsnapped a battered cardboard guitar case, revealing a Martin guitar, a beauty. The instrument, acoustic, was made from a variety of woods. It sported an inlaid mother-of-pearl design in a herringbone pattern around the sound hole and along its neck. A fine piece of workmanship.

"From the fifties," he said, admiring it. It had no strings.

"I also bought two midcentury chairs," he said. "We can pick them up when we make the rounds collecting your stuff."

"Midcentury" is a term taking hold, meaning the fifties. That's the nineteen fifties. But the sixties and seventies are sliding in under that definition, too. To me, that's the stuff my grandmother's house was full of. It held no appeal for me. I asked if the chairs were upholstered in avocado leatherette.

"White with gold boomerangs," he said. Yuck.

"All in all, a good morning's work," Mr. Hogarth said. Then he was off to consult with Baker about the picnic. "Don't forget," he reminded us. "We have to get together again at noon. I'll bring picnic assignments."

This was a good time to pack today's collected treasure away in TJ's rental truck. All three of us got in the truck, and TJ drove us back to the Girls' Field. Monica pointed out a tent where she saw an amber necklace that really tempted her. She thought it might go well with the brooch she purchased. I told her that now was the time to get it, but she needed to think about it.

Together, we made quick work of picking up the heavy furniture and large pieces I had accumulated. TJ's chairs were less bulky than mine, and they were in excellent shape. But I still couldn't see the attraction.

Then we picked up my car and TJ followed me to Al's, where we packed all we could into the truck for the trip back to the Cape. Since the truck couldn't hold everything, I picked the items I was willing to leave behind and we settled them back into the storage space.

"We'll come back one day next week," I told TJ. "We can pick up this stuff, and anything else I buy over the next two days." When we finished, we all tramped into Al's kitchen. It was quiet. Al was not in sight, but she couldn't have been too far away. The kitchen smelled of recent baking.

I offered to make TJ and Monica a pot of coffee, but they both quickly demurred. Everybody makes a joke about my "bad" coffee. I know they're just teasing, but sometimes it bothers me. I didn't have time to be offended, though, because we heard Al coming down the stairs.

She made coffee, but announced that except for a few broken cookies, she had nothing tasty to offer us, as she had just sent several trays of sweets off to the picnic. The broken cookies were wonderful, but the conversation was odd. Al told Monica that she had known Philip from the day he was born, and Monica coaxed her into telling "baby stories" about him. Where was I when these events were unfolding? I had to have been there; Philip was my firstborn, but none of it sounded familiar to me.

The stories went on a little too long, and we had to dash back to Brimfield to meet Mr. Hogarth and pick up our picnic assignments. We were a few minutes late, but Mr. Hogarth was relaxed and in a good mood.

"Have you decided what to do about food?" TJ asked.

"For me there's no deciding necessary," Mr. Hogarth answered, "I always have the same thing at this picnic: Canadian pork pie, apple pie, and lemon meringue pie."

His eyes pulled almost shut and his shoulders shook. "It's . . . what . . . you . . . call"—and from his carefully pronounced words, his timing, and his not too well smothered snort, I knew the joke that was coming—"a well-rounded diet," Mr. Hogarth said. The snort collapsed inward and became a cackle. He enjoyed his little joke as much as if he had never heard it before, much less repeated it, thousands of times. "A well-rounded diet," he repeated happily.

TJ, who has spent a lifetime around politicians, rewarded him with an easy laugh. He also cocked an eyebrow, and glanced sideways at me.

"That's the menu," I agreed. "You can have anything else that appeals to you, but pork pie, apple pie, and lemon meringue are always served at this picnic."

"It sounds majorly excellent," TJ said.

"All four of us will pick up the pies. We'll each carry two," Mr. Hogarth said.

"That's a lot of pie," I said.

"Baker is expecting quite a large crowd."

I turned to him, and he gave me a look that I couldn't quite read. We all walked over to the Quinsigamond Quilters pie booth. My favorite. Someone in that booth makes a Canadian pork pie that is to die for. It draws me back again and again.

Several booths sell homemade pies during the antiques marketplace. Women's clubs of one sort or another do this to raise money for good causes. The Quinsigamond Quilters start late. Their booth hadn't opened yet, but their area was mobbed. We snaked our way in as close as we could to the front of the booth. The crowd that had gathered hadn't bothered to form a line; they had instead thronged against the counter without pattern.

The ladies seem unaware of their contribution to the congestion around their booth. They stock it after the surrounding booths have been open for a while. They unload their cars with painstaking diligence, one pie, one trip. If a pie lady has baked or collected five pies, she makes five trips back and forth from her car to the pie booth. When she arrives at the booth with a pie, the assembled group makes a space for her to walk through. When she passes, they close ranks in a different order.

Most of the ladies are senior citizens, some extraordinarily senior. They are ladies in an old-fashioned, New England sense of the word. Looking as delicate as feathers, but working with rigorous industry and ramrod dignity. Finally, the booth was stocked.

"Why aren't they opening?" Monica asked.

"Each lady has to find her knife and her spatula. They all have favorites," Mr. Hogarth answered.

We all watched attentively as search and discussion groups formed to decide which utensil would be used by whom. I watched the ladies closely, and began to fantasize that they were playing pie lady roulette with me. I wanted to scale the counter, grab a knife, and start cutting the damned pies before midnight. Finally, they were ready. The people in front of us shouted their orders, and the pie ladies cut the pies. Carefully, very carefully.

Knives must be wiped on a damp cloth between each cutting. Paper plates must be separated, pried carefully from the stack. TJ and Monica were doing a little eye rolling as we moved closer to the counter. The fragrance tantalized.

The pies are lovely; they arrive in shades from pale, warm beige to a toasty nut brown. They have crusts that are crimped, fluted, twirled, or sculpted in some way that suits the baker's idea of pie beauty. Some, direct from the oven, are still warm and redolent of the fruits and spices bursting from within.

Pies are usually sold by the slice here, but an exception is made for Mr. Hogarth, whom the ladies admire greatly. All of a sudden we were there, and all the ladies flocked toward us, fawning over Mr. Hogarth. They handed the pies over to us, not boxed. But they had trouble letting go of Mr. Hogarth until the crowd behind us started rumbling complaints. Then, finally, we were on our way.

We placed all eight of the pies on the van's floor, empty now except for Supercart, folded into its smallest position. Monica rode with me, TJ followed in the packed rental truck, and Mr. Hogarth followed in his own car, as he was heading elsewhere after the picnic.

Baker had chosen the park at the reservoir, a perfect spot. Remote from the antiques marketplace, it's usually a nice, quiet place to get away from the crowd. We drove in, and I was surprised to see so many vans and pickup trucks lining the narrow entrance road; it was unusual, because the park has a nice little parking lot just above the dam. But the parking lot turned out to be the site of the picnic, and it was perfect.

There were probably thirty people there, and more were arriving. We descended, carefully balancing our pies, in mincing single file, down to the only level spot in the park.

A dozen tables had been set up end to end down the center of the narrow parking area. They were of different styles—some were antique, some just old. Sturdy old oak rubbed shoulders with elegant mahogany, round ones, square ones, and rectangles, in a variety of heights. A few had tablecloths spread on them.

The two tables in the middle of the line seemed to be where all of the food was being gathered. The pies took up a lot of room, and we edged some over to an additional table. The assortment of food was fantastic, leaning heavily toward desserts. The assortment of chairs was varied, too, not many antiques among them.

Coylie, his orange curls a beacon in the sunlight, stood between his two lawn chairs, waving us over to the table farthest from the entrance, the last table in the line. There was a huge old upholstered wingback chair set up at the end of that table, and he directed Mr. Hogarth into it. It suited him. He gave the appearance of presiding at the head of all twelve tables.

Monica, TJ, and Coylie crowded in close to him. He had certainly made a hit with all three of them, acolytes under his spell, hanging on his every word. They made room for me, too, and I put my sweater on the bench to save the place, but I stood there soaking up the ambience. I watched as two more tables were carried down to the other end of the line.

I decided to sample the food and circulate among the crowd before I settled down. The food offerings had spread to even more tables, and the array was magnificent. The picnic had never approached this variety before, never mind the quantity and quality of the menu. I took a paper plate, filled it with more than it should carry, and strolled over to Muriel, who had waved from several tables away. She smiled and told me it was a wonderful picnic. I admitted that I'd had less to do with it than in any other year.

"Everyone knows it's your picnic, Lucy. Baker told us we could bring food, or tables, or chairs. This table is mine, and the next one is Mildred's. We use them to display our wares in our booths."

So that's how he arranged it. I had never thought of assigning furniture. With my mouth full, I pointed to the little phyllo-wrapped triangles on my plate. She tried one and grinned. They looked like spanakopeta, but they were filled with sweet custard and sprinkled with pistachio nuts. Heaven.

We sat in the warm sunshine, and when a Volvo pulled up and parked in front of the line of cars, I pointed out John Wilson. "He's becoming known for his fund-raising at the museums," I said.

"I've never met him," Muriel said. "But I've heard of him. My old boss once considered him for his fund-raising skills. That didn't last long, because one of the trustees put the kibosh on the suggestion."

"Did he say why?"

"It was his opinion that Wilson micromanages everything."

"He's a fussy sort," I said.

"He may be fussy, but it was his practice of keeping all of the information to himself that was the main issue at the museum," she said.

"Hard to work with someone like that," I agreed.

"Especially in money matters."

I nodded. "He's a bit pretentious, too," I said, quietly savoring, for a moment, the fact that he'd been wrong about the Matilde jewelry.

We watched him walk down the hill. He looked about as casual as I'd ever seen him. Khaki pants, loafers, a blue oxford button-down shirt, pale yellow sweater tied over his shoulders. Neat-looking.

Muriel giggled a little. I looked at her.

"That sweater," she said. "I get silly every time I see someone wearing a sweater tied on that way. I start wondering if I should try to begin a trend by wearing my panty hose tied around my legs."

We shared an idiotic grin, and turned back to watch Wilson as he walked down the hill, then strolled toward the head of the tables. There he sat in the space I'd saved near Mr. Hogarth.

I was comfortable here, and intended to visit several people before I returned. I sat nibbling with Muriel and saying hello to folks around us, until I saw Natalie walk in from the driveway with an old-fashioned picnic basket over her arm. She looked spectacular.

I stood up and waved to her. She nodded and signaled that she'd join us, and headed for the food section of the tables. She took a bowl from her basket, probably potato salad since she's famous for her potato salad, and a dish of something else I couldn't quite see, and then she headed our way.

"You've missed this whole Brimfield," I said after the introductions.

"It was unavoidable," she said, and offered no further explanation.

I was just about to grill her about her new flame, when the next arrivals caused such a stir within our little circle that I stopped to take it in. It was Baker and Al, acting positively bewitched with each other.

Natalie, who knew both, absorbed what was happening immediately. She waved them over and engaged them in a sugary conversation about the beautiful day, the beautiful weather, the beautiful picnic. She smiled slyly over her shoulder at me.

She was not going to tell me about her new flame. I was going to have to wheedle it out of her when she finally forgave me for phoning at four a.m. She's so willful sometimes that it's impossible to deal with her.

26

I circled the tables, visiting with people I had missed, reaping compliments for the first picnic I hadn't actually put together. That done, I returned to my own brood.

Monica borrowed the van for another look at the amber necklace. I gave her the keys, reminded her to return by three o'clock so she could ride back to the Cape with TJ, and took her place at the table. Mr. Hogarth tapped a thermos. "Ginger tea, or coffee?" he said.

"I like ginger anything, but the tea sounds especially good to me today," I said.

"Too New Age for me," Mr. Hogarth said. "None of that stuff can beat good strong coffee for a pick-me-up."

TJ and Coylie were ready for second helpings. When they asked if they could bring us anything, we all declined.

"Nice young fellows," Mr. Hogarth said as they moved off. "And that daughter-in-law of yours is a gift. It's good to see young people so interested in antiques."

I nodded. "They're lucky they have you to nurture them."

He smiled hugely. "Lucy, you know how much I love having someone to coach. I enjoy that part as much as I enjoy the business of antiques."

"I do know," I said. "It's wonderful having your guidance, even now, but in the early years it saved me from so many mistakes." I looked at the crowd clustered around the tables. There were about fifty people here now. "I wonder how many of us here today are your alumni."

He scanned the crowd, then turned back to me. "I see a few, but the two of you were my star pupils."

I turned to Wilson. "You too?" I asked.

He nodded but said nothing.

"I even tried to instill a little sense into your rascal friend, but he wasn't interested," the old man said. Wilson got red in the face, but the old man continued. "I wonder now if I misread that kid."

"Why don't you just leave it alone?" Wilson snapped.

Mr. Hogarth looked over his glasses at Wilson. "Consider it done," he said quietly.

"Who are we leaving alone?" I asked.

They both turned and stared at me. They seemed surprised that I was sitting there. I was a star pupil a minute ago. When my stellar intelligence finally kicked in, it dawned on me that Mr. Hogarth was talking about Monty. Of course!

He must know about Monty's old trouble. That's what'd been bothering him. He'd been holding a grudge all this time.

"Monty?" I said. Mr. Hogarth nodded curtly.

Wilson was irritated, and Mr. Hogarth couldn't seem to let go. It was hard to imagine Wilson and Monty as friends; they were so different that I looked at Wilson again, considering who they might have been back then.

Could they have done something foolish as young men? Monty had been the one caught in a bad situation. It was no stretch to visualize Wilson convincing someone, a young Monty, say, into taking blame for him. I snapped out of that train of thought when I became aware of Wilson's discomfort at my staring.

TJ and Coylie returned with more food and chatter, and Wilson, noticeably irritated, gathered his things and moved on. As he drifted away I watched. He chatted briefly with Natalie, said a few quick hellos to other people, and then he climbed up the hill to his car.

Wilson, Monty, and Mr. Hogarth? I asked Mr. Hogarth how they all knew one another way back then, but his mood had soured, and he told me what I already knew, that antiques was a small world. I'd catch him in a better mood later; I'd like to know more about their relationship.

Some of the other picnickers were leaving, and I decided I'd better visit anyone I had missed. Baker and Al had settled at the far end of the tables, and I headed their way. Natalie was about halfway between us, so I detoured around the other side, avoiding contact until I could figure out a way to get back into her good graces.

When I arrived Al was saying good-bye to Baker. She had to return to the B&B to prepare for the evening crowd. Baker had a spot of egg salad on his chin. Al wiped it off with her napkin. She patted him on the cheek and turned and walked up the hill to the car. Baker sighed and held his hand to his cheek, gazing after her. I couldn't believe this. They'd known each other less than twenty-four hours.

"That's your car she's driving off in," I said.

"I know," he said.

"How are you getting around?"

"I thought you'd give me a ride back, but if not, someone around here is sure to be going that way."

"As long as you can wait until the picnic is over, and the cleanup is done," I said, hoping to seem over-worked.

"I'll help pick up," he said.

He was such a good person, and he had really made this a great picnic, truly lightening the burden for me. "It was a great idea to have people bring the furniture, Baker."

"Al told me to do it that way," he said. "She also told me how to handle the food assignments. She's taught me so much," he said. Another sigh.

I looked at him. He was perfectly serious. He turned to me and said, "I can't thank you enough for introducing us, Lucy."

My God.

"Will you write about Monty in the next *LIAR*?" I asked, bringing him back to earth.

"Yes, of course. I thought of weaving aspects of the antiques market into Monty's story. It's clearly affected the tone of this show. But on reflection, a simple appreciation might be best. Without a solution to the murder, I'm not sure how I'll sum up the story."

"Well, some things are looking up, at least for Billy. A friend of Coylie's may be able to provide an alibi for him," I said.

"Well, figure out the rest of it and I'll have my story," he said.

I told him what Shirley said about Monty meeting the buyer for the pickle castor just before he was murdered. "The pickle castor guy must be the killer," I said.

"It may have just been a deal Monty had lined up."

"It very likely was a deal," I said. "But anyone legitimate would have come forward by now. I'm going to ask Billy what he remembers." In fact, I hadn't talked to Billy since I had left him in Matt's capable hands.

When Monica returned at three, more people were leaving. She didn't buy the amber necklace after all. She decided to leave it behind, but she still struggled with that decision. TJ was ready to go, but Monica dithered around saying good-bye to everyone she had met. Bubbling with gratitude, she hugged and thanked me for her wonderful day. Okay, okay, so everyone has had a fine time, now let's get on with it. She finally got into the truck with TJ, and they slowly pulled away. I waved good-bye. Lord, it took them forever.

Now I could hardly wait for the picnic to be over, but the cleanup plodded along. People and furniture flowed out of the park in a slow but steady stream. When my final trash bag was filled, only a few of us remained, and those who stayed were helping.

I'd go see Billy face-to-face. He must have known what was happening around Monty's Contents in the days before the murder. I should have talked to him sooner. I was thinking about what to ask him, when I was startled by Natalie's voice.

"Were you going to ignore me forever?" she said.

I swung around, surprised. "I thought you had left," I said.

"I didn't, and we've played cat and mouse long enough," she said. "Are we going to chat?"

Now? I looked at my watch. Almost four o'clock. I had to get to Worcester to see Billy. From there I planned on driving back to Boston to get my first decent night's sleep of the week.

"Yes, of course I want to chat," I said. How long could it take? "I'll be finished here in five minutes. Shall we have coffee somewhere?"

"It's a little complicated," she said.

What isn't?

"I have an appointment to see some ivory netsukes

in Sturbridge," she said. "It will probably take me until, say, five, to be on the safe side. How about meeting me at the Ugly Duckling at about five fifteen?"

No way. The Ugly Duckling means dinner, not just coffee, and there's no way I could get to Worcester and back by five fifteen. And hanging around here for over an hour, then eating dinner, then going to Billy's—I didn't know. I just didn't know.

"I thought ivory was illegal," I said, stalling.

"New ivory is illegal, elephants are endangered, and certain old ivory is off limits, too, but there's still a legal market for most of the antique stuff."

"Well, I have an appointment, too," I lied. It was sort of an appointment, even if Billy didn't know about it yet. "I can *probably* get back by six." Even that would be a tight squeeze if I had to go looking for Billy. But she was already agreeing to meet me at the Ugly Duckling. I'd better not complicate things further.

We wished each other luck; she assumed that I had an antiques deal lined up, too. So, I'd come back here from Worcester, only a couple hours out of my way, we'd chat, everything would be all better between us, and I could still get back to Boston and get some sleep.

Baker joined us. Oops, I had forgotten that I said I'd drive him back to Brimfield. But I didn't have to. Natalie offered to get him to Al's, which was just slightly out of her way on the drive to Sturbridge.

I drove away from Brimfield, hardly noticing the explosions of greenery along my route. How could this be referred to as merely green? And yet, I was nearly at the end of Dead Horse Hill before I woke to the panoply of greens being squandered on me.

At some level, though it's never been mentioned, I knew that Silent Billy lived in the little room at Monty's Contents. I found him in the office, which was still a-tumble with the mess I'd seen the other day. The door had been replaced, but the disorder within the room hadn't changed.

"Just finished up," he said, nodding toward the room. Maybe this was how it was supposed to look.

"Can I ask you a few questions, Billy?"

He nodded his shaggy head once, said, "Okay," and motioned me to follow him to the workroom, where he took his place at the workbench.

"Police think I did it," he said.

"I know you didn't. I may even have information that will help."

"Matt said you found the guy with the broken frame."

"Frankie, yes. If the murder can be pinpointed to when you were with Frankie, you're golden. If not, we should know anything that can help."

Billy nodded, and I plunged in. "What did Monty say about the pickle castor, Billy?"

"Pickle castor?"

"Monty was meeting someone about a pickle castor the morning of the murder," I said.

"Why?"

"I was hoping you knew, Billy."

He nodded, shrugged his shoulders, looked mystified. His confusion seemed genuine. Why? He was around here every day; he must know something. Monty was not secretive. Reading his moods was easy, and he was known to say what was on his mind. I had to get Billy talking.

"Did Monty stay at the campsite?" I asked.

"No. He hated camping, needed a comfortable bed."

"Okay, so you were up there alone. What time were you supposed to meet him?"

"At five. By the Patio. Got woke up early."

"I heard about that, Billy. How long did you stay there after you woke up?"

"Four thirty, quarter to five."

Close enough to what Frankie said. We could confirm the time of Frankie's call home on the cell phone, and the time of Monty's death by the report of Monty's stomach contents. Oh, my God, Monty's Contents. I got a little queasy. Had to hurry up and think of something else.

"What was going on around here?" I asked. "Was there something that, looking back, now seems different?"

"No."

Wrong question. What else could I ask?

"Billy, did you know Monty before he hired you?"

"Nope. A guy got us together about six years ago."

"What about the candlestand Billy. Was there something unusual about it? Why did Monty send it to Baker, rather than leave it here or bring it to Brimfield?"

Bingo. Well, that got a reaction. Billy looked like a deer caught in the headlights. Face frozen, eyes open wide, neck pulled back, ready for flight. Not what I expected, but a reaction that said I was onto something.

"Trouble, a mistake," he said.

"The candlestand?" Where were we headed?

"I made a lot of mistakes." And, not waiting for comment, he went on. "One mistake got me into prison." Beads of sweat appeared on his forehead as he struggled toward something.

"Another mistake was that table."

"The table?" I asked. He nodded. The candlestand must be the table that Edgar mentioned. Billy was overwrought, but I held my tongue, and he went on.

"That's my drawer."

"You repaired it?"

"Yes, and a good job, too."

Billy was defending his work on a fine piece of furniture. Baker told me that both the candlestand and the repair were excellent, but he hadn't seen Billy's mark.

"Did you sign it?"

"Couldn't. Monty went nuts when he saw it."

Monty would know that the candlestand was a fine piece of furniture. I know Monty didn't want Billy to waste his time repairing cheap furniture, so why all the complaining? Still, I hesitated to interrupt, thinking

Billy was getting to something, some information I needed. But now he clamped his mouth shut, and rubbed his hands over his face.

There must have been more. Billy must have known more. "Was there something else?" I asked.

"No, it was the table. Said he knew that table."

"Whose table was it?" I asked.

Billy hesitated. "A kid in trouble. Kid didn't know a damned thing. Wanted it fixed before his mother knew it was broke."

"Who was the kid?"

"Don't know," he said. He ran both hands through his hair. "Kid said he needed it fixed right away. I helped him out, and Monty came back, saw it, and went nuts. He said I made a deal with a swindler."

"Who?"

"Didn't say. Said it could land me back in prison, said I never should have touched it. He nagged and complained, and told me the kid had nothing to do with it. Said the kid was a sucker and I was a patsy."

"So why did he send it out to Baker?"

"He told me that Baker was going to make things right."

"But why?"

"Museum piece."

"Monty always said that, Billy," I said.

"No, it was *from* a museum," he said. That was it. Billy was finished. Another museum piece.

I drove back toward Brimfield, trying to make time among the commuters jockeying for the best stretch of road. The candlestand was from a museum, not merely the kind of museum piece that's the product of wishful thinking. It probably still belongs in a museum. Why else would Monty make such a big deal about it?

I was only fifteen minutes late for Natalie, but she was miffed again.

I was tired. Too damned tired to play games. "Natalie, I'm just back from trying to get information out of Silent Billy. It was like removing slivers, and just as productive. I'm tired, and I'm out of ideas."

"Did you accuse him of murder, too?"

"I didn't, and I didn't accuse you, either, as you well know. But let's not go there. Please. If we're going to have a nice visit, let's have it. If we've gone beyond that, let's call it quits for today, and maybe we can start fresh tomorrow. Right now I'm done for."

I flung my backside into the chair across from her. It surprised me by being comfortable. I straightened up and wiggled myself deeply into its lap. When I looked across the table, I was surprised by the look on her face. She must have understood the mess I was mired in. She took my hand and patted it.

"I'm sorry," she said. She seemed sincere, and I relaxed a little. "I've been so self-centered that I didn't realize my teasing would cause you pain."

I laughed. That was so like her, to apologize even though I deserved so much of the blame. I felt guilty enough to apologize for my lateness today, and for missing her on that first day of Brimfield. "And I'm sorry I called you at four o'clock this morning," I said.

"You should be sorry about the wake-up call. That was cruel and inhumane treatment," she said, laughing.

"So, what's happening?" I could feel my edginess falling away.

"I thought you'd never ask," she said. "I've been occupying myself with analyzing a stimulus bill," she said.

That only stopped me for a moment. "His name is Bill, and you're certainly looking stimulated," I said, and felt like a quiz show winner when she nodded and giggled.

And thus we started. I was cheered as she described, in Natalieze, the situation. In English it might be called love. In Natalieze it was a meltdown. Her happiness over the meltdown was so evident that it lifted me up out of my own troubles.

I, in turn, told her what I surmised about the Baker and Althea meltdown.

"It's so perfect, Lucy. I don't know why I didn't see it before it happened."

"Really? I never would have picked those two for each other."

It was fun to visit, and we lost track of time over our excellent dinner. But it was our souls that found nourishment in the desserts we shared, oozing of white chocolate, rich dark chocolate, caramel, and custard.

I didn't mention Hamp's upcoming retirement, and I stayed away from the murder. I didn't want to burden her when she was in such a good mood. When I finally remembered to tell her that the pickle castor was still available, she was only mildly interested. That first morning of the antiques show she had been upset, but now that she'd given herself permission for the meltdown, it was forgotten. She laughed when she heard the outrageous price Shirley was asking.

"I'll bet the McGirr Museum wouldn't pay that much for it now. She should open her own museum," she said as we walked into the parking lot. "A Pickle Museum." And on that note we said good-bye and drove off in opposite directions.

I got back to Boston at ten thirty. There was one message under the door. Hamp. I knew I had to call him tonight. I didn't look forward to it, as I still had no idea what to say about the retirement.

"I hoped you'd come home tonight, Lucy," he said when I called.

"If I had, I know I'd never drive back to Brimfield tomorrow morning," I said. The three-hour drive is too much as the exhausting week progresses.

"One day away from Brimfield shouldn't be a calamity," he said.

He doesn't feel that my business is a business. He sees it as a way for me to keep busy, and to also earn money for "extras," such as small household luxuries, upgraded vacations, and such. It hasn't been that for some time.

"I wouldn't ask you to take a day off from school, Hamp."

A pause. "Okay, you're right. But we need to make plans, because this retirement is happening soon."

We hung up at midnight. I pulled out the old sofa bed but couldn't get comfortable. The bright green numbers on the tiny clock lit the room brilliantly. I drifted in and out of sleep, my mind spinning with retirement, murder, stolen antiques, museums. When I finally slept, the alarm screamed the news that it was four o'clock, time to get moving.

The drive on the turnpike at that hour usually soothes me. The empty road, the promise of a new day, hints of treasure to be found. But the pickle castor and the candlestand taunted me, magnifying my tiredness. Both belonged in museums. Both were important to Monty.

Neither item was on anyone's stolen list, but they were stolen, I was sure of it. He hid the candlestand, but the pickle castor was right out in the open. He needed to accompany the buyer to the sale of the pickle castor. Why? Because he was going to make things right. He was going to confront the thief, and that's when the thief killed him.

27

I was early enough to be near the front of the unruly line for today's opening and would have an excellent shot at the good stuff. I was exhausted; the week's exploits were catching up with me. Mr. Hogarth was just ahead of me, embedded in an amorphous clump of people, and he was bursting with energy and excitement.

"I spent the night at my daughter's. We had a wonderful visit," he said. No wonder he was refreshed. His daughter is the only family he has, but she runs a big corporation and their time together is limited.

"You should have stayed the weekend," I said.

"No way. I have to do this opening, and tomorrow is the last day. I never miss my Sunday cleanup," he said, cackling.

No new fields open on Sunday, but it would be crowded with people who came for the festive atmosphere. For a shrewdie like Mr. Hogarth, Sunday at Brimfield offers a different opportunity: high-priced bargains. His bargaining on the final day of the marketplace is for top-of-the-line antiques that didn't sell during the week: antiques brought here for specialized collectors. On the last day the reality of dragging things back home encourages flexibility in sellers.

This is where Mr. Hogarth shines. He is able to approach a dealer and offer a price high enough not to be offensive, but low enough to be a good deal. He'll go home tomorrow with a few rare and beautiful treasures, and he'll have paid bargain prices. I emulate him whenever I can. Today, though, I wasn't thinking straight, and I was so tired that I felt sick.

"All I want to do is get through this field, grab the best stuff I can, and leave," I told him.

I was still uncertain where, exactly, I'd go when I finished here. I probably *should* go home to the Cape, where I could comfort Hamp and assure him that retirement is good, and that he'd enjoy it. But if I did that, it was unlikely that I'd return tomorrow.

On the other hand, when I finished this field it would be early enough that I could get to Boston and finally get a great night's sleep. If I did that I'd be able to return to Brimfield tomorrow fresh and rested, give it one last shot, and still get home to the Cape at a decent hour. A decent hour tomorrow was almost as good as a decent hour today.

My indecision nagged as I shopped the crowded field. Fortunately, nods and quick hellos were enough to pass for social skills this morning. We all knew we were down to the wire.

I spotted Wilson, again empty-handed.

"So, what's the story on you and Monty, way back in the day?" I said. He'd probably have a different version than Mr. Hogarth.

Wilson scowled. "There is no story. We hardly knew each other," he said. He turned on his heel and walked away stiffly.

Well, maybe I was a little abrupt. I should have thought about what I'd say to him, but I was too tired to think straight. I finished my trek through the field, which yielded enough goodies to fill Supercart.

Mr. Hogarth was packing up his truck when I finished loading the van. When I complained of my tiredness, he delivered a lecture admonishing me to take a nap in the van before driving anywhere.

I didn't need a nap. I always miss my sleep during Brimfield Week. This week's three or four hours a night made it exceptionally thin, but I could handle it. Maybe I *was* feeling the tiredness more. Maybe I was coming down with something. Maybe fifty was going to be a harder age than I expected.

When he realized that I didn't intend to follow his advice, he insisted on getting coffee to wake me up for the drive. I agreed to the coffee. It would get him on the road and off my case, and it would make my stomach wretched enough to keep me awake throughout the drive.

Finally, it was time for him to leave. I acted revived,

thanked him, and waved good-bye. Hardly able to keep my eyes open, I climbed into the van. It was full because I hadn't folded Supercart into its smallest position. I leaned over to fold it down, heard something behind me, felt a strong push, and then nothing. Nothing at all.

I'm aware of a faint humming sound, but I can't place it. It's dark, I hurt, and the floor moves. Vibrates. Can't think—I slip away.

The humming stops, the vibration stops, and the hurt returns, separates into individual pains. I'm trapped, wrists tied in back, legs tied together in front. My mouth is taped.

My head throbs; my hair is plastered to my face. It's sticky with . . . Oh, no, this is bad. Very bad. It's blood. I can smell it. I move my shoulder away from the wall, and new pain stabs through my rib cage, leaving me breathless.

I lean my head down and begin to bring my knees up, but instantly snap back. Explosions of pain jab through my head, fire rips through my chest. I recoil, freeze still as stone, concentrate on clamping my haunches to the floor. The pain recedes. I think of Hamp and the kids.

My sweet, beautiful babies, they'll be motherless. They scared me so much at first. They came so fast, and so soon. Philip only three months after our wedding. What a ruckus that was. Our wedding. On April Fool's Day. Our folks in an uproar, hotly contesting which of us had ruined the other's life. And me simpering with love, and relief.

And our second baby boy, tiny sweetheart, ten months after the first. Our parents finally warmed up, at least to-

ward the babies. Cooing at our perfect little family. The twins, almost a year later, startled all of us. Another darling boy, and an angelic little girl. Our mothers, suddenly united, visited the hospital together, grim.

They instructed me to take the pill. I was grateful for their sudden interest. The pill had swept the country by then. I inquired about it, and was advised that serious side effects were surfacing. I thought it over. When I went back to the doctor to announce my decision, I was already experiencing a side effect of not having taken the pill. Nancy was born barely ten months after the twins, the week before my twenty-first birthday. The sweetest little cherub, and the last of the lot. Five babies before our third anniversary.

I wake again, aware that I'm trapped, and in pain, but dying? A wave of sensibility sweeps over me, but it's gone before I can grasp it. I'm in trouble. I know where I am. I just can't pull its name to mind. The floor, rough, wooden, shivers a little whenever I move. That familiar noise at each move. I shift my weight again, squirm, try to reduce the pain.

I jiggle the rope that binds my wrists. Try again to slip out of it. No dice. It scrapes my skin, but I hardly feel it, hardly feel my hands at all, except that they're so cold. The cold trickles into the rest of my body. I shiver, and finally realize that I'm not done for.

I finally understand the noise, but just as I remember, the world topples over, and I'm thrown against a side wall. My backside slides forward, and my knees fold upward, sending shafts of pain through me. I feel myself slipping back.

No. No, stop this. Work it out. Pay attention to getting

free. Don't think of the pain. Get a grip on yourself. You're not dead yet, so call off the funeral. That noise again. I know that noise.

Supercart. I'm in Supercart. Something is draped across its top. A tarp, maybe? A blanket? It's dark inside, but thin lines of weak light seep between the boards. I was in the van; now I'm in Supercart. That's it. It's Supercart's springs I hear when I move.

My purse is gone. I can't guess how long I've been here. I need to think. Fully awake now, and aware of my surroundings, I need to figure out how to get out of here. I will not let this be the end.

I'm on a hillside. Supercart just rolled downhill when I jostled it. The roll down the hill has pitched me into a different position. I move carefully, define the pain. A broken rib, maybe. My head explodes at each movement. I'm not sure how bad the head injury is, but I was unconscious for a while. Then I drifted for another while. I must have bumped it when I was dumped into Supercart.

I slump, catch my breath, end up with my right thigh leaning against a lump. My wad. Still here. Big help cash is now. But keys! There are keys in my stash. Keys are good.

I work at getting the keys. Wrists firmly secured behind me, freezing fingers endeavoring to move in ways they were never meant to, I become aware of my determination to get myself out of this mess.

I struggle with the pocket I "invented" long ago. It doesn't want to open. Blasted Velcro. I blessed it when I first saw it. No more wrestling with zippers. Denim skirts, my *uniform since I was chasing after kids, were excellent for my experiments.*

I found the right place to keep a fairly large stash hidden. By opening the skirt's side seam, and inserting a small pocket about three inches above my knee, below the regular pocket, I'd solved the problem of getting at the cash easily.

I grasp the key with the sharpest teeth, hold it in fingers that can hardly feel, and saw back and forth against the rope. Work at it. It'll take a week this way. Keep working. The key drops, and I retrieve it. Doggedly work a rhythm into my sawing. Finally, I feel the rope begin to give.

Joy! My right wrist is free, then my left. I flex my fingers and stretch my arms. I rub both hands back and forth on the denim, bringing feeling back to my fingers. In a minute I'll have the rest of my bindings off.

Stop. Stop. Oh, God, I hear something. Someone's coming. Yes, it's footsteps all right, coming closer. My killer. No doubt now. This is no social call. He means to finish me off. I have to act.

I'm not going out of this life without a fight. My legs are still tied together. I grasp the keys in my hand, maneuver them until all three protrude from between my knuckles, making a weapon I'd heard of long ago and never needed.

When he uncovers me, I'll gouge his face off. Do what damage I can to get out of here. If I can't get out, I'll at least damage the swine. Here he comes. Here now, he's moving the tarp overhead. Come on, you ugly rat snake. Anger bubbles up from deep inside me. With it comes strength.

I'm ready, and as bright moonlight spills into the cart, my right arm shoots straight up. My fist full of keys heads *straight toward his face, his head silhouetted above me. I jab at that face, waving my hand wildly at the same time. I feel it scrape against the devil, hard. I jab and twist. Oh, God, I should have spotted his face better but, but . . .*

A piercing scream splits the seconds into a thousand instants, all shattered, all interminable. The shrill shrieking is wrong, all wrong. Is that me? It can't be me, my mouth is taped. I didn't have time to get the tape off.

Then I heard the voice.

"Lucy? It's me."

What? Leaning over the edge, overhead, was Monica. Monica? What in God's name was Monica doing here?

She was shaking, her voice unsteady. "My God, Lucy, I was sure you were dead." Her hand gripped her chin, and in the bright moonlight a black shadow oozed through her fingers and dribbled down her arm.

The keys. I'd gotten her with the keys. I couldn't see how bad it was.

"I'm alive," I said, fumbling the tape away from my mouth. No need to tell her I'd been holding a wake for myself minutes earlier.

"Get me out of here."

"Yes, I'll get you to a hospital," she said.

We grappled awkwardly with the rest of my ropes. "I don't need a hospital. I have to get to the old man," I said. Then I noticed that her wound spurted each time she spoke, or moved. It looked lethal. Guilt embraced me.

"I'm sorry, Monica, truly sorry. You need a hospital

more than I do," I said as my bindings finally came apart. I scrambled to stand up in Supercart, aware again that I had to get out of there in a hurry.

"How in the world did you find me?" I asked. And, lurching to my feet unsteadily in Supercart, I lost my balance, and flung my arms around her. Monica, misunderstanding, hugged me tightly, patted my back, and whispered "there-theres." The kid was comforting me.

I was so startled to find myself being comforted that I burst, blubbering, into howling sobs. I clung to her, wallowing in her comfort. In a while, my wailing subsided, I ceased my sniveling, and with Monica's help I climbed out of Supercart.

Free again.

28

<hr style="width:20%"/>

We came to our senses, and I asked for her cell phone.

"I left it on the kitchen counter, still plugged into the charger," she wailed.

"Then let's get out of here."

We drove away, each babbling over the other's story, trying to make sense of what seemed a random hash of events. "But how did Supercart end up over here?" she asked.

"I'm not sure. I think I was driven over in the van, and then dumped into Supercart."

She clutched her chin with one hand and steered the car with the other, trying to explain how she'd tracked me down.

I didn't quite understand yet. I tried to stop interrupting. "But how did you find me? Why aren't you back at the Cape?"

"I almost didn't find you, Lucy. I came back for the amber necklace. It was after three by the time I got here. The necklace had been sold, and I stopped at Coylie's to ask if he'd seen you.

"He hadn't seen you, only your van. He said the van had been missing, then returned, but he wasn't sure when," she quavered on.

"I waited for a while. Then I left a note on the wind-shield and looked around the fields. I didn't yet realize anything was wrong, but later the note was still there, and I finally looked inside. Antiques were there, but Supercart was gone.

"That's when I knew that something wasn't right. I drove out to Al's to see if you'd landed there by some fluke. She hadn't seen you all day. You hadn't stored anything in her barn. She said that was unusual.

"So I came back to Brimfield, where everything was the same. I needed time to think, so I went to the little restaurant in town, and after I lingered over a cup of tea, I felt better. The sun had gone down by then, so I called home."

Oh, no, bad move. "What did you tell them at home?"

"Not much, Lucy. As a matter of fact, I didn't quite lie to Philip, but I didn't quite tell him the truth, either. When I'd determined that you weren't at home on the Cape, I told him that I was thinking of staying the night with you in Boston." She looked over at me, guilt in her eyes, blood dribbling from her chin.

"Good work," I assured her. "No need to get him all upset over nothing."

"This is nothing?" she asked.

"No, but the worst is over. We can finish up and get out of here, and there's no need to make things worse for ourselves with the family. But how did you find Supercart?"

"When I came out of the restaurant it was dark," she said. "I checked the van again. Nothing had changed, but in the dark everything looked different. I looked for Coylie, thinking he might have an idea. At the picnic yesterday he mentioned that it would be a nice spot for camping. So I drove over, parked, and sat here.

"Coylie's truck was nowhere to be seen, and I didn't see much else in the dark. After a while my eyes adjusted, but by then I'd stopped looking, and I may have dozed. I was ready to give up. And then, right before my eyes, your big red exclamation point became visible. It took shape in the trees on the hill right in front of me, only it was black, not red, in the moonlight."

I held up a hand to stop her babbling. "What exclamation point?"

"Supercart, Lucy. The big red exclamation point you painted on Supercart. It was there under the trees on the hill, right in front of my eyes, but it didn't register with me as Supercart until it started rolling down the hillside."

Useless now to explain away that red paint as swatches for choosing the color of our shutters. Maybe it did look like an exclamation point.

As Monica drove along the deserted road and told her story, I rubbed life back into my legs and checked

my injuries. A couple of ribs in trouble, my left shoulder throbbing but functional, and my old hip injury
competing for attention. The walnut-sized lump on my
forehead had stopped oozing and was strangely numb,
but it seemed to provoke a sort of flashbulb effect
whenever I turned my head.

I checked her wound covertly. It made me sick. It
would leave a jagged scar where I'd split her skin. I'd
hacked a cleft into that chin that I understood, pro-
foundly, would haunt me.

It was going to be hard, very hard, explaining all
this to the family. Then, too, there'd be Monica's reaction, when she finally got a good look at what I'd done
to her. I'd need time to work out the story I'd tell them
later, but right now I needed some simple cooperation
from Monica.

"What I'd like," I said, "is for you to drop me off at
Mr. Hogarth's, then continue on down the road a few
miles to do two things. The Jones-Toner Medical Center is there. It's a walk-in place, and you can get your
chin treated there."

Monica looked over at me. "And what will you be
doing?" she asked.

I told her I wanted to see Mr. Hogarth for a minute.

"You're going to drop in on him at midnight?" she
asked, and paused a second before realizing that I
didn't intend to respond. "And what else?" she went
on. "You said you wanted me to do two things."

I couldn't think fast enough to give her a foxy explanation for asking her to send the police to Mr. Hog-

arth's. I preferred keeping her in the dark, and out of further trouble. But she already suspected the game was afoot, so as we drove along the rural road closer to Mr. Hogarth's, I offered her a quick answer. I worked it out as I spoke.

"There's trouble at Mr. Hogarth's place."

"Lucy, you don't think the old fellow is the killer, do you?"

"I'm not sure exactly what is going on, but he's been acting funny lately. I just want to check up on him, and I'd like to keep you out of harm's way."

She kept her eyes on the road, and said, "I'll go to the hospital when you go to the hospital, but first let me tell you that I didn't drive up here from the Cape to miss out on this part."

That girl is stubborn—I can see trouble ahead for Philip because of it. But there was no time for debate now; we were approaching Mr. Hogarth's.

We drove right past when we spotted two cars parked near the lamp shop entrance. At the sight of the second car, my stomach flip-flopped. Were we already too late? Monica pulled off the road at the curve beyond his house, and then she pulled up to the road's edge, facing out. Good thinking.

She wouldn't wait in the car, and I couldn't waste time arguing with her. The best I could do, to impress on her that *I* was leading this venture, was to command her not to slam the door as we slipped out of the car. She didn't answer me, but she didn't slam, either.

The house was dark. In the lamp shop, at the front of the house, thin light seeped around the edges of the windows. The tiny flashlight on Monica's key chain provided just enough light for us to make our way through the shrubbery and underbrush. When we reached the gravel path, we slowed, trying to mask the crunching underfoot. We stopped at the shop door and looked. In the dim light, the drawn shade, several inches away from the other side of the glass, did little to hide what was happening inside. It was terrible.

Mr. Hogarth was alive, but it was bad. He was tied to a chair, his hands behind him, his face a bloody mess. Wilson, gripping a flashlight, smacked it against Mr. Hogarth's head. The flashlight triggered a rush of understanding. It was that flashlight, not the shove into Supercart, that had caused the wound in my forehead.

The intake of breath from Monica, next to me, brought me back. We heard Wilson. "You have five seconds to tell me where that candlestand is."

"I don't know what you mean," Mr. Hogarth groaned.

"You've hidden it. Monty said he was putting it in the safest place."

"It's not here," the old man said. "And neither is the pickle castor."

"I know where the pickle castor is. Monty called a month ago and said he'd found it. I didn't even remember it, I'd taken it so long ago. No one's even looking for it by now. But Monty recognized it from one of my early museums.

"I went along with him, said I'd buy it back fair

and square, then donate it back to the McGirr. I swore I never did it again, after that pickle castor. But when he came up with the candlestand a few days ago, he knew I was still at it, and I knew he could make big trouble."

"It was you all those years ago," Mr. Hogarth said.

"What does it matter? What's done is done," Wilson said, and he raised the flashlight over Mr. Hogarth's head.

"Someone will figure it out," Mr. Hogarth said.

"You lie, and what did you tell that busybody about the stolen artifacts?"

"I didn't know about them until now. It was the box of lace that finally made me realize I've been wrong."

The flashlight came down again on Mr. Hogarth. I had to do something. I knew I couldn't overpower Wilson, and Monica and I together were not likely to be much better. But we might stall him long enough for the police to get here.

I turned to her. "I'll go in this door and try to divert Wilson from the old man. Do you think you can slip into the back door of the house without being heard, and call the police? Then come into the shop and help me hold things down?"

"Sure," she whispered. And without another word, she turned and disappeared into the dark along the side of the building.

I had to move. It was time to enter the shop. I took a breath. I didn't know if Monica had made it into the house, but I had to open the door in front of me. I hoped that I wouldn't have to break the glass to open it, and I was lucky. The silly thing was unlocked, and it opened quietly. So far, so good. I stepped into the shop, looking around for a weapon. Nothing in sight.

Wilson, his back toward me, hissed at the old man. His stance was rigid, his words strained.

"Do you think I'm going to let a bunch of junk collectors put me in prison over a few misplaced baubles? The minute those idiots get wind of goods taken from my museums, they'll start looking at my fund-raising. I am not a crook," he screamed.

Mr. Hogarth was slumped in the chair facing me. I was plainly in his sight line, but he didn't bat an eyelash, didn't change expression, didn't give me away. "John, I'm so disappointed in you," he said. He closed his eyes, and lowered his head, chin to chest. "I was so wrong about Monty all these years."

Wilson raised his hand, the flashlight poised for another strike. "Where is that goddamned candlestand?"

I had to act before the flashlight came down on Mr. Hogarth again. I had no weapon. I knew I needed one, but I also needed to be quick. My anger surged, overwhelmed me, and for reasons I'll never figure out, I screamed at him.

Did I think my scream would scare him to death, and that he'd stop this siege? Did I think he'd quit beating the old man, and then we could all sit down and discuss his hateful ways? In fact, I didn't think at all. Furthermore, the instant I started screaming, he spun around and exploded at me. He struck out with the flashlight, with his feet, with his whole body.

The man's face was electrified with fury. I felt myself thrown back against a table, and cracked in the head. I wanted to run away but couldn't. Wanted to stop and figure out how to get out of this. Wanted him to stop hitting me. I felt light-headed. The cut on my forehead reopened; I felt blood running down my face.

But I kept screaming. I scratched, and screamed, and screamed, and screamed. I got him, too, with my fingernails. I could hardly see for the blood in my eyes, but I clawed out, and kept clawing, until I felt myself scratch across something terrible. Did I scratch his eye? My God, his eye. I think I got his eye.

Now it was Wilson screaming. Dear Lord, don't let it be his eye. My stomach twisted.

He stepped backward and I jumped to my feet. With relief, I saw that Monica had slipped in from the house. She held an old metal lamp base, a perfect weapon. She held it like a baseball bat. Wilson swayed in front of me, and then he slid down on one knee, howling. I looked out through a bloody mist, and focused, just in time to see Monica swing the heavy metal lamp base into the space where Wilson had been, and into my face. Then I didn't see anything.

29

I'm sure I heard her whack Wilson in the head, too. I was conscious. She claims I was not, and that she was sure she had killed me. But I *know* I heard the sound of that lamp base as it whumped against his head. Furthermore, when the police arrived a few minutes later, Monica and I were both on our feet, clutching each other. Doesn't that prove I was conscious?

We were both bleeding and hysterical. I, allegedly thanking her for breaking my nose, and she, just as allegedly thanking me for not being dead.

After a moment or two of confusion with the police about who was who, Mr. Hogarth, still tied to the chair, satisfied them that it was Wilson, still on the floor, whimpering, who had caused the mayhem we all wallowed in.

The whole business was extremely messy, and I've lost a tiny piece of my memory, but they say it should come back. I remember nothing of the ambulance ride to the hospital, or the celebration that everyone claims took place later in the emergency room, when Mr. Hogarth limped out of his cubicle, unaided, sporting a heavily bandaged head, and what was surely the beginning of a pair of black eyes.

The hospital summoned Hamp and Philip to bring us home, and I avoided questions by faking sleep when they arrived, but before long I must have actually slept, because the next thing I remember is waking up in my bed at home. I didn't feel too perky and would have drifted off again, but I heard sounds in the kitchen.

It was still dark, not yet dawn, but I heard something out there. In fact, it got downright noisy, so I needed to see what was happening. I was surprised to find most of the family gathered.

"Good morning," I said, and they all turned and started speaking, but stopped, and gazed at me instead. I realized that I probably looked battered; I surely felt an assortment of aches and pains. I saw the sympathy in their faces, and knew I'd take advantage of it to stave off accusations that I'd rushed heedlessly into another mess.

"I'd better get ready for Brimfield," I said. "Today is the last day."

"Brimfield is over, Lucy," Hamp said. He worked a piece of dough on the counter, folding and pressing it, and folding it again.

Was he telling me not to go back there? I have to

admit that I didn't feel like it this morning, but if Hamp was suggesting what was best for me, maybe I should make a stand.

As I realized what a dumb move that would be, Monica came toward me. "Lucy, I'm so sorry. I'm truly sorry." She bit her lower lip, and winced as her stitched chin lifted. I could see that it hurt.

"I'm sorry, too, Monica. I thought you were my killer." She laughed, and winced again.

"Come sit down, Ma," Philip said. "Brimfield was over hours ago. You've played Sleeping Beauty long enough; it's dinnertime."

He was serious. So that's what Hamp meant. I'd missed the whole day. I couldn't believe it.

"I'd better get cracking. I'll bet you're all starved. I've got some nice rice cakes. I'll melt some carob over them, and we can—"

"God, no, Ma," Philip said. Philip hates carob.

"Don't worry, Philip. I have a new mint and coconut topping for you. You'll love it." It's been such a long time since we all sat at the table together. Every time I start getting a meal ready the family scatters. They all have their own lives.

"Sit down next to me, Mummy. I'll make you feel better."

Nick, my silliest child, pulled up a chair and motioned me over; he calls me Mummy. Nick is as silly as Philip is serious. I still can't understand how children in the same family can be so different from one another. But Nick always makes me feel good, perhaps because I see so much of myself in him.

He threw his arm over my shoulder in a friendly gesture, but I stiffened in pain. He took my hand and patted it; then he sang to me. His version of Brenda Lee singing "I'm Sorry" always cracks me up. He told me that Spence and Nancy were on their way home. All of us—it'd been so long. I remembered setting off for Brimfield less than a week ago, happy to leave them behind.

"Dad's making scallion pancakes; he's taught Monica how to make the dipping sauce."

"I can do that," I said, and amid a chorus of nos they assured me that I should sit back down and be waited on. This was so nice and cozy.

"Baker has been calling you all day."

"What for?" I asked, and right on cue, the phone rang. I reached, picked it up, and the whole family shouted, "Hello, Baker!"

It was turning into a party around here.

Baker explained that he was wrapping up his Brimfield story, and asked if I could fill him in on some details. I agreed, but when I tried to explain, I was lost; I just couldn't put it all together. I got so frustrated that I could feel tears stinging my eyes, and handed the phone over to Monica.

I heard her telling Baker about Supercart, and the ride to Mr. Hogarth's, and most of it came back to me. The whole family quieted down and listened to Monica when she told Baker about our terror at Mr. Hogarth's.

When she hung up she told me that Mr. Hogarth told Baker he feels terrible about his belief in Wilson over the years. That even as the evidence began to mount, he clung to the idea that Monty had masterminded the theft long ago, and had involved Wilson in his scheme, rather than the reverse.

The family sat staring until Hamp put a plate of sizzling scallion pancakes in front of us. We all grabbed some; they were wonderful. We savored them and let Wilson's vile work slip into the background.

When Hamp told us that his next course, moo shi chicken, would be along soon, I had to decline. I needed a nap. And for the next few days I did plenty of napping. Everyone tiptoed around and treated me like the princess I always wanted to be.

So it's over. Wilson is where he belongs, and his fund-raising activities are also being investigated. The family has survived what Monica and I have come to call Our Mishap, and we're all back at the Cape, snug and sound, ready to begin living happily ever after.

Epilogue

THE LEARNED INFORMER'S ANTIQUES REVIEW

SPRING EDITION Vol. 18, No. 2

A KILLING AT BRIMFIELD

by Baker Haskins

The big news at last month's Brimfield Antiques and Collectible Shows was sad news. Montgomery "Monty" Rondo was murdered in the predawn hours prior to the show's official opening. He appears to have been strangled with a strip of lace.

Mr. Rondo was the owner of Warehouse

Used Furniture in Worcester, a used furniture business. In addition, he was a well-regarded antiques picker, supplying fine antiques to businesses around New England.

John Wilson, of Lodgefield and Martha's Vineyard, has been charged with the crime. Mr. Wilson was most recently the curator of the Jeffries Jade Museum of Goodtidings, Massachusetts.

Jay Goode, District Attorney for Center County, reports that the charges against Wilson also include kidnapping and aggravated assault upon Mrs. Lucy St. Elmo, and aggravated assault upon Mr. Pettigrew Hogarth. Mrs. Monica St. Elmo, daughter-in-law of Lucy St. Elmo, was also injured in the melee that preceded the arrest of the suspect. Theft and fraud charges may also be brought against Mr. Wilson as the district attorney's investigation continues.

Mr. Pettigrew Hogarth, business acquaintance of both Wilson and Rondo for many years, theorizes that the murder may have been triggered by the resurfacing of some recently stolen antiques that may be related to a theft that happened many years ago. Mr. Rondo appears to have taken the blame for a theft that Mr. Wilson committed when both were young men. Hogarth now believes that Rondo felt that, in taking the blame, he could free Wilson to rise in the world with a clean slate, whereas he, Rondo, understood himself to have extremely limited horizons.

Knowing of Wilson's connection to the original stolen goods, it is likely that Rondo became suspicious that his former friend was at it again when he discovered a pickle castor about a month ago, and realized it was taken from one of Wilson's previous museums. Further investigation by Rondo appears to have uncovered Wilson's more recent theft of a candlestand. This discovery put Rondo into the situation that led to his murder.

Rondo's partner, William F. Sylund (known as "Silent Billy" to many Brimfield old-timers), has announced that Mr. Rondo has left a sizable sum of funds to be placed into a scholarship fund that Rondo founded recently, called Unlimited Horizons, for the purpose of educating troubled youths.

Police are interviewing directors of other museums where Mr. Wilson has been employed, seeking information about past thefts from their institutions. The *LIAR* has learned that objects meant for preservation and safekeeping were placed in museum archives, where they often become "lost."

Museum thefts may be the tip of the iceberg, however, as the focus now shifts to Wilson's fund-raising activities. It has come to light that at least one of Wilson's previous employers is investigating the possibility of embezzlement. An undercurrent of other allegations has surfaced, and audits are under way.

Regardless of the outcome of the Wilson trial, we can say, from our personal experience and from those who also knew him, that Monty was known to be an impeccably honest dealer and a "diamond in the rough." We will miss him.

LUCY'S COLLECTING TIPS FOR BEGINNERS

Don't buy it unless you love it. There are wonderful things out there, in every price range. Don't buy an object just to have another one in your collection, or especially because it *might* increase in value.

Learn everything you can about the objects you love. There are books on almost any category of collectible or antique. Consult the annual antiques price lists. By the time they are printed, the prices are slightly out-of-date, but they are excellent sources for identifying antiques and collectibles, and they allow you to compare values.

Visit antiques shops, flea markets, and shows to familiarize yourself with objects. Each place is different. Some will be far more comfortable and appealing to you than others.

Cultivate the antique dealers who sell the kind of things you love. They're fonts of information, and they love to share it, but please, consider their time, too; don't ask them for information when they're busy with customers.

Buy the best quality available in your price range. Look for damage, or signs of repair work, as you accumulate your collection. Hold back on cleaning, and "improving" the objects. Although they have survived this long, many have not had to withstand dishwashers and microwaves.

If the price is too low, beware! When a beginner comes across a bargain that seems too good to be true, it probably is. Don't expect to make a killing in antiques until you've made yourself an expert.

Use your collection. Don't just hide it away.

Happy hunting!